Grissom took off running, kicking up snow as he struggled to sprint through the drifts. Without thinking, Sara plunged after him.

"Grissom! Wait up!"

But he did not slow for her.

She didn't know why they were running, where they were going, or what had set Grissom off; but she suspected what it was and knew she wasn't going to like it.

Grissom just kept running, his head swiveling from side to side, and when he finally stopped, it was so sudden she almost barreled into him.

She let out a squeak, and lurched to the right to avoid colliding with Grissom, who turned and sprinted left into the woods.

Sara slipped, gathered herself, then tore off after him again. "Grissom!"

He fell to his knees then, maybe ten yards in front of her, as if seized by the urge to pray. When she caught up and bent to help him, she realized he was scooping up handfuls of snow, and throwing them at a burning body, smoking and steaming in the snow.

CSI:

CRIME SCENE INVESTIGATION ™

COLD BURN
a novel

Max Allan Collins

Based on the hit CBS television series
"CSI: Crime Scene Investigation"
produced by Alliance Atlantis in
association with CBS Productions.
Executive Producers: Jerry Bruckheimer,
Carol Mendelsohn, Ann Donahue,
Anthony E. Zuiker
Co-Executive Producers: Sam Strangis, Jonathan Littman
Producers: Danny Cannon, Cynthia Chvatal &
William Petersen
Series created by Anthony E. Zuiker

POCKET STAR BOOKS
New York   London   Toronto   Sydney   Singapore

An Original Publication of POCKET BOOKS

A Pocket Star Book published by
POCKET BOOKS, a division of Simon & Schuster, Inc.
1230 Avenue of the Americas, New York, NY 10020

ISBN: 0-7434-4407-8

First Pocket Books printing April 2003

10 9 8 7 6 5 4 3

Front cover illustration by Franco Accornero

Printed in the U.S.A.

For information regarding special discounts for bulk purchases, please contact Simon & Schuster Special Sales at 1-800-456-6798 or business@simonandschuster.com

For Anthony E. Zuiker—
without whom . . .

M.A.C. and M.V.C.

*"With method and logic
one can accomplish anything."*

—HERCULE POIROT

*"Data! Data! Data!
I can't make bricks without clay."*

—SHERLOCK HOLMES

1

LIKE THE BEACON OVER BETHLEHEM, THE FALLEN BUT bright star called Las Vegas had long ago guided wise guys from the east to this unholy city where Christmas of a sort was celebrated year-round. Ever since Ben "Bugsy" Siegel had died for the sins of tourists everywhere, men had journeyed across the desert, lured by the glowing neon temples called FLAMINGO and SANDS and CAESAR'S, summoned by celestial bodies with names like Liberace and Sinatra and Darin, to worship at the altar of the elusive fast buck.

Right now, with Christmas less than a month away, gamblers were high-rolling into town like a horde of last-minute shoppers, bucking the odds and dreaming of a green Christmas.

Driving through the Lake Mead National Recreation Area in the predawn darkness, Ranger Ally Scott—like most residents of Las Vegas—was contemplating the upcoming holiday in terms that had nothing to do with gambling. That is, except for the gamble she would take buying anything for her perennially hard-to-shop-for father. Then there was her sister Elisa . . . a gift certificate, that would just be cold.

Which was exactly what Ally was at the moment. She didn't have the Park Service Bronco's heater on and the vehicle's interior wasn't any warmer than the night she plowed through, the temperature hovering around a crisp forty. Ally had bundled herself up in her heavy jacket and Thinsulate gloves, but like so much of the Las Vegas population she had grown up somewhere else. Iowa in her case—so she damn well knew the difference between *real* winter and what Las Vegans only *thought* was winter.

Thin, practically scrawny, and barely over the mandatory Ranger height minimum, Ally enjoyed the relative chill of the December Vegas night as she tooled along the two-lane blacktop that snaked its way through the entire twenty-mile length of the Lake Mead facility.

The flat-brimmed campaign hat covered most of Ally's blonde hair, the rest ponytailed back and tucked inside the collar of her jacket.

Ally had joined the Park Service right out of college and had spent the six years since then working her way up the ladder. Barely a year ago, after bouncing from station to station in the Southwest, she'd landed this plum assignment, here at Lake Mead. Now and then, she drew the night shift like this, but she didn't mind. She was comfortable in her own company.

Headlights slashing the darkness, the Bronco rounded a curve, and the ranger felt (more than actually saw) a blur of motion to her left. Slamming on the brakes, she jolted the vehicle to a stop just as a creature tore across the road in front of her and disappeared into the blackness to her right.

Coyote.

Out here, the lights of the city were a glow on the horizon; otherwise, under a moonless desert sky scattered with half-hearted stars, the landscape remained a mystery. Still, Ally felt something—off to the passenger side of the Bronco.

With the windows rolled up, she could hear nothing, yet her well-trained senses were tingling. *Was* that . . . something? Some muffled sound, out there in the night . . . ?

She shoved the gearshift into park, let out a deep breath, and pretended the goosebumps on her arms were from the cold. Opening the driver-side door, she dropped onto the blacktop and stilled as she listened, intently. At first, only the wind whipping through the foothills, like the ghost of a mule train driver thrashing his team, broke the silence. Then, between lashes of wind, Ally heard something else. . . .

Something animal.

The ranger unsnapped her holster and rested her hand on the butt of her Smith and Wesson model 10, like a western gunfighter ready for the worst. Though most cops these days carried automatics, Glocks, Brownings, the Park Service still issued their rangers traditional, standard Smith and Wesson six-shooters

with four-inch barrels. Ally wished she had something
with a little more stopping power and, considering her
prowess with the weapon, several more rounds at her
disposal.

Stepping cautiously, quietly around the open door
and walking to the front of the Bronco, Ally could see
nothing, although her ears picked up something,
something that might have been a far-off conversation. No words could be made out, but the ranger
thought she heard voices. . . .

Then, in one chilling moment, she understood
what the "talk" was. The coyote that'd crossed her
Bronco's path was over there, and the creature wasn't
alone—a minor critter convention was under way.
Ally didn't bother pretending that the shiver up her
spine was caused by the wintry wind.

Ally clambered back into the Bronco and slipped
the gearshift into reverse, backing the vehicle, blocking the road, and cranking the wheel so the front
beams threw their small but insistent spotlights up
onto the desert hillside.

Six . . . no, seven coyotes huddled around and
hunkered over a large white lump on the ground.
For just a moment, the shape was abstract in the
harsh headlights. Then Ally knew. As acid rose in her
stomach, Ally Scott recognized the lump as human
flesh—the nude body of a woman, sprawled on her
side.

The body wasn't moving.

Even with the presence of the coyotes, Ally held
out hope that the woman might still be alive, that
this was an unconscious body and not a dead one,

despite the scavengers. She again hopped down from the Bronco, pulling her pistol to fire a round into the night sky.

The shot splitting the night and then echoing across the desert did get the attention of the animals, the coyotes' heads popping up, turning in her direction . . . but it didn't spook or disperse them.

Ally lowered the pistol and fired off another round, only a foot or so over the heads of the coyotes this time. The critters jumped and moved away, a few feet, claws scratching the desert floor, but most still lingered near the prone nude form.

And that pissed Ally off.

She charged right at them, screaming and firing off several more shots, and the animals finally took the hint, relinquishing their prize, and scampering like evil puppies into the night.

Making more noise than necessary, to help make sure the scavengers didn't return, Ally pulled off a glove and knelt next to the body. The woman—a brunette—appeared to be dead, after all. She lay on her side, as though she were sleeping . . . but she wasn't. Reaching down, Ally touched the woman's neck and, trained cop though she was, drew back her hand quickly as if she'd touched a hot stove.

What she had sensed was quite the opposite—the flesh felt more like cold rubber than anything warm and human. The woman's lank hair felt damp—had the woman crawled up here from the lake? Was this some skinny-dipping party gone awry?

Ally's stomach flipped and the ranger knew

that her supper was about to make a return trip. She started panting on purpose, like a dog, just like her orthodontist had taught her back when she was a teenager getting braces. While Dr. McPike had taken that mold of her mouth, he'd instructed her that panting would help her overcome her gag reflex.

You just never know, she thought, *when these little life lessons are going to come in handy.*

Ally searched for a pulse—finding nothing stirring under the cold, clammy flesh. This was a dead body, clearly . . . and that put Ally right smack in the middle of what she knew damn well was a crime scene. The urge to drag the body back to the Bronco was nearly overwhelming, but Ally knew not to disturb the scene any more than she already had, rushing in to chase off the coyotes.

Pistol still in her hand, Ally backed carefully to the vehicle, her eyes sweeping the dark beyond the body and the Bronco beams, just waiting for the first coyote to creep back into the wash of the car's headlights, for her to pick off. She knew, too, that if this was a murder, the perpetrator could possibly still be in the area . . . though she doubted that. The coyotes wouldn't have made their move until they were alone with the corpse.

Her eyes still searching the hill, Ally reached inside, plucked the mike from its dashboard perch, pulled the long cord out so she'd have an unobstructed view of the body and pushed the talk button.

"Dispatch," she said, "this is mobile two."

No response from the base.

"Dispatch, this is mobile two. Aaron, it's your wake-up call! Get off your ass—I found a dead body."

The low-pitched male voice sounded groggy, which was hardly a surprise. "Ally? What the hell did you say?"

"Call the city cops, Aaron—we got a d.b."

A summer intern brought back on temporarily to help out during the holiday vacations, Aaron Davis had little experience beyond handing out maps to tourists and flirting with teenage girls come to swim in the lake.

"Aren't we supposed to notify the FBI, Ally?"

The mild irritation Ally felt was a relief compared to the creepiness that had come over her, touching that cold corpse.

"We will, Aaron," she said with feigned patience, "but the Fibbies won't make it for days." She sighed. "The Vegas P.D. will be here within the hour. Call 911."

"But we're the cops, aren't we, Ally?"

"Well . . . I am."

"You mean, cops can call 911, too?"

"Aaron . . . just make the call. Then you can go back to sleep."

"You don't have to be mean," Aaron said.

She clicked off then and the ridiculousness of the conversation made her laugh. She laughed and laughed, tears rolling down her cheeks, and then she thought to herself, *Laughin' like a damn hyena,* and that made her think of the coyotes.

And then she didn't laugh any more.

She just watched the still white lump of flesh, guarding it from scavengers. Ally Scott could protect the dead woman from the coyotes, no problem; but if the woman was a murder victim, it would take a different breed of cop to find the animal who had done this.

2

STANDING AT THE EDGE OF THE BLACKTOP, CATHERINE Willows—Las Vegas Metro P.D. crime scene investigator—let the headlights of the Park Services Bronco, blocking the road, give her her first view of the body.

The dead naked woman lay on her left side, arms folded chastely across her bosom, legs pulled up in a tight, fetal ball. At this distance, no signs of violence were apparent and Catherine wondered if this death could somehow be natural. According to the ranger, the woman's hair was damp and, even from here, Catherine could make out the dampness of the ground beneath the corpse. Maybe the woman had been swimming in the lake; perhaps this was a romantic tryst that had got out of . . .

Catherine stopped herself. Unlike her boss and colleague Gil Grissom, she almost always allowed herself to play with theories before all the facts were in. But she knew the practice could be dangerous if left unchecked, particularly this early on.

On their first case together, Grissom had said, "It's a

capital mistake to theorize before one has data.
Insensibly one begins to twist facts to suit theories, instead of theories to suit facts."

"That sounds like a quote," she'd said.

"It is," Grissom had said, with no attribution, just
glancing at her with that little half-smile and smug
twinkle of the eye she now knew so well.

Even so, the tryst notion was one of the few logical
explanations that came readily to mind to answer the
musical question, what was a nude woman doing
wandering around the Lake Mead National Recreation Area in the middle of the night . . . ?

Two squad cars, their rollers smudging the night
with alternate smears of red and blue, blocked the
road a hundred yards on either side of the scene.
Detective Jim Brass's unmarked Taurus sat on the
shoulder of the road near where Catherine and her
partner tonight, Warrick Brown, had left their Tahoe.

Ever the gentleman, Warrick was pulling their
flightcase-like field kits out of the back of the SUV
while Catherine had stepped to the edge of the road
for an overview of the crime scene. Her hair whispered at her ears, thanks to the gentle desert wind—
which had a bite to it, as the sting at her cheeks
attested.

Captain Brass ambled up next to her. Despite the
temperature, Brass wore no topcoat, just a plaid sport-
coat over a gold shirt with a blue-and-gold striped tie.
When she had first known the detective, Brass had
been a rumpled sort, with the unkempt aura of the recently divorced; but time passed and the detective had
long since spiffed up.

A small cloud huffed out as he spoke. "Dead nude woman."

As if that were the beginning and the end of it.

Catherine asked, "No ID?"

"Nude, Catherine," he said, dryly. "She wasn't strolling around buck naked with her purse."

"I don't go anywhere without mine."

"Nonetheless . . . we got nothing here."

"Not yet." Catherine smiled at him, teasing just a little. "Warrick and I'll have a look, if you don't mind."

"Knock yourself out."

Following her flashlight's beam, she slowly walked over the sandy ground, careful not to disturb any potential evidence as she approached the corpse.

Brass remained on the edge of the road.

She heard Warrick behind her, field kits clanking. Then he was beside her, asking, "How's it read?"

Tall, with a shaggy, modestly dreadlocked haircut, Warrick Brown had skin the color of coffee with just a hint of cream stirred in. He was a man with a ready smile, though Catherine knew him to be serious and even inclined to melancholy.

He watched as Catherine played the flashlight along the woman's back, as if painting an abstract picture. Then she crouched and shone the beam on the woman's disturbingly peaceful face: the eyes closed, a puggish nose above full colorless lips . . . but no sign of violence, no immediate cause of death visible.

"She doesn't have much to say yet," Catherine said. "Fortunately, the coyotes were just getting started when that ranger interrupted 'em—this could be a lot worse."

"Maybe not from Miss Nude Vegas's point of view," Warrick said, in his deadpan way. "Dumped, y'think?"

Catherine nodded. "Probably dropped here, yes—other than paw-and-claw prints, no signs of a struggle on the ground. But, damn . . . who is she?" Then to the corpse, "Who are you?"

"She went out of this life," Warrick said softly, "same way she came in—naked."

Catherine frowned. "Maybe not . . . I think I saw some sort of impression, maybe from underwear. Still, it's not a lot to go on."

"Well, you know what Gris would say."

She nodded. " 'Just work the evidence.' "

"That's it."

"Well, even if that's what 'Gris' might say, allow me to point out that while we're 'working' the evidence, our fearless leader and his trusty aide will soon be sucking up room service in a first-class hotel."

Graveyard shift supervisor Grissom and another CSI, Sara Sidle, would be leaving early this morning for a forensics conference at a mountain lodge in upstate New York, where they would be teaching. Though forty degrees might be cold in Vegas, Catherine knew that where Grissom and Sara were headed, a minus sign would likely be in front of the temperature before the weekend was over. She really didn't envy the pair a bit.

Warrick made a clicking sound in his cheek and said, "Explain to me again why we're not there?"

"I didn't go because I declined the opportunity."

"You declined? A paid vacation?"

"Yes. Unlike some people, I have a life, and I didn't

want to leave my daughter with a babysitter for that long."

"I have a life."

"Let's say you do. Even so, you hate the cold."

Warrick sighed. "Yeah, well. That cushy hotel, it's got heat, doesn't it?"

Catherine allowed that it probably did.

"And the classes are indoors, right?"

"Grissom's will be," she admitted. "There may be some outdoor crime scene stuff, but you don't bring people in from Vegas to teach criminalistics in the snow."

"Thank you. You make my point—I'm tellin' you, Cath . . . that could've been us on that trip."

She nodded. "If I hadn't declined . . . and you weren't such a baby."

"Hey—that's cold."

"See? Bellyachin' about the weather already."

Finished with her examination of the corpse, Catherine rose and faced her partner. "Time to go to work, before I start thinking you don't love your job."

He shook his head. "You can love your job, and still need a little R&R."

"Well," she said, as they headed back to the Tahoe, "how about, for fun, you find us a usable tire track on the shoulder of the road, before all these people tromping around turn Lake Mead into a dust bowl."

Catherine snapped off photos as fast as the flash would recharge, little pops of daylight in the night, two photos of each angle, for safety, covering the body five ways: from the right; the left; top of the head down; bottom of the feet up; and overhead.

Warrick poked around the side of the road, occasionally bending, now and then taking his own photos. Finally, satisfied he'd found all the pertinent, usable tire tracks, he spritzed them with hair spray to hold them together, then got his field kit and mixed up some goo—casting powder and dental stone—so he could cast some of the different tracks he'd marked.

Catherine didn't think about it, but nobody spoke to them while they processed the scene—and this was not unusual. Crime scene investigators, working their scientific wonders, created in those around them a quiet reverence, as if all the kneeling she and Warrick were doing was praying, not detecting.

Or maybe it was the dead woman, in the midst of the CSI rituals, who inspired the silence.

Over on the blacktop, Brass interviewed the ranger who'd found the body, while the uniformed men stood around and did their best to look official. Truth was, once the CSIs had shown up, a uniformed cop at a crime scene usually had just about the most boring job in the law enforcement book.

Under the bright light of some portable halogens, Catherine went over the corpse as carefully as she could—nothing seemed wrong, other than a few nibble marks on the arms and legs where the coyotes had begun. No signs of struggle, no skin under her fingernails, no black eyes or bruises—nothing to say this woman wasn't just sleeping, except for the absence of breath.

An indentation showed the curve of the victim's panty line, but Catherine could find not so much as a thread for evidence. It was as if the sky had given birth to Jane Doe and let her fall gently to the sandy ground—stillborn. Finally, as night surrendered the desert back to the sun, Brass approached with cups of coffee for the two criminalists.

"Life's blood," Catherine said as Brass handed her the steaming Styrofoam cup.

Warrick saluted with his and took a sip. "Here's to crime—without it, where would we be?"

Brass raised both eyebrows and suggested, "In bed, asleep?"

They watched as the ranger climbed into her Bronco—she paused to nod at them, professionally, and they returned the gesture—and then she slowly pulled away.

Using her coffee cup to indicate the departing vehicle, Catherine asked, "She seemed competent."

"Yeah," Brass said with a nod. "We got lucky, having her find our girl."

"She see anything?"

"Nearly hit a coyote with her Bronco." Brass shrugged one noncommittal shoulder. "About all she saw was coyotes, gathered around the corpse."

"Singing Kum-bayah," Warrick said dryly.

"Did those little doggies mess up your crime scene much?"

Catherine shook her head. "Hardly any marks on the body."

Eyes tightening, Brass asked, "What's that tell us?"

"Our vic probably did not just wander out here and die," Warrick said.

Brass looked at him.

"She's barefoot," Warrick continued, "and there's

no bare footprints anywhere. You don't have to be an Eagle Scout to figure, if she was wandering dazed and nude, coyotes woulda got to her before she made it this far into the middle of the park. Somebody dropped her off."

Brass returned his gaze to Catherine. "That how you see it?"

"Makes sense to me," she said. "Lady Godiva's probably a dump, all right . . . but if the coyotes were around her and the ranger scared them off, she couldn't have been on the ground for very long, or else there wouldn't have been much left after the coyotes chowed down."

Frowning, Warrick asked the detective, "Ranger didn't see or hear a car?"

"Nope," Brass said. "She did mention that five bucks buys a car a five-day pass to the Lake Mead recreation area. Tourists can come and go as they please, whenever they please."

Warrick said, "Ever wonder what it's like to do this job in a town not crawling with tourists?"

"Oh but that would be too easy," Brass said. His sigh started in his belly and dragon-breathed out his nose. "Could be any car and it could be anywhere by now. You said there were no bare footprints—how 'bout shoeprints?"

"No," Catherine said, "whoever brought her in must've blotted them out, when they were leaving."

Almost to himself, Warrick said, "Ten million tourists a year visit this place."

"Yeah," Brass said grumpily. "Fish and Wildlife guy told us so, last time we had a dead naked woman out here."

Last autumn a woman's torso had been dredged from Lake Mead.

"We caught that guy," Warrick reminded Brass.

"How about cars?" Catherine asked. "How many in the park now?"

Brass offered up a two-shouldered shrug. "No records. It's a vacation spot—casual. Your guess is as good as mine."

Catherine frowned. "So they never know who's in the park?"

"Just happy campers—happy *anonymous* campers."

"So," Warrick said. "We have a dead naked woman . . . no ID, nothing around the body, and the only evidence we have is a track off a tire that could belong to just about any vehicle."

A grin put another crease in the rumpled detective's face. "And that's why you guys make the medium-sized bucks."

They exchanged tired smiles, which faded quickly as the trio watched two EMTs struggling to maneuver the gurney bearing the black-bagged body down to the road. The EMTs loaded the black bag—the woman finally clothed, in a way—into the back of the ambulance, closed the doors with two slams that made Catherine start a bit, then climbed in around front. The flashing lights had been on when the vehicle barreled in, and now came on again, automatically; but the driver shut them off, and the vehicle rolled away.

No hurry, not now.

"What's next?" Warrick asked.

Glancing at her watch, Catherine said, "We call it a night."

"We haven't even identified her yet," Warrick said to Catherine, but his eyes cut to Brass. "First twenty-four hours—"

"We don't even know," Brass interrupted, "if we have a homicide. . . . And if we did, can you point at any evidence that's time-sensitive here?"

Catherine shook her head.

After a moment, so did Warrick.

The detective held up his hands in front of him, palms out, his way of saying this was neither his fault nor his problem. They all knew that Sheriff Brian Mobley had put the kibosh on overtime except homicides, and even then on a case-by-case basis. Mobley was eyeing the mayor's seat in the next election and wanted to be seen as fiscally responsible, and that meant cutting most OT.

Catherine said to Warrick, "If it was up to me, we'd work this straight through—since homicide seems a possibility."

Brass, who'd had his own share of battles with the sheriff over the years, said, "We're all slaves to policy. You're on call, as usual—something pressing comes up, your beeper will let you know."

"I think our vic deserves better," Warrick said.

"Is she a vic? Do we even know that, yet? . . . Get some rest, come in tonight and look at this again, with a fresh eye."

In the rider's seat of the Tahoe, Catherine sat quietly, letting Warrick brood, and drive.

Truth be told, for Catherine the moratorium on overtime was sometimes a blessing of sorts. Sure, she wanted to find this woman's killer . . . if the woman had been killed . . . as much as Warrick or God or anybody; and she knew damn well the longer they waited, the colder the trail.

On the other hand, Mobley's penny-pinching gave her the chance to spend a little more time with daughter Lindsey after school. As much as she loved her job, Catherine loved her daughter more, and Lindsey was at that stage where the girl seemed to have grown an inch every time Catherine saw her.

But this was a homicide. She wouldn't say it out loud just yet, but she knew in every well-trained fiber of her being that some sicko had left that woman out here as meal for the coyotes.

And that just wouldn't do.

When she came in that night, right after ten, Catherine Willows was already dragging. She'd slept through the morning, catching a good four hours, but did housework and bills in the afternoon, then spent the evening helping Lindsey with her homework. The latter, anyway, was worth losing a little sleep over.

Until Sheriff Mobley's recent fiscal responsibility manifesto, the CSIs had worked whatever overtime was necessary to crack the case they happened to be on. Catching a case on the night shift meant that certain tasks just couldn't be accomplished during their regular shift. And the level of cooperation with the day shift was less than stellar—Conrad Ecklie, the supervisor on days, considered Grissom a rival, and Grissom considered Ecklie a jerk. This did not encourage team playing between graveyard and days.

Now, with OT curtailed, the CSIs just had to try to

cram more work into a normal shift. Although the new policy might pave the way for Mobley's advancement, Catherine knew that rushing to cover so much ground in such a short time could lead to sloppiness, which was the bane of any CSI's existence.

Her heels clicked like castanets on the tile floor as she strode down the hall toward the morgue. When she arrived, she found what she had hoped to find—Dr. Robbins, hard at work on her case. His metal crutch stashed in the corner, the coroner—in blue scrubs, a pair of which Catherine would put on over her own street clothes—hovered over the slab bearing their Jane Doe, a measuring tape in his hands, sweat beaded on his brow.

The balding, chubby-cheeked coroner, his salt-and-pepper beard mostly salt by now, was the night shift's secret weapon. His sharp dark eyes missed nothing and, despite having to use the metal crutch after a car crash some years ago, he moved around the morgue with a nimbleness that ex-dancer Catherine could only envy.

"Getting anywhere?" she asked lightly.

He shrugged without looking up. "Catherine," he said by way of acknowledgment, then answered her question with: "Early yet."

For all the time she'd spent studying the dead woman under her flashlight beam, Catherine moved in eagerly for a good look under better conditions. Crime scene protocol had meant Catherine had left the woman in her fetal position; now the nude female was on her back on a silver slab.

Her flesh ashen gray, Jane Doe had a pageboy haircut, wide-set closed eyes and full lips that had a ghastly bleached look. A nice figure, for a corpse.

"Funny," Catherine said.

"What is?"

"She kinda looks like Batgirl."

Robbins glanced up, then returned to his work.

"From the old TV show," Catherine explained. "Not that you'd—"

"Yvonne Craig." Robbins flicked her a look. "You don't want to play Trivial Pursuit with me, Catherine."

"I'll keep that in mind. Sex crime?"

"No evidence of it. When she died, she hadn't had intercourse in a while."

Catherine gestured to the woman's waist. "What about the visible panty line?"

"She died clothed—marks from a bra too."

"Cause of death?"

"Asphyxia, I would venture." He thumbed open one of Jane Doe's eyelids and revealed red filigree in what should have been the white of an eye. "She has petechial hemorrhaging in the conjunctivae."

Catherine leaned in for a closer look. "That's asphyxia's calling card, all right. Strangulation?"

"Strangely, doesn't appear that way—no ligature marks, no bruising."

Catherine pondered that a moment. "So . . . you've ruled out what, so far? Suicide?"

He smiled. "Unless you know a way she might have killed herself, then stripped off her clothes."

"Where are we, then?"

He shrugged. "As I said . . . early. Printed her and gave them to Nick to run through AFIS."

Nick Stokes was another of the graveyard shift CSIs. He'd been working his own case last night, so he hadn't joined them on the trip out to Lake Mead.

"Nick's in already?" she asked.

"Few minutes before you. Closed his case before he went home last night and was looking for something to do."

"We all feel a little lost without Grissom around," she said, attempting to be sarcastic and yet not completely kidding.

"Couple of odd things that will, I think, interest you," he said. "Have a look. No charge. . . ." He pointed to the victim's right arm.

Catherine moved around where she could get a better view. The victim had an indentation in her left arm above the point of the elbow—a faint stripe, resembling a hash mark.

"And here," Robbins said, pointing to the victim's left cheek, which had been out of sight at the crime scene.

"Any ideas?" asked Catherine as she looked at a small, round indentation that appeared as if the tip of a lipstick tube . . . or a bullet, maybe . . . had been pressed into the woman's cheek.

Again Robbins shook his head. "I was hoping you might have one. . . . Found postmortem lividity in the buttocks, lower legs and feet, as well as the left cheek. I checked your photos and they show her lying on her left side."

Catherine shrugged. "That's the way we found her."

"Well, it almost looks like she was in a sitting position, after she died." Robbins then abruptly changed the subject. "Tell me—how cold did it get last night, anyway? What did the temp get down to?"

Thrown by this seemingly out-of-left-field question, Catherine shrugged again, more elaborately this time. "Chilly but no big deal. Forty, maybe."

Robbins shook his head again, but this time it was more an act of bemusement than disagreement. "Body's pretty cold—colder than I would have expected."

"She was cold to the touch last night, too."

"And the hair was wet, you said?"

"Yeah—damp."

"Does it seem reasonable to you that someone might have been swimming in the lake on a night that cold?"

"No . . . but we run into people doing a lot of things that don't seem reasonable, Doc."

"That's true. That much is true. No pile of clothing found?"

"Not a scrap."

"Interesting."

And with this, he fired up the bone saw and got ready to start the more in-depth procedures.

Frustrated, Catherine wandered off to find Nick. She checked the AFIS computer room—no sign of him. Wandering the aquamarine halls of the facility, a glass-and-wood world of soothing institutional sterility, she passed a couple of labs and Grissom's office before she finally tracked Nick down in the break room. He sipped his coffee and took a bite of doughnut as Catherine walked in.

"Hey, Nick," she said, trying to sound more nonchalant than she felt. Solving Jane Doe's murder would be a lot easier if they could ID her quickly.

Using the Styrofoam cup, Nick gave her a little salute as he finished chewing his doughnut.

Catherine dropped into a chair across the table from him and waited, knowing the doughnut just might be Nick's dinner. The break room always seemed to be undergoing some sort of massive cleanup, but no matter what either they themselves or the janitorial staff attempted, the room still smelled like one of Grissom's experiments gone awry. The refrigerator against the far wall held items that looked more like mutant life-forms than food, and the coffeepot was home to a sludgy mass that reminded Catherine too much of things she'd seen on the job.

She asked, "Any luck with AFIS?"

"Nope," he said, then took another bite of doughnut.

"So we don't know any more about her now than we did this morning?"

He shook his head. "I put her into the Missing Persons database, but . . ." He made a sound that was half snort, half laugh. ". . . you know how long that can take."

Catherine nodded glumly.

Warrick came in, wearing a brown turtleneck, brown jeans, and his usual sneakers. "Hey," he said.

"Hey," said Catherine.

Nick nodded and finished chewing the last of his doughnut. "I'm on the Jane Doe with you guys, now."

"More the merrier," Warrick said. "Anything new?"

Catherine said, "Robbins thinks asphyxia—but not strangulation, and not a sex crime. How about you?"

"Nothing on the tire mark so far, but the computer's still working."

A familiar voice squawked on the intercom. "Catherine, you in there?"

She spoke up. "Yes, Doc—with Nick and Warrick."

"Well," the voice said, "I have something to show you."

They exchanged looks, already getting to their feet, Catherine calling, "We're on our way!"

Nick slugged down the last of his coffee and the three of them moved silently but quickly to the morgue. When they walked in, in scrubs, they found Robbins bent not over the corpse—opened like a grotesque flower on the slab nearby—but a microscope. Immune from Sheriff Mobley's overtime edict, the doc regularly put in punishing hours, a habit that was helpful to the CSIs in this current Scrooge-like climate.

"Notice anything odd about this body?" he asked, directing the question to Catherine, senior member of the group.

"Nothing we haven't talked about already," she said, with a glance over at the autopsy-in-progress. "For some reason her hair was wet, and she was cold, but why not? It was chilly out last night."

Robbins nodded and gestured with an open palm for her to take his place at the microscope. "Yes, but was it this cold?"

Sitting down, Catherine gave Robbins a look, then pressed her eye to the eyepiece of the microscope. On the slide he'd prepared, she saw what appeared to be a flesh sample with several notable oddities—specifically, distortions in the nuclei of some cells, vacuoles and spaces around the nuclei of others.

Catherine looked up at Robbins. "Is this what I think it is?"

He nodded. "Your Jane Doe was a corpse-sickle."

Warrick and Nick exchanged glances.

"Say again?" Warrick prompted.

"A frozen treat," Robbins said again, in his flat, low-key way. "What Catherine is looking at under the microscope is a tissue sample from Jane Doe's heart."

"She *froze* to death?" Warrick asked, his usually unflappable demeanor seeming sorely tested.

Robbins shrugged one shoulder. "Still working that one out. Suffocation is cause of death, but I don't know the circumstances for sure."

First Nick, then Warrick took turns gazing into the microscope.

Robbins said, "Notice those discolorations, vacuoles and spaces?"

Warrick nodded, eyes glued to the slide.

The doctor continued: "Ice crystal artifacts."

"So she was frozen," Nick said, trying to process this information. "But maybe after she was dead."

"Frozen God knows when . . . and rather carefully frozen, at that."

Warrick's eyes were wide and his upper lip curled. "And then what?"

"And then," Robbins said, "thawed . . . which is why her hair was damp. Catherine, the ground beneath the body was damp, I believe?"

She nodded. "Wet underneath and in a small area downhill from where she lay."

"Suffocated," Warrick said. "Then frozen."

Robbins did not answer immediately. But, finally, he said, "Yes."

Catherine's mind was racing. She expressed some of her thoughts: "And because Jane Doe was frozen, we can't pinpoint when she died."

Robbins grunted a small laugh. "Pinpoint isn't an issue. It could've been a week ago, it could've been six months, or even longer, for that matter."

Nick was shaking his head. "Well, hell—how did we not notice she'd been frozen?"

The doctor raised a finger. "As I said . . . she was 'carefully frozen.' Someone took precautions to avoid freezer burn. Wetted her down—a spray bottle would be enough. Kept wetting her down, all over, as the freezing process continued. And that is what kept her from getting freezer burn."

"So," Catherine said. "Our killer knew what he was doing."

"Or she," Nick put in.

Robbins sighed, nodded and then explained his theory.

Jane Doe has probably been either sedated or restrained or both. She's still clothed at this point, then something clean cuts off her breathing, plastic over her nose and mouth maybe, and she's out within five minutes. . . . Dead in not much more than that.

The killer strips her, then seats her inside a chest-style freezer. Could be an upright, but a chest freezer would be easier; then he . . . or she . . . cranks the freezer up to its highest setting . . . but is careful to use a pitcher or a squirt bottle, maybe even a hose, to wet down the corpse. The killer checks on her at least once a day, and wets the body every time he checks the progress of the freezing. After some unspecified time, the killer pulls her out and allows her to defrost naturally . . . then dumps her body in the Lake Mead National Recreation Area.

Warrick's eyes were tight with thought. "If he . . . or she . . . thought we'd be fooled into thinking we had a fresh body, then—"

"Then on that effort, our killer failed," Catherine said. "But even so, we've still had the time of death stolen from us, here."

"Exactly," Robbins said.

"So . . ." Catherine lifted her eyebrows, smiled at her colleagues. ". . . if we can't determine when she died, let's start with who she was."

"Which'll lead," Nick said, arching an eyebrow, "to finding out who wanted her dead."

"Which'll lead," Warrick said, with finality, "to putting the bastard on ice."

3

INITIALLY, THE IDEA OF A GETAWAY WEEKEND WITH HER BOSS had appealed to Sara Sidle, for all kinds of reasons. But somehow in the thirteen hours between when she'd left her apartment and fallen gratefully onto this cloud of a bed in a posh hotel, she had gotten lost in some newly discovered circle of Hell.

Grissom had picked her up just after 10 P.M., the time they normally would have been heading into the lab. Instead, they drove to long-term parking at McCarran and schlepped into the airport with their carry-ons as well as two suitcases of equipment for their presentation; the attendees would mostly be East Coast CSIs with the instructors flown in from around the country. Typically, the boyishly handsome, forty-something Grissom wore black slacks, a black three-button shirt, and a CSI windbreaker.

"That's the coat you're taking?" she had asked. Sara had a Gortex-lined parka on over her blue jeans and a plain dark tee shirt.

He looked at her as though a lamp had talked. "I've got a heavier one in my bag."

She glanced at his two canvas duffels, both barely larger than gym bags, and wondered how he got a heavy coat into either of them. Deciding not to think about it, she got into the check-in line right behind her boss. Both were using their carry-ons for clothing, and checking their suitcases of equipment on through. No need to freak out the security staff, who would not be prepared for X-ray views of the sort of tools, instruments, chemistry sets, and other dubious implements that the CSIs were traveling with.

Sara spent the flight from McCarran to O'Hare squashed in the middle seat in coach—Grissom took the window seat, not because he was rude, she knew, but because it was his assigned seat, and Grissom never argued with numbers.

Sara dug into an Agatha Christie mystery—the CSI could only read cozy mysteries, anything "realistic" just distracted and annoyed her with constant inaccuracies—and Grissom was engrossed in an entomology text like a teenager reading the new Stephen King.

The whole trip went like that—the two of them reading their respective books (Sara actually went through two) with little conversation, including an O'Hare breakfast that killed some of their four-hour layover in Chicago. Then it was two hours to Dulles in D.C., another forty-five minutes on the ground, and a ninety-minute flight to Gordon International, in Newburgh, New York. Grissom was better company on the trip than a potted plant—barely.

They were met by a landscape covered with four or five inches of snow that, judging by its grayish tint, appeared to have fallen at least a week ago. The cold air felt like the inside of a freezer compared to what they'd left behind in Vegas, and as the pair stood outside the airport waiting for the bus that would haul them and their gear the twenty miles from Newburgh to New Paltz, Grissom glanced around curiously, as though winter in upstate New York was one big crime scene he'd stumbled onto.

Sara, on the other hand, felt at home—spiritually at home, anyway. The temperature here, just above thirty, took Sara back to her days at Harvard; the frigid air of winter in the east had a different scent than the desert cold of Vegas.

At the curb in front of the New Paltz bus station, an old man in a flap-ear cap, chocolate-colored Mackinaw, jeans and dark work boots, waited next to a purring woody-style station wagon, the side door of which was stenciled: MUMFORD MOUNTAIN HOTEL.

Carry-ons draped over them like military gear, Grissom and Sara made their cumbersome way toward their down-home chauffeur. As soon as the codger figured out they were headed his way, he rushed over and pried one of the suitcases from Sara's hand.

"Help you with that, Miss?"

But he'd already taken it.

"Thanks," she said, breath pluming.

The Mumford man was tall, reedy, with wispy gray hair; his hook nose had an "S" curve in the middle where it had been broken more than once.

After slinging Sara's bag in the back, he turned and took one from Grissom and tossed it in. The man's smile was wide and came fast, revealing two rows of small, even teeth.

"Herm Cormier," he said, shaking first Grissom's hand, then Sara's. "I've managed the hotel since Jesus was a baby."

"Gil Grissom. Honor to be picked up by the top man himself."

"Sara Sidle. We're here for the forensics conference . . . ?"

"Course you are. You're the folks from Vegas."

Grissom smiled. "Is it that easy to spot us?"

Cormier nodded. "Your coat's not heavy enough," he said, with a glance toward Grissom's CSI windbreaker. "And you both got a healthy tan. We got nobody comin' in from Florida or California for this thing, and I knew two of you were coming from Vegas. . . . Plus which, all but a handful of you folks won't be in till tomorrow."

Grissom nodded.

"You, though, Miss," Cormier said, turning his attention to Sara, "you've been around this part of the country before."

Though anxious to get into that warm station wagon, Sara couldn't resist asking: "And how did you reach that conclusion?"

The old man looked her up and down, but there was nothing improper about it. "Good coat, good boots, heavy gloves—where you from, before you lit in Vegas?"

"San Francisco."

"No, that ain't it." His eyes narrowed. "Where'd you go to college?"

She grinned. "Boston."

Cormier returned the grin. "Thought so. Knew you had to've spent some time in this part of the country."

The driver opened the rear door of the wagon and they were about to climb in, when another man sauntered up. A husky blonde six-footer in his late thirties, the new arrival had dark little eyes in a pale, bland fleshy face, like raisins punched into cookie dough. He wore a red-and-black plaid coat that looked warm, aided and abetted by a black woolen muffler. In one black gloved hand was a silver flight case—this was another CSI, Sara thought, and that was his field kit—and in the other a green plaid bag that jarred against the competing plaid coat.

"Gordon Maher," he said to all of them.

Cormier stepped forward, shook the man's hand and made the introductions, then said to the new arrival, "You must be the forensics fella from Saskatchewan."

They piled into the station wagon, Grissom and Maher in the back, Sara and Cormier in the front. Despite the snow blanketing the area, the roads were clean. As the station wagon wended its way through the countryside toward Lake Mumford, Sara allowed herself to enjoy the ride, relishing the wave of nostalgia she felt, watching the snow-touched skeletal trees they glided past.

Harvard had been where Sara first took wing, first got out from the shadow of her parents. She sought out kindred spirits, overachievers like herself, and soon she was no longer seen as too smart, too driven, too tense.

The very air in this part of the country smelled different to her now—like freedom, and success. She didn't know when she fell asleep, exactly, but suddenly Cormier was nudging her gently. The car was parked on the shoulder and, when she looked around, Sara realized that Grissom and Maher had gotten out.

"Thought you might like to catch the hotel and lake," Cormier said, "from their best side."

Slowly, Sara got out of the car, the chill air helping her wake up; she stretched. Grissom and Maher stood in front of the car, staring at something off to the right. Going to join them, she looked in that direction as well, shading her brow with her hand as she gazed down the hill through the leafless branches at an ice-covered lake surrounded mostly by woods.

In preparing for this trip, Sara had understandably assumed Mumford Mountain Hotel would perch atop a mountain. Instead, the lodge hunkered in a valley between two mountains, overlooking the lake—and from this distance, situated as it was on the far side of the frozen expanse, the sprawling structure brought nothing so much to mind as a gigantic ice castle from the fairy tales her mother had read to her as a child.

It wasn't beautiful, really, more like bizarre—and mind-numbingly large, which was especially startling out here in the middle of nowhere. A hodgepodge of five interconnected structures, Mumford Mountain Hotel might have been a junkyard for old buildings: in front, near the lake, sat a squat dark-wood ski chalet; to the right and behind the chalet, a huge gray castle complete with turrets and chimneys rose seven stories. That gothic monstrosity was flanked by two functional-looking green four-story buildings that might have been the boys' and girls' dormitories at an old private school.

The one on the right had a deeply sloped, gabled roof, while its fraternal twin at the other end had a flatter roof with a single sharp point rising like the conical hat of a Brothers Grimm princess. If those buildings didn't supply enough rooms for Mumford's guests, a last building—what looked like a two-story gingerbread house—had been cobbled together on the far right end. The whole unlikely assembly seemed to shimmer under a heavy ice-crystal-flung dusting of snow.

"The Mumford Mountain Hotel," Cormier said, pride obvious in his voice.

"Can't say I've seen its like before," Maher admitted, arms folded against himself. "What's the story on the various building styles?"

"Well, that castle part came first—then wings were added, to suit whoever was running the place at the time. The hotel just sort of grew over the years. It's hard for people to get an idea of how big she is, when they're up close. I like to give folks the chance to see it from a distance, get a little perspective."

Sara said, "You could get lost in that place."

Cormier nodded, breath smoking. "Over two hundred fifty guest rooms, grand ballroom, complete gym, meeting rooms, tennis courts, golf course."

"The lake get any action in the winter?" Maher asked.

Again Cormier nodded. "They'll clear the snow off and play hockey on it when the weather gets a mite colder."

Soon they were back in the car and following the narrow road that wound down the mountain and ended at the check-in entrance of the hotel, which was alongside the building—otherwise the guests would have had to maneuver the flight of stairs to the actual main entrance and the vast covered porch where countless rocking chairs sat unattended. A light snow began to fall as Cormier directed several bellboys to unload the station wagon, piling the guest luggage onto carts, a process Grissom watched with suspicion—his precious tools and toys were in those bags.

They checked in, having just missed lunch, but Grissom shared with her a fruit basket the conference chairman had sent, and Sara left him at his room, where he was eating a pear as he unpacked. She headed down the wide, carpeted hall for her own accommodations, eating an apple along the way. She felt like Alice gone through the mirror into a Victorian wonderland—dark, polished woodwork; soft-focus, yellow-tinted lighting; plush antique furniture; wide wooden stairways; and little sitting areas with fresh-cut flowers and frondy plants and their own fireplaces.

Now, midafternoon, having gotten the nap she so desperately needed (sleeping in the car had actually made her feel worse), Sara felt an irresistible urge to go exploring—there were only a few hours left before sun-down. She wondered if Grissom would feel the same.

Of course he wouldn't.

He was probably curled up with that damned bug book again. Not that she didn't understand his almost hermit-like behavior—she was a loner herself. But ever since the Marks case, Sara had tried to force her-self out into the world more, to have a life beyond the crime lab, after noting the work-is-everything, stay-at-home, shop-out-of-catalogues existence that had contributed to the death of a woman way too much like herself.

She had come to Mumford with a plan to embroil Grissom in an outing and Sara Sidle was nothing if not thorough. Quickly she changed from her traveling clothes into black jeans, a heavier thermal undershirt and a dark flannel blouse. She slipped into her parka, snatched up her camera, briefly considered taking along her collapsed portable tripod, then decided not to be encumbered. Maybe later. She locked the door behind her and went to Grissom's room.

Her first knock inspired no answer, and she tried again. Still nothing. On the third, more insistent knock, the door opened to reveal Grissom, entomol-ogy text held in his hand like a priest with a Bible—it was as if she'd interrupted an exorcism.

"Hey," she said, chipper.

"Hey," he said, opening the door wide. "You look rested."

Wow—that was one of the nicest things he'd ever said to her.

Encouraged, she tried, "You wanna go for a walk?"

He glanced toward the window on the far side of the room, then turned back to her. "Sara—it's snowing."

She nodded. "And?"

He considered that for a while.

"I don't do snow," he said. He was still in the black slacks and black three-button shirt. Gesturing with the bug book, he said, "It's cozy, reading by the fire. You should try it."

That almost sounded romantic. . . .

He frowned at her and added: "Don't you have a fireplace in your room?"

". . . I finished my books already."

"The first thing the pioneers did was build shelter and go inside. Out of respect to them, I—"

"Did you know there are 274 winter insects in eastern New York state alone?"

He stilled, but clearly sensed a trap. "You made that up."

Grinning, she handed him the printout. "Snow-born Boreus, Midwinter Boreus, Large and Small Snowflies and the Snow-born Midge . . . just to name a few."

After a quick scan of the page, he said, "If you've got your heart set on it, I guess I'll get my coat."

To Grissom's credit, the coat he withdrew like a rabbit out of a hat from his canvas carry-on—a black, leather-sleeved varsity-type jacket, sans letter or any other embellishment—was heavier than the windbreaker, though still not really sufficient for this weather. He slipped some specimen bottles into the pockets, zipped up the coat, yanked on black fur-lined leather gloves and they were off.

The first hour or so they spent hiking through the snow-covered woods, Grissom stopping every now and then to look for insects on the ground and on trees. Sara—who found Grissom's behavior endearingly Boy Scout-ish—snapped off about a dozen nature shots, barely putting a dent in her Toshiba's 64-mg memory card; but after a while the snowfall made that impossible. It was getting heavier, and Sara knew they should head back.

But she was having too good a time. The wintry woods were delightful, idyllic. A charmingly gleeful Grissom actually found several specimens that he had carefully bottled for transport back to the hotel. He was close to her, their cold-steam breath mingling, showing her one of his prizes, when they heard it.

A pop!

They swung as one toward the forest.

Frowning, Sara asked, "Hunters?"

Grissom shook his head, but before he could speak, four more pops interrupted.

Shots—no doubt now in her mind, and clearly none in Grissom's, either.

Even though the shots were in the distance, they both found trees to duck behind.

"If it's hunters," he said, looking over at her, "they're using handguns."

"Where?"

"Can't tell. . . . Over there, maybe," he said, pointing to their left. Without another word, he took off walking in that direction, and Sara fell in behind him.

"Should we really be moving toward the gunfire?" she asked.

He threw her a sharp sideways glance. "It's our job, Sara."

"I know that, but we're not in our jurisdiction and we're not armed. What are you going to do if we meet the shooter?"

They were moving through the trees, twigs and leaves snapping underfoot; and the snow was coming down now, really coming down.

"What if it's a hunter?" she asked. "We aren't in bright clothing—Grissom! Stop and think."

He stopped. He thought.

Then he made a little shrugging motion with his eyebrows. "Maybe we ought to turn around," Grissom admitted. "Could be someone just doing a little target practice."

"Good. Yes. Let's do that."

But he made no move to go back. Snow now covered their boot tops and threatened their knees. They were deep in the woods, deep in snow, somewhere on the slope behind the hotel—they could still make out its towers through the skeletal branches and haze of snow. Soon it would be dark, and they'd have to navigate by the lights of the hotel.

Looking at Grissom, Sara realized that his varsity jacket wasn't doing him much more good than his windbreaker would have. The CSI supervisor was working to hide it, but he obviously was shivering. His cheeks were rosy, the snow in his hair making it appear more white than gray.

Still, she knew him well enough to know the cold wasn't what was on his mind.

Just ahead, a round wooden pole peeked above the

drifting snow, bearing two signs: one, pointing left, read Partridgeberry Trail to Lakeshore Path (whatever that was); the other, pointing to the right, said Forest Drive.

"Either of these paths get us back faster?" Grissom asked.

Sara shrugged. "As long as we can see the hotel, we're okay."

"But we can go back the way we came, right? You do know the way."

She twitched a sheepish smile. "Well, to be honest . . . when we were looking for those snowflies, and we cut through the woods . . ."

"Sara, if we're lost, say we're lost."

"We're not lost," Sara insisted. "If you look through there, you can see the hotel."

He turned to look at the path they'd carved coming up the trail. Already the snow filled in their tracks and, if they tried retracing their steps, the guesswork would soon begin. . . .

"Look, I've got my cell phone," she said. "Why don't we just call the hotel and tell them where we are?"

Without answering, Grissom looked down where the Partridgeberry Trail ought to be, then back in the direction they'd been going, then sharply back toward the Partridgeberry Trail, his nose in the air, sniffing the wind.

"Grissom," Sara said. "This is no time to be a guy. Asking for directions is nothing to be ashamed of."

He kept sniffing.

She continued: "Let's just phone the hotel and tell

them we're . . ." Something about the look on his face stopped her. "What?"

His nose still high, the snow turning his eyebrows white, he asked, "You smell that?"

Now Sara sniffed the air. "Grilling, maybe?"

"In this weather? No . . . I recognize that smell!"

And Grissom took off running, kicking up snow as he struggled to sprint through the deepening white stuff. Without thinking, Sara plunged after him; it was like trudging through sand.

"Grissom! Wait up!"

But he did not slow for her.

She didn't know why they were running, where they were going or what had set Grissom off; but she suspected what it was and knew she wasn't going to like it.

Grissom just kept running, his head swiveling, and when he finally stopped it was so sudden she almost barreled into him.

She let out a squeak, and lurched to the right to avoid colliding with Grissom, who turned and sprinted left into the woods.

Sara slipped, gathered herself, then tore off after him again. "Grissom!"

He fell to his knees, maybe ten yards in front of her, as if seized by the urge to pray. When she caught up and bent to help him, she realized he was scooping up handfuls of snow, and throwing them at a burning human body.

The snow hissed and steamed when it struck the flames. Swallowing quickly to avoid being sick, Sara dropped to her knees and joined him in flinging handfuls of snow at the burning body.

Finally, after what seemed like hours, but was probably only a couple of minutes, of heaping snow on the body, the fire was extinguished. For the most part, the flames seemed to have been centered on the chest and face of a male who lay on his back, his arms at his sides, his legs slightly splayed.

Reaching carefully, avoiding the still steaming torso, Grissom felt the man's wrist for a pulse.

"Damnit," Grissom said bitterly, as if this were his fault. "Dead."

"What happened here? Not spontaneous combustion, certainly."

Grissom took a quick look around. "No. There are other sets of tracks here." He pointed further down the hill toward the hotel. "Give me your cell phone; I'll call 911. You start taking pictures of everything—fast. The way this snow's coming down, this crime scene will be history in fifteen minutes."

"It's a digital camera. . . ."

They both knew that in some states, photographs taken on a digital camera were inadmissible in court—digital doctoring was simply too easy.

"It's what we have," Grissom said. "We can both testify to that. Get started."

A comforting sense of detachment settling down on her, Sara tossed Grissom the phone and got to work.

She'd start with the body, then work her way outward from there. She logged the facts in her head as she took her photos. He was a white man between nineteen and twenty-five, judging from his young-looking hands—tall, maybe six feet, six feet one, 175 to 185, dark hair, most of it burned off, wearing a navy blue parka, mostly melted now, over a tee shirt (black possibly, but that might have been the charring), jeans, boots and, surprisingly, no gloves.

Sara devoted a couple dozen shots to the body—already planning to erase the nature photos, if need be—and was careful to capture as much detail as she could. Then she moved to the tracks in the snow. They were already filling in; she took close-ups and distance shots, wishing she had the tripod after all, using one of her gloves to show scale.

Five sets of tracks: three sets coming from the hotel, two sets going back. With the way the snow was coming down, Sara couldn't even tell if the other sets were the same approximate size, let alone whether they had been made by one set of boots or two. And her hand was freezing.

Grissom walked up to her. "How's it going?"

"Lost cause," she said, glumly. "Boot holes are filling up—no way to get a decent picture."

"That's the least of our problems," Grissom said. His voice was tight; he was either irritated or frustrated—maybe both. "I just got off the phone with the Ulster County Sheriff's Office."

"On their way?"

"Not exactly. Deputy says they might have a car out here . . . tomorrow."

She brushed snow off her face. "That's not funny."

"Am I laughing? It's snowing so hard they've closed the roads."

"Well . . . I guess that's no surprise."

"Add to that, they've had a major chain reaction accident up on Interstate 87. . . . All the available deputies and state troopers are working that scene."

"Shit." She was hopping now, trying to stay warm.

"So we're on our own."

"On our own. . . ."

Grissom gestured toward the smoldering human chunk of firewood. "Our victim was already dead when the fire started, or he would have been face down."

"I'm too cold to think that one through. Help me."

"Sara, nobody alive stays on his back in the snow with his face on fire."

"I see your point."

Grissom headed back to the corpse. "We need to try to determine cause of death."

She fell in with him, slipping her camera in her parka pocket. "Okay. But with this snow coming down, we can't treat the body with the respect it deserves."

"That's a given."

They bent down over him, one on either side, and began carefully wiping away the snow, which already threatened to bury him.

"No visible wounds other than the burns," Sara said. "Were you thinking those gunshots we heard—"

"I'm not thinking anything yet. Just observing." Slowly, Grissom rolled the body onto its right side. He pointed to a spot in the middle of the victim's back. "Entrance wound."

"Looks like a .38."

"Or a little smaller."

Sara, teeth chattering, let out a nervous laugh and Grissom looked up sharply at her.

"Sorry," she said, and held up her gloved hands in surrender. "My bad . . . I was just thinking of something you taught me when I first joined CSI."

"What?"

She sighed a little cloud and said, "First on the scene, first suspect. . . . And this time it's us."

He reacted with an eyebrow shrug. "Other prime suspects include people the victim knew, relatives, friends . . . and we're strangers."

"Lots of people are killed by strangers."

He nodded, looking toward the tracks in the snow. "How do you see this?"

Sara squinted, thinking it quickly through. "Well. . . . He's being followed by two people . . . with a gun, or guns. They've brought him out here to kill him."

"Then why all the shots? I only find one wound."

"All right," Sara said, processing that. "Two people chasing him, missing him, finally one of them got him, then they set him on fire."

A branch cracked behind them and Sara reflexively reached for the pistol that wasn't on her hip as she spun toward the sound.

"Whoa, Nellie!" Herm Cormier said, holding up his hands in front of him. "It's just me and Constable Maher."

Sara noted that Cormier had a .30-06 Remington rifle slung over a shoulder, the barrel pointed down. He'd traded in the Mackinaw for a heavy fur-lined coat; a stocking cap came down over his ears, and he wore leather gloves.

Maher was encased in a parka and wore a backpack. He too wore gloves and a stocking cap. "What the hell happened here?" he asked.

"Gunshot wound to the back," Grissom said. "At some point the victim was set on fire . . ."

"Jesus H. Christ," Cormier said, his voice hollow. He had stepped around them, and now stood looking down at the charred body in the snow.

Sara asked, "You know him, Mr. Cormier?"

Shaking his head and turning away, an ashen Cormier said, "Hell's bells, he's burned so damn bad, I . . ."

"But do you know him?" Sara pressed.

Cormier choked like he might heave, then swallowed and said, "I can't rightly tell."

"How about the clothes?" Grissom asked.

Glancing at the body, then turning away again, Cormier said, "That don't help. . . . We better call the sheriff."

Grissom filled them in on that score.

"Did you check for a wallet?" Maher asked.

"Just getting ready to," Sara said. "You want to give me a hand?"

Maher propped the body on its side while Sara patted the pockets; nothing.

Looking from one man to the other, Grissom asked, "What are you two doing out here?"

Swiveling toward Grissom, Cormier said, "Jenny— that's the little gal at the desk Ms. Sidle spoke to about the weather—she told me you two were out walking . . . and that she'd told Ms. Sidle the snow wouldn't be too bad. Turns out this could be one of them hundred-year storms."

"Really," Grissom said.

Cormier nodded. "Weather Bureau's predicting as much as twenty-four inches in the next twenty-four hours."

Maher piped in, "Mr. Cormier decided he better come find you two. I overheard his conversation with the desk clerk and, since I track in the snow for a living, I offered to come along."

"We better start gettin' back," Cormier said.

Sara dusted snow off herself. "How are we going to get this body back to the hotel?"

Cormier said, "For now, we got to leave it here."

"We can't do that," Sara said. "That body is evidence, and this crime scene is disappearing as we speak."

Cormier shrugged. "Ms. Sidle, we try to carry him with us, he could end up being the death of us all. These storms get worse 'fore they get better."

"But . . ."

"This is a murder," Grissom said, gesturing about them. "What about the evidence?"

Maher stepped forward now. "Dr. Grissom, excuse me, but I've been working winter crime scenes my whole career. The evidence is going to be fine."

"In a blizzard."

Maher nodded, once. "The snow will help preserve it, not destroy it. But you and Ms. Sidle are right—we can't just leave the scene unguarded. For one thing, predators could come along and make a meal of our victim."

Sara asked, "What do you suggest?"

"I suggest," Maher said, "we take turns guarding the scene—the three of us. I can help you work the crime scene after the storm breaks."

Sara had no better idea, and when she looked Grissom's way, she could almost see the wheels turning in the man's head. The only two people she figured for sure weren't suspects were Grissom and herself.

Everybody else was a candidate.

But her gut said to trust Maher. He'd come to the conference alone and, like them, didn't seem to know anyone here.

"Any other options?" Grissom asked.

Maher shook his head. "We stay out here now and Mr. Cormier's right. There'll be five deaths to investigate."

Grissom said, "All right—how do we get back?"

Sara said, "Grissom . . . are you sure about—"

"Constable Maher is the expert here, not us. We'll have to take his word for it."

Maher turned to the hotel manager. "Mr. Cormier, I'm going to need your rifle."

"Why?"

"So I can take the first shift."

"I'm not as keen on this idea," Cormier said, "as you and Mr. Grissom."

Maher pointed toward the hotel. "In two hours, I want you to lead one of these two back up here to relieve me. You can find this spot, in the dark, right?"

"Course I can, no problem . . . but that ain't the

issue. This weather, it's beautiful from a distance . . . up close, it can get goddamned ugly."

"Can't leave the crime scene unsecured," Maher insisted.

Grissom said, "Mr. Cormier, please."

Reluctantly, Cormier held out the rifle.

Maher said, "Hold that just another minute, eh?"

The Canadian withdrew something shiny from his backpack. He unfolded what looked to be a large silver tablecloth.

"Space blanket," he explained with a smile. "Good for holding in the heat. Thought one of you might need it. Dr. Grissom, if you could give me a hand. . . ."

Grissom took one side, Maher the other, and the pair covered the corpse.

"This will help preserve the site," Maher said. "Once the snow stops we can investigate the scene."

"But it'll be under two feet of snow by then," Sara pointed out.

Maher gave her a lopsided grin. "And that's a bad thing?"

"Of course!"

His smile straightened out and widened. "Ms. Sidle, I know a few tricks—if we were in the desert, wouldn't you?" Then a gust of snowy wind blew through, and seemed to carry off Maher's smile. "I don't want this man's killer to get away any more than you do."

Grissom surprised her by putting a hand on her shoulder. Sara stared at the fingertips touching her coat. She tried to analyze her feelings, but suddenly felt paralyzed. Then, with the wind picking up to a near howl, she heard Grissom's voice from what sounded like far away. "Whoever did this won't get away from us."

"Now," Maher said, "I need you to take the long way out of here—back the way you two must have come, judging from the tracks."

Finally, Cormier handed over the rifle to the constable. "Sure I can't talk you out of this lunacy?"

"Positive. Just remember, I need you to bring one of them back here to relieve me."

Nodding, Cormier said, "All right, but it's crazy."

Maher turned to Grissom. "I know you two don't have much experience with winter, but we're going to have to guard this scene until the snow stops."

Sara stepped up. "All night?"

"However long it takes."

Grissom said, "Makes sense. Two-hour shifts sounds good. I'll come up next, then Sara."

Maher nodded.

Cormier said, "We better get going—be dark soon, and we don't want to spend those two hours getting down to the hotel."

Maher took a small black box out of his coat pocket. "GPS," he said.

Sara knew that it would be easier for them to find this spot again with the use of Maher's global positioning unit.

"That's a small one," she said, admiringly.

"Yeah, brand new, eh? Just breakin' it in." He punched a few buttons and handed the gizmo to Grissom. "Use this to find your way back," the Canadian advised.

"Anything else?" asked Grissom.

"Yeah, bring coffee on the return trip—for me and you."

Sara asked the Canadian, "Any suggestions for when we get back to the hotel?"

"Check around the buildings for footprints. If the killer or killers went all the way down this slope, they had to come out somewhere. If they went straight down, the tracks'll probably start around the back of the building."

"All right," Grissom said.

Cormier seemed to be working hard to keep his back to the corpse, even though the space blanket and the beginnings of a layer of snow already covered it. And when Maher gave him the high sign to start back up the trail, Cormier was obviously eager to go. Sara and Grissom dropped in behind him.

"How do we know," Sara asked Grissom quietly, making sure Cormier, whom they'd lagged behind somewhat, couldn't hear, "that we can trust Maher?"

"We don't."

"Then why . . . ?"

"If we accept him at face value," Grissom said, "he's a real boon to us—an expert on winter crime scenes, which we're not."

"Granted. But, not counting us, he and Mr. Cormier were the first on the scene . . . making them suspects."

"Well," Grissom said, "if we've left the murderer behind with the body of his victim, he will try to cover his tracks . . . and not just with snow."

"You mean . . . he'll give himself away."

"Yes. We didn't mention that you'd taken extensive

photos of the victim and the crime scene, before he and Mr. Cormier got there."

Sara smiled slyly at her boss. "And we won't mention it, will we?"

Grissom answered with a smile and a shake of the head, and as they trudged after Cormier, toward the towers of the hotel, their cozy, shared conspiracy almost made her feel warm.

Almost.

4

Seated on a stool in a musical equipment shop on Tropicana Avenue, Warrick Brown strummed the C.F. Martin DSR guitar, forming a mellow C major 7 chord.

"Sweet," Warrick said. "How much you say, again?"

Sitting on a Peavey amplifier nearby in a MUSIC GO ROUND tee shirt, Mark Ruebling stroked his chin thoughtfully. "They're going for $2,499 new . . . I can let you have that beauty for $1,400."

The shop had opened a little over four months ago, and Warrick had been one of the first customers through the door. Always on the lookout for good musical gear, he'd liked how Ruebling, the owner, gave him fair value for trade-ins and didn't try to gouge on new items.

Like the DSR Sugar Ray, for example, a solid-body mahogany; Warrick knew—having been to the Martin company's website—that the store owner spoke the truth about the retail price. Still, nobody sold anything full retail these days, and fourteen hundred was a lot of green.

Warrick had been getting heavier and heavier into his music, partly because what had been the other great passion of his life—gambling—he now knew was a sickness. He already had an acoustic guitar, a decent, funky old Gibson he'd picked up in a pawnshop; but not one anywhere near as fine as this Martin.

"That's a tempting offer, Mark."

The store owner nodded, his chin still in his hand.

"But," Warrick said, "you know I been trying to deal with my temptations."

Ruebling smiled slyly. "Not all temptations lead to sin, my friend."

"True. But even at that price, it's a sinful lot of money for a public servant . . . How about I think on it, get back to you?"

"No problem. I'll hold it for you, few days. Just let me know what you want to do."

Now it was Warrick's turn to nod, playing it coy and low-key, when both of them knew damn well he'd end up taking the guitar. But maybe Mark would carve off another C note or so. . . .

And in the meantime Warrick could work on convincing himself that spending that much money wouldn't break him. Funny thing was, Warrick had never worried about having enough money back when he gambled. Like all degenerate gamblers, he always figured he'd win and then there would be plenty to spread around.

Reading his customer's mind, Ruebling said, "Seems to me, Warrick, cleaning up and livin' the straight life has turned you kinda conservative."

"Gotta be, with you so liberal with my money."

The two men exchanged smiles, as Warrick handed the guitar back to Ruebling, then checked his watch—time to head in.

Warrick liked how late the stores stayed open in this town—even a graveyard shift zombie like him could do a little shopping on the way to work. Growing up in Vegas made him prejudiced, Warrick knew, but there was nowhere else in the world he would rather live . . . even though with his gambling jones, no other place could be worse for him.

Generally Warrick showed up at CSI a half-hour early, with Nick maybe five or six minutes behind him. He went straight to the break room, poured himself a cup of coffee and strode to the locker room to change. The leather jacket he wore into work would never see a crime scene. He changed pullover sweaters as well, trading this month's tan one for last year's gray one.

Locker closed, he plopped onto the bench, sipped from his coffee and imagined himself in his living room playing that Martin acoustic. The thought gave him a warm feeling—like hitting twenty-one at blackjack. He closed his eyes and leaned back, his head resting against the cool metal of his locker.

"Asleep on the job already?" Nick's voice.

Keeping his eyes closed, Warrick said, "Let a man daydream."

"Is that possible on night shift? . . . What's she look like?"

"You must know, I'm playing my new guitar I haven't bought yet."

"Oh boy—the Lenny Kravitz fantasy again?"

Warrick opened one eye and looked up at Nick,

who stood over him with a smile on half of his face. "Now, Nick, don't be dissin' Lenny."

"I wasn't dissin' Lenny. I would never diss Lenny. . . . You, maybe. But not Lenny."

Warrick opened the other eye and couldn't stop from smiling. "You're gettin' an early start. . . . Seen Catherine yet?"

Nick shook his head, going to his own locker. "I came straight in here." He quickly changed shirts, then the two of them went off in search of Catherine Willows, currently their acting boss.

They spotted her moving briskly down the corridor just outside the layout room. Warrick took one look at her and thought, *If she can afford that wardrobe, I can swing that Martin.* Today—tonight—fashion-plate Catherine wore an oxblood leather jacket with a silk scarf of white, gold and maroon flowers. Nick fell in on one side of her, Warrick the other.

"Where we headed?" Warrick asked.

"Where is it always lively around here?" Catherine asked rhetorically.

"The morgue," Nick said.

"Right you are, Nick," Catherine said. "Our vic is still the only body of evidence we have . . . though that's about to change."

"I like change," Warrick said. "I'm in favor of change."

She brandished a file thicker than a Russian novel. "We've ID'ed our vic," she said, flashing a triumphant smile. "And you're never going to guess who she is."

"Gris doesn't let me guess," Nick said.

Warrick said, "Amelia Earhart?"

"Not that big a media star," Catherine admitted, as they walked along. "Does the name Missy Sherman ring any bells?"

"One or two," Nick said. "Missing housewife, right?"

"Had her fifteen minutes of infamy, a year or so ago," Warrick added. "She our ice queen?"

"She is indeed," Catherine said. "Missing Persons database coughed up her prints, this afternoon."

They stopped and she showed them a photo of the Sherman woman—it was their frozen victim, all right, and she was warmly beautiful, dark bright eyes flashing, pert-nosed, with a vivacious smile. Warrick had the sick feeling he often had, toward the start of a murder investigation, as he registered the reality of the human life, lost.

"So, then, day shift told the husband?" Nick asked.

"No," Catherine said, and put the picture away. She started walking again and Warrick and Nick fell in like nerds in a high school hallway tagging after the prom queen. "They're under the same OT restrictions we are—if it's night shift's case, it can wait till night shift."

"Jesus," Warrick breathed. "Guy's sitting at home, his wife's dead and nobody tells him 'cause of budget cuts?"

"We have to specifically request day shift help—in triplicate," Catherine said, with a humorless smile.

"I don't want to tell the husband," Nick said. "It's not CSIs' job to tell the husband."

Catherine nodded and her reddish-blonde hair shimmered. "I have a call in to Brass—we want to be there for that, though. Anyway, I want to go through the file one more time, before we have a look at Mr. Sherman."

They stepped into the anteroom of the morgue, the area where the CSIs would wash up and get into their scrubs, if an autopsy were going on. Warrick said, "You know the case, Cath? All I remember is, housewife evaporates, details at eleven."

"You're fuzzy on it," Catherine said, " 'cause Ecklie's people worked that one—Melissa 'Missy' Sherman, married, white female, thirty-three, no children. She and her husband, Alex, lived in one of those new housing developments south of the airport."

"Which one?" Nick asked.

"Silverado Development." She thumbed quickly to a page in the file. "Nine six one three Sky Hollow Drive."

"I lived in Vegas all my life," Warrick said, "and I have no idea where that is."

"Across from Charles Silvestri Junior High," Catherine said.

"Home of the Sharks," Nick put in.

Warrick and Catherine just looked at him.

"Football," Nick said, as if that explained it all.

"That's twisted, man," Warrick said, then asked Catherine, "was hubby ever a serious suspect in her disappearance?"

"Well, you know he was a suspect," Catherine said. The spouse always was.

"But," she continued, "serious? Let's just say Ecklie and the day shift detectives didn't find anything."

Warrick smirked humorlessly. "Ecklie couldn't find the hole in the doughnut he's eating."

"No argument," Catherine said, "but apparently this was a fairly mysterious missing persons case. That was part of why the media was attracted to the story—June Cleaver vanishes."

Warrick frowned. "And nothing at all on Ward?"

"They were college sweethearts at Michigan State, got married and moved out here when Alex Sherman graduated from college. Missy finished her finance degree at UNLV."

"Maybe they're not Ward and June," Nick said. "Maybe they're Barbie and Ken."

Catherine shrugged. "Looks like a perfect life, till the day she and her girlfriend went out shopping and for lunch, after which Missy was expected to drive straight home."

"Instead, she drove into the Bermuda Triangle," Warrick said.

Nick asked, "Wasn't the car found?"

Catherine nodded. "In the parking lot at Mandalay Bay, a 2000 Lexus RX300. That's an SUV. She and her friend ate at the China Grill . . . then poof."

Nick's eyes narrowed. "You mean, she never even made it to the car?"

"Oh she got that far. Ecklie's people found a doggy bag in the Lexus. But after that . . ." Catherine held her hands up in a who-knows gesture.

The trio found Dr. Robbins behind his desk, where he was jotting some notes; he looked up as they neared.

"Hey Doc," Catherine said. "Got ya an ID on Jane Doe."

Robbins gave her a satisfied smile. "Melissa Sherman. We've met."

Catherine frowned. "Did somebody call you with the missing persons info?"

The coroner's smile expanded. "No. Some of us are just good detectives."

"You figured out this was Missy Sherman?" Warrick asked. "Where do you keep the Ouija board?"

"In her stomach," Robbins said. "That is, the clue was in her stomach. And what's interesting is, it gives us a more reasonable window for time of death. Freezing or no freezing."

Catherine was nodding, half-smiling, as she said, "Let me guess—Chinese food."

Robbins tapped the tip of his nose with his index finger. "Undigested beef and rice in her stomach. When she was killed, the body stopped working and the freezing kept the contents from decomposing."

"And the Chinese food led you to Missy Sherman how?" asked Warrick, not sure whether he was annoyed or impressed.

"It reminded me of the doggy bag they found in her car when the Sherman woman went missing. I checked the original evidence report and it stated Missy Sherman's doggy bag contained Mongolian beef and rice. That, in turn, prompted me to recall we'd gotten a copy of her dental records when she first disappeared . . . just in case, you know, a body turned up, as it too often does in these cases . . . and I just finished matching those dental records to the body you brought in yesterday."

"Wow," Nick said. "Good catch, Doc."

"You are the man," Warrick admitted. "And now nobody can say we don't have a homicide."

Catherine already had her cell phone in her hand. She punched the speed dial and waited. After a few seconds, she said, "Jim, it's Catherine. We've ID'ed the body from Lake Mead: Missy Sherman—that missing persons case from—"

She waited while Brass spoke, then looked at her watch, and said, "You want to go at this hour?"

Brass said something else, then Catherine said, "All right—we'll meet you there."

Punching the END button on her phone, she turned to Warrick and Nick. "Brass was out on a call. He'll meet us at the Sherman place."

Before long, they were turning right off Maryland Parkway onto Silverado Ranch Boulevard; then the Tahoe swung into the Silverado Development and followed a maze of smaller streets back to Sky Hollow Drive, a neighborhood peaceful under a starry sky with a sliver of moon, asleep but for a few windows flickering with TV watching, and Warrick could've sworn he could hear the muffled laughter from the Conan O'Brien show audience.

A handsome mission-style stucco, 9613 was a tall, wide two story with a tile roof that seemed more pink than orange under the mercury-vapor streetlights. Large inset windows were at either end of the second floor with a smaller window, a bathroom maybe, in the center. A two-car garage was at left, flush with the double archways of a porch at right, leaving the dark-green front door in shadows.

For so nice a home, the lawn was modest—true of all the houses in the development—and had turned brown for the season, though evergreens along the porch provided splashes of green while blocking the view of the front-room picture window, whose drapes were shut, though light edged through. An upper-floor window, with closed curtains, also glowed.

The temperature again hovered around the forty-degree mark, just crisp enough to justify Warrick and Nick putting on CSI jackets. Brass, in his sportscoat, didn't seem to notice the chill; this was typical of the detective, Warrick knew, as the man had spent a large chunk of his life in New Jersey, where a winter like this would rate as tropical.

They did not go up to the front door immediately. Instead, the detective and the three CSIs stood in the street next to the black Tahoe parked behind Brass's Taurus, and got their act together.

"What do we know about this guy?" Nick asked.

"I remember this case," Brass said. "I wasn't on it, but I sat and talked to the guys working it, often enough."

"What did they say about Sherman?" Warrick asked.

Brass shrugged. "Guy did all the right things—full cooperation, went on TV, begged for his wife to contact him or, if she was kidnapped, for the kidnappers to send a ransom demand. You probably saw some of that."

Nick was nodding.

With a shake of the head, Brass said, "They say Sherman seemed genuinely broken up."

"What does your gut say?" Warrick asked the detective.

"Just wasn't close enough to it to have a gut reaction. But in the car, on the way out here, I called Sam Vega—he caught the case, was lead investigator."

They had all worked with Detective Sam Vega when he did graveyard rotation. He was a smart, honest cop.

Catherine asked, "What did Sam have to say?"

"Well," Brass said, "at first, as convincing as Sherman seemed, Sam figured this was a kidnapping . . . but then when no ransom demand came in, he started looking at the husband again."

"Was Mrs. Sherman unhappy in her marriage?" Nick asked. "Could she have just run off, to start over someplace?"

Brass shook his head. "By all accounts she was a happy woman with a happy life, and if she was going to run off, why leave a doggy bag in the car?"

"People rarely carry leftovers into their new life," Catherine said.

Brass went on: "If she did run off, consider this: Missy Sherman took no money, no clothes, never called anyone from her cell phone, never e-mailed anybody—this woman just flat out disappeared, and didn't even bother with the puff of smoke."

"So she didn't run off," Warrick said.

"Anyway," Brass went on, "the longer this case dragged on, the harder Vega looked at the husband. This guy came up so clean, water beaded off him."

Catherine asked, "What was Sam Vega's bottom line on the husband?"

"Sam says Sherman seems like a right guy, who hasn't done anything weird or different or outa line, since Scotty beamed the poor bastard's wife to nowhere. No new girlfriend, no attempt to collect on the wife's life insurance policy, which wasn't that substantial, anyway—nothing."

"How'd he pay for that hacienda?" Warrick asked, with a nod toward the formidable stucco house.

"Very successful computer consultant," the detective said. "He's got some real estate too."

Nick asked, "What kinda real estate?"

"Apartments. Sherman makes good money. Pretty much pool the four of our salaries, and you got his annual income."

They stood there, contemplating that.

Then Catherine said, "Maybe we better stop loitering in the street before somebody in this nice quiet neighborhood calls the cops about the riffraff."

They followed Brass to the dark-green front door of the Sherman home; the four of them barely fit on the shallow porch. From the living room, they could hear voices—loud, animated.

"Movie," Nick said.

"Sounds like *Bad Boys*," Warrick said.

"Bad what?" asked Brass, wincing.

"*Bad Boys*," Nick said. "You know, Will Smith, Martin Lawrence—they're cops . . ."

"If they're cops," Brass said, "I'm a police dog."

Warrick and Nick exchanged he-said-it-not-us glances.

Smirking sourly, Brass turned back to the door.

Warrick was listening to the sounds from within. "That's a high-end sound system. He's watching a DVD."

"I'll be sure to put that in my report," Brass said, and rang the doorbell.

They waited. The loud movie voices ceased, then a few seconds later the door cracked open; one brown eye behind one wire-framed lens peeked cautiously out. "Yes?"

Brass held up his badge on its necklace. "Mr. Alex Sherman?"

The eye narrowed, examining the badge; then the door swung open wide, revealing another eye and the rest of his wire-framed glasses, and the rest of him.

Alex Sherman—six-two, easily, and in his mid-thirties—wore his black hair short, razor cut, and with his high cheekbones, dark brown eyes and straight nose he had a vaguely Indian look, though he was only moderately tanned. In his stocking feet, he wore gray sweatpants and a green tee shirt with a white Michigan State logo; his build said he worked out.

"What can I do for you, Detective?"

"May we come in?"

Sherman motioned for them to enter, eagerly, saying, "It's about Missy, isn't it? Is it about Missy?"

They stepped into a foyer with a small, round table next to the door and a framed black-and-white photo of Missy Sherman on top of it.

"Is there somewhere we can sit down, Mr. Sherman?" Brass asked evasively.

Anxious, Sherman led them to the right into a living room smaller than the Bellagio casino, though Warrick would've needed a tape measure to be sure. A massive wide-screen plasma TV monitor hung on the far wall; beneath it a small cabinet held stereo and video components with speakers scattered strategically around the room. A tan leather sofa ran under the picture window, its matching chair and hassock angled toward the television; to the right of the sofa was an easy chair in rough fabric with a faux Navajo design.

Sherman sat on the sofa, Brass next to him, while the others fanned out in front of them. Brass quickly identified himself and the CSIs by name.

"This is about Missy," Sherman said, "isn't it?"

"I'm afraid so," Brass said. "We saw a light on upstairs—is someone here with you?"

"No—I turn that light on so I don't have to walk up to the bedroom in the dark. Now, what news do you have about my wife?"

Brass paused; he swallowed. "I'm sorry, sir. Your wife was found—"

"You've found her?" Sherman said, jumping in, dark eyes wide.

"Her body was found, Mr. Sherman. Early this morning by a park ranger at Lake Mead."

"She's dead," he said incredulously, clearly not wanting to believe it.

"She's dead, yes."

Sherman covered his mouth with a hand, and then the tears began. And then he flung his glasses to the end table beside him, hunkered over and began to sob.

Warrick looked at the floor.

Catherine handed the man a small packet of tissues. Warrick could only admire her—she was always prepared, wasn't she?

After perhaps thirty seconds, Sherman said, "Missy can't be . . . why, after all this time . . . ? I thought . . . I hoped . . . you hear about amnesia, and . . ."

More comments, only semicoherent, tumbled from him, but within another thirty seconds, the sobbing had ceased, and he seemed to have hold of himself.

Brass asked gently, "Is there someone you'd like us to call for you? You probably shouldn't be alone now."

Sherman's reply had building anger in it. "I shouldn't be *alone* now? I shouldn't have had to be *alone* for all these months, but I was! Why didn't you find her last year? Maybe she'd be alive! She would be here, with me. . . . Missy's everything to me. You people, you *people* . . . !"

Catherine stepped forward, hands raised before her. "Mr. Sherman—we're very sorry for your loss. It's not good for someone who's had a blow like this to be alone."

Sherman appeared startled that someone had interrupted his tirade, and in such a compassionate manner; and that brought him back.

In a low, trembling voice, he said, "I'm sorry . . . I'm really sorry. I shouldn't be angry with you. I'm sure you did everything you could. . . . Where's Detective Vega?"

"We're with the night shift," Warrick said. "Detective Vega works days, right now. He'll be informed, and I know he'll be concerned. I'm sure he'll talk to you."

Nodding, lip trembling, Sherman said, "He . . . He tried . . . tried very hard."

Then Sherman just sat there, collapsed in on himself, like a child trying not to cry.

How Warrick hated this part of the job. But he knew that Gris would only remind him that the CSIs worked not just for the victims, but for their loved ones. Warrick and his associates couldn't make the pain of losing a wife or a sister or a friend go away; but at least they could try to provide some answers and—

when the system worked the way it was supposed to—a modicum of justice.

Nick appeared from somewhere with a glass of water and handed it to Sherman, who took a short sip, then a longer drink. Hand shaking, he set the glass on the end table. "Thank you, Officer."

Nick just nodded.

"I love my wife very much," Sherman finally said. His voice had a quaver, but he had regained some composure. "And for a whole year I've had only questions with no answers. I just wanted Missy back alive. I should have known that after this long . . . Ever see that movie, with John Cleese?"

Brass frowned at the seeming non sequitur. "Sir?"

"He's trying to get somewhere and can't make it on time, just one damn thing after another . . ."

"Clockwise," Catherine said.

"Is that what it's called? Well, in that movie, John Cleese, he says, 'It's not the despair . . . I can handle the despair. It's the hope!' "

And Sherman began to laugh, only the laughter turned to tears again. But briefly, this time. "Like the big dope I am, I just kept hoping."

"In your position, we all would, Mr. Sherman," Catherine said. "We all would."

"And sir?" Warrick said. "You'll have plenty of time now, to come to grips with this. Don't beat yourself up."

Catherine glanced at Warrick, a bit of surprise in her expression, then said to Sherman, "You will make it through this. And, for what it's worth, we will be working very hard to find out who did this."

Sherman looked up at her, his forehead tightening. "You make it sound . . . She was killed?"

Brass said, "Yes, sir."

"Oh my God . . . oh my God . . ."

They let him cry. Warrick watched Catherine and Brass exchanging a series of looks that were a silent conversation about whether they should press on with any questioning, or if Sherman's grief made that impossible.

Brass seemed to want to stay at it. To give the man a chance to get himself together.

The tears slowed, then stopped. Sherman dried his face with some of Catherine's tissues. "There was a time when I . . . I can't believe I'm admitting this, but there was a time I actually wanted her to be dead."

Catherine said, "Mr. Sherman, you should—"

"If her body was found, that at least would mean the end of wondering. I sit here, sometimes all night, watching mindless movies, trying not to think where she might be. The later it was at night, the more horrible the possibilities. Now . . . now, that it's finally happened, I have a thousand questions, a million questions. Who would do this to Missy? *Why?*"

"This investigation is just starting," Brass said.

"It's not—You don't consider it just an old case that . . ."

"No. It's very much on the front burner. We hope to be able to answer some of your questions soon."

Swallowing hard, turning sideways toward the homicide cop, Sherman asked, "Was she . . . ? Did someone . . . ? Was . . . ?"

Brass didn't seem sure what Sherman meant, but

Catherine said, "She was not sexually assaulted, Mr. Sherman. She died of suffocation."

"Suffocation . . . Missy?" Leaning forward and grasping Brass's hands, startling the detective, Sherman implored, "Jesus Christ man, what can you tell me? Where has she been for the last year? Who had her?"

"She wasn't strangled, sir," Catherine said. "We're not sure of the circumstances, where her suffocation is concerned. But she was not strangled."

"And we can't tell you where she's been all this time," the detective said. "But she appears to have been killed shortly after she disappeared."

"You said . . . Lake Mead. A ranger found her?"

Brass nodded.

"But that's . . . such a public place!" Sherman was growing outraged again. "How could she not be found, in over a year?"

Catherine stepped forward, crouched in front of the man and touched one of his hands, as if he were a small child she were comforting. "We understand how difficult this is for you, Mr. Sherman. But even though your wife was killed over a year ago, the person who committed that crime—or some associate of the murderer—only this morning placed her body in the park. That makes this a very new, active case . . . and we need to get right to work."

Sherman swallowed, nodded. "Anything you need. Anything."

"Well . . . to begin with, we must ask you to go over this one more time. It's been a long time since anyone looked at your wife's case with fresh eyes. And since we didn't work the case before, maybe we can find something that got overlooked the first time."

Gazing at her, his eyes still damp, Sherman nodded that he understood. "Where do we start?"

Catherine rose and backed up a little, giving Brass some room as the detective took over again. "From the beginning," he said. He withdrew the small tape recorder from his sportscoat pocket, adding, "And with your permission, we'll record this interview."

Turning sideways again, to look right at the detective, Sherman said, "No problem, Detective uh—what was your name, sir?"

"Brass."

Sherman took several deep breaths; he had another long drink of water. Then he said, "Whatever you need. Ask whatever you need to."

"All right. You last saw your wife when?"

"Thursday, December 6, 2001. That morning, before I went to work."

"Was everything all right that morning?"

Shrugging as he said it, Sherman said, "Fine. Great. We were a happy couple, Detective Brass."

"Tell us about that morning."

"Well . . . Missy was going shopping with her friend Regan Mortenson; then they were supposed to finalize plans for the four of us to have dinner and a movie Saturday night."

"The four of you?"

"Missy and me . . . Regan and her husband, Brian."

"You two couples socialized frequently?"

Sherman nodded. "They've been our best friends for, oh . . . years. I don't think I would have made it through the last year without them. Regan's always stopping by to check on me, Brian and I have lunch, oh, twice a week, anyway."

"How and when did you meet them?"

"Missy and Regan went way back. Hell, they were sorority sisters at Michigan State—Tri Delts."

Warrick repressed a smile, reflexively remembering the old joke from his days at UNLV. Don't have a date? Tri Delt.

"After we moved out here," Sherman was saying, "Regan came out a year later. They weren't just sorority sisters, Missy and Regan, they really were like sister sisters. Anyway, Regan met Brian out here, and they got married."

"Brian Mortenson," Brass said, more for his own benefit than Sherman's.

"Yes. Great guy. Wonderful guy."

"And what does he do?"

"He's Events Coordinator for the Las Vegas Convention Center, sets up their programs and conventions . . ."

Heavy-duty job, Warrick thought.

Brass nodded. "And his wife?"

"Regan? She solicits funding for Las Vegas Arts."

"Is that a job, or volunteer work?"

"Volunteer."

"How long have you known Mr. Mortenson?"

"Oh, ten years, easily. . . . We met not long after Missy and I moved to Vegas. In fact, we introduced them, Regan and Brian. He and I were playing basketball at the health club we both belonged to; still do. He was sixth man at Bradley, Brian was."

Brass shifted on the couch. "Back to the day in question. You say Missy was here when you left for work."

"That's right."

"Presumably, then she went shopping with Regan."

"No presumably about it. Ask Regan—they went shopping, and had lunch together."

"And when did you first suspect something was wrong?"

"Almost immediately. From when I got home from work, I mean. If Missy wasn't planning to have supper, she'd have said something. And if there'd been a change of plan, she'd have called on the cell, or at least left me a note."

"So you were concerned."

"Well . . . not overly. Didn't get too worried at first. Her car wasn't here, I figured she ran up to Albertson's for something."

That was a local grocery chain.

"Or maybe ran out to get some carry-out," Sherman was saying. "If she got too busy to fix supper, she'd sometimes stop for Chinese or Italian."

Brass nodded. "How long before you started to worry?"

Sherman considered that. "I waited . . . maybe an hour. Then I called Regan. She said she hadn't seen Missy since lunch. I couldn't think of where she might be."

"Then what?"

"I called our usual take-out places—they hadn't seen her. I started in on all of her friends that I could think of, and none of them had seen her, either."

"Is that when you called the police?"

"No. I called Regan again, to see what kind of mood Missy'd been in. Regan said normal, fine, real good spirits. And then the paranoia set in . . . I mean, we were happy, but we had our arguments."

"Such as?"

"Well, I'd been on her about credit cards; she was buying a lot of clothes. I handle the finances, and she was kind of, you know, irresponsible at times. I told all this to Detective Vega."

"You'd had words about it recently?"

"Not . . . words. We bickered about it, not the night before she disappeared, but the night before that. Still, that was enough to get me stewing. I even went upstairs to see if her clothes were still in the closet. You know, thinking maybe she'd left me or something—not for real, just ran to her mom's or one of her sister's in a huff maybe. But everything was there."

"Did you call her family? Her mother, her sisters?"

He nodded glumly. "None of them had heard from her."

"So, Mr. Sherman—when did you call the police?"

Looking a little uncomfortable, Sherman said, "I heard that you can't file a missing persons report until someone has been gone twenty-four hours."

Brass shook his head. "Not always the case."

Sherman shrugged. "Well, that's what I believed. . . . So I waited all that night and didn't call 911 until the next morning."

Her voice low, Catherine said to Warrick, "That's why day shift got it instead of us."

Brass was asking, "What did you do that night, while you waited?"

Sherman sat slumping, his hands loosely clasped. "I . . . tried to think of where she might go and went driving around looking for her car. First, the grocery store, Albertson's, the one over here on Maryland Parkway." He pointed vaguely off to his right. "If she was mad at me, maybe she was driving around the city, pouting. . . . She could pout, at times. So I just started driving around, all over the place. The Strip. I started with Mandalay Bay where she'd last been seen."

"That's where officers found her car," Nick put in, "the next day, right?"

Sherman nodded vigorously. "Yes . . . but I didn't see it there. Somehow I missed it."

Warrick noted this: the first real inconsistency, the only striking anomaly in the husband's story, so far.

"2000 Lexus," Brass said. "Nice car."

"You wouldn't think I could've missed it, but I did. In my defense, I was pretty worked up at this point . . . frantic. And it is a huge parking lot."

Brass nodded. "So, you just drove around all night?"

"Not all night. Only till about ten . . . and then I came home. I suppose I hoped that she'd've come home while I was out . . . but, of course, she hadn't."

"So what did you do then?"

"What I always do when I want to get my mind off my troubles—put in a movie." He sat up and a faint near-smile crossed his lips. "Missy and me, we're kind of movie buffs. . . . You can see the home theater here, pretty elaborate. We watched a lot of movies."

"So," Warrick said, "you just popped a DVD in and waited."

"Yes," Sherman said, looking up at Warrick. "I

didn't want to worry—I didn't want to be ridiculous. But I kept looking out the front window every five minutes to see if she was pulling up. At some point, I finally just dropped off to sleep. When I woke up and found she still wasn't home, I called 911 right away."

"Then the police took over," Brass said.

"Yes."

Brass said, "Thank you, Mr. Sherman," and clicked off the recorder.

"Is . . . is that it? Is that all?"

"Actually, Mr. Sherman," Brass said, "we would like to take you up on your offer to help."

"Certainly. . . . Anything at all."

"Good. Because I'd like to have our crime scene investigators take a look around."

Warrick winced—that was a poor choice of words, considering . . .

Sherman flushed. "Crime scene . . . ? Are you saying that after all I've been through, I'm a suspect, now? In my wife's murder?"

Brass began, "Mr. Sherman, please . . ."

His spine straight, his eyes wild, Sherman almost shouted: "You come to tell me she's dead after a year of me praying for a fucking miracle that she might be alive and I open up my heart to you and you have the goddamn audacity to accuse me?"

"Mr. Sherman, no one's accusing you of anything—" Warrick protested.

"It sure as hell sounds like it! Crime scene my ass!"

"Sir," Nick said, "we know it's been a year, and that things have changed, but we have to look."

"I don't have to let you," he said, almost petulantly. "You need a search warrant, don't you?"

"You don't have to let us," Brass acknowledged. "But I was taking you at your word, when you said you wanted to help."

For several long seconds, Sherman just sat there, his hands balling into fists that bounced on his knees; he was clearly struggling to decide what to do.

Catherine crouched in front of him again. "You loved your wife—we can all see that. But if there's so much as a shred of evidence in this house that might lead us to her killer, wouldn't you want us to find it?"

Slowly, the fists unballed. "Of . . . of course."

She kept her voice low, soothing. "Then let us do our job. We want to catch your wife's murderer as much as you want us to. But to do that, we need to examine everything pertinent to the case . . . and that includes this house. Unless you've gotten rid of her things, Missy's home will have a lot to tell us about her."

Sherman swallowed and sighed . . . and nodded. "I understand. I'm sorry I lost my temper. It's just . . ."

Catherine touched his hand. "No problem."

"And I haven't gotten rid of her things, I could never do that. Everything's exactly the way it was the day she left. I haven't moved so much as her toothbrush. I always hoped the door would open and she'd walk in and we'd just pick up from where we left off. . . ."

He began to cry again.

Several awkward moments crawled past, as the CSIs looked at each other, wondering if they should get started or not.

Then Sherman said, "If . . . if it will help, take all the . . . all the time you need. You won't be keeping me up. It's not like I'll be sleeping tonight."

Diving right in, Warrick asked, "I have to ask this, sir. Do you own a freezer?"

"Not a stand-alone freezer. Just the little one in the top of the refrigerator."

"Not a chest-style freezer, either?"

The man shook his head.

"Ever had one?"

"No." He looked curious about their questions, but pale, and Catherine could almost see him deciding he didn't want to know why they were asking.

They went out to the Tahoe and got their equipment; inside the house, they split up. Catherine took the bathroom and the master suite; they didn't want Sherman getting upset about one of the men pawing through Mrs. Sherman's things, so Catherine volunteered for that duty. While Brass talked informally with Sherman in the living room, Nick and Warrick divided up the rest of the house. Nick started in the kitchen, Warrick in the garage. As with most houses in Vegas, there was no basement.

Warrick didn't expect to find anything in the garage, really, at least not as far as the freezer was concerned. Even if Sherman had at one time had a freezer, and used it to freeze his wife, it would be long gone by now. But the criminalist did check the floor for telltale marks of a freezer or any other appliance having been dragged across; nothing. A small workbench with a toolbox atop it hugged the near wall. Warrick looked it over and checked the toolbox but again came up empty.

Missy's Lexus, returned by Ecklie's people months ago, sat on the far side, Sherman's Jaguar parked beside it. The garage had sheet-rock walls, a large plastic trash can and a smaller recycling receptacle in the corner nearest the double overhead door. One of those pull-down staircases led to a storage space above the false ceiling. Walking around the cars, Warrick saw some gardening tools and a lawn mower against the far wall.

The place seemed only slightly less sterile than a hospital. Shaking his head at the cleanliness, Warrick tried the door of the Lexus and found it unlocked. Even though the Chinese food had sat in the car for some time, the smell was gone. In fact, Warrick noticed, the car smelled new. Too new—it had been professionally cleaned. Looking down at the carpeting, then studying the seats closely, confirmed his diagnosis: the SUV was cleaner than the day it had left the showroom.

After closing the door, he walked around between the cars and pulled the rope for the pull-down stairs. He climbed the flimsy ladder, pulled out his mini-Mag and light-sabered it around the darkened storage space. A few cardboard boxes dotted the area, mostly close to the opening, and when Warrick touched them, they seemed empty.

Moving the beam from right to left, he paused occasionally, looked at something a little closer, then slid the light further along. Nothing seemed out of the ordinary. Putting the butt of the mini-Mag into his mouth, he leaned over and undid the folded flaps of the nearest cardboard box. Inside he saw the Styrofoam packing that came on either end of the DVD player he'd seen inside. The next box had held the receiver for the home theater system. It too contained only original packing. Warrick finished quickly and rejoined the others back inside.

The search had taken nearly two hours and they had nothing to show for it. As they packed up and prepared to leave, Warrick wandered into the living room where Brass and Sherman still sat. "Mr. Sherman, I take it you had your wife's car washed?"

Sherman started. "Why, yes . . . yes I did. At one of those places where they really give it the works. Did I do something wrong? The other officers told me I could, they said they were finished with the Lexus and it was covered with what they said was fingerprint powder. I mean, the car was really filthy."

Warrick nodded. "You didn't do anything wrong, sir."

"You guys about ready?" Brass asked.

"Catherine's done and Nick's just putting the drain back together in the kitchen. We're done."

Brass rose and shook Sherman's hand. "I'm sorry for the intrusion, but I'm sure you understand. And we are very grateful for your cooperation."

"Whatever you need. Whenever you need it."

Catherine trooped in, looking beat.

Sherman sat up. "Any luck?"

Dredging up a smile, Catherine said, "Too soon to tell. Thank you again, sir."

All of them thanked their host and paid their sympathies, then followed Brass outside onto the sidewalk. The houses around them were dark now, and silent.

"Anything?" Nick asked Catherine, his voice a strained whisper.

She shook her head and, with her eyes, posed the same question of Warrick.

"Nothing," he whispered. "Can't blame him for wanting to wash the fingerprint crap and luminol outa his vehicle."

Nick was shaking his head, his expression discouraged. "A year's a long time," Nick said.

Brass heaved a sigh, then said, "I'll talk to the Mortensons tomorrow—maybe they can tell us something."

"It's no wonder we found ice inside Missy," Warrick said, "with a case gone this cold."

And they got in their vehicles and drove back to HQ.

5

WALKING SINGLE FILE THROUGH THE SNOW, HERM CORMIER remained in the lead, followed by Sara, with Grissom bringing up the rear. They had trudged through a winter landscape tinted blue by twilight, though by the time they could see the hotel again, night had swallowed dusk, and the lights of the wonderfully ungainly conglomerate of buildings glittered in the darkness as if the lodge were a colossal jewel box.

By the time they reached the back parking lot, Sara's breath was coming in short, raspy gulps. Despite the cold, she was perspiring, her hair lank and wet against her cheeks, forehead and nape of her neck, and inside her coat she could feel a trickle of moisture down her back. Mostly it was from the exercise of the forced march down the mountain; but some of it was excitement, nerves.

Less than a dozen cars were scattered about the mostly deserted lot, all of them covered by various depths of powder, ice particles sparkling back the reflected lights of the hotel. The snow showed no sign of letting up—if anything, it seemed to be coming down harder now, as if God couldn't wait to sweep their evidence under a gigantic white rug.

"Is Maher going to be all right out there?" Sara asked, as they stopped in the lot, convening in a little huddle. "Storm's getting worse. . . ."

"The constable knows what he's doing," Grissom said. "He's better suited to thrive under these conditions than we are."

With a chuckle, Cormier said, "Constable Maher lives in weather like this, Ms. Sidle. . . . He'll be fine. We just don't want to leave him up there alone for too long a spell."

A spell? she thought. This guy was a fugitive from a Pepperidge Farm commercial.

Sara, who was usually game for anything in an investigation, was not looking forward to her own shift at the snowy crime scene. And she found it difficult to accept that the cold and snow would preserve the crime scene; she was glad to have those photos to fall back on, digital or not.

"Any idea how long this'll keep up, Mr. Cormier?" Grissom asked, looking up into the falling snow, white shimmering along his eyelashes.

Squinting up into the snow himself, the hotel man said, "Storm like this'll usually blow itself out, oh, in a day or so . . . no more'n two."

"What happens to the conference?" Sara asked.

Shaking his head, flinging snow, Cormier said, "It may be just you two and Constable Maher. Not many were coming in early . . . instructors like you folks mostly . . . and those that come in today on later flights, well they sure as H aren't gonna join us. Only a few other guests got here before the downfall commenced . . . but when we get inside, I'll check the register, just the same."

"You don't expect anyone to trail in tomorrow," Grissom said.

As if the storm had its own answer for Grissom, a howl blew through the parking lot, stirring up a new storm of snow.

"We won't see anyone else make it in for at least twenty-four hours . . . unless it's by sled or sleigh."

Grissom wiped moisture from his face and asked: "Did anyone leave, after the storm started?"

Cormier shook his head again. "Can't rightly say—guests usually check out no later'n one or one-thirty, but somebody mighta had somewhere to go tonight, in town maybe, and when the snow started, tried to beat the storm to where they were goin'."

"You can check, though."

"I'd have to—I don't know who come and went, while we were in the woods."

"The victim could've been a guest."

"That's a fact."

Sara said, "And the killer or killers may well still be in the hotel."

Cormier said, "Seems reasonable, too. Don't cherish the thought, but I can't rightly argue with it."

"You have neighbors?" Grissom asked. "Anyone live in a cabin nearby, for example? Is there a private home tucked away up here?"

"No. The hotel owns all this land—everything your eye can see, Mr. Grissom."

Glancing around at the billowing storm, Grissom said, "My 'eye' can't see much right now, Mr. Cormier."

"Well, if the sun was shining, and I made that statement, it'd still be no exaggeration."

"Any of the staff live on the premises?"

"Only my wife and me—rest're in New Paltz, and drive up here to work. Just before we went lookin' for you two, I let the bellboys and the housekeeping staff go on home . . . and I'm pretty sure none of the night shift even tried to make it in."

Grissom glanced at Sara, then said to the hotel manager, "Who does that leave, Mr. Cormier?"

"Well, let's see. . . . Me and the Missus, Jenny, the desk clerk, Mrs. Duncan, the head cook, and maybe two or three more of the kitchen staff, maybe a dozen or so other guests, and the three of you."

The wind wailed.

"We have to consider them all suspects," Sara said.

"It's not as many as I thought we might be dealing with," Grissom admitted. His gloved hands were in the pockets of the black varsity jacket. "But questioning them indiscriminately won't get us anywhere."

Sara nodded, sighing, "We could use Brass about now, couldn't we?"

Cormier, not understanding, said, "Oh I wouldn't say that, Ms. Sidle—I got the utmost confidence in you folks . . . and the constable, of course."

Grissom smiled a little and said, "Thank you, Mr. Cormier. But what Sara means is, interrogation isn't our strong suit. We follow the evidence."

"Although if it leads us to a suspect," Sara said, "we

will interrogate that person, to the best of our abilities. It's just not our specialty." Then she turned to Grissom and said, "Trouble is, the evidence is two miles that way . . ." She pointed up the mountainside. ". . . under a foot of snow."

Grissom twitched a smile. "Some of it is. But that's not the only evidence. . . . The killer got to that body the same way we did—he walked."

"Or killers," Sara reminded him. "We saw two sets of tracks coming and going before they got buried, too. That is, two sets besides the victim's."

Grissom nodded. "And from what direction were the tracks coming?"

"Well, right down here." Sara thought back, imagined the footprints she'd photographed. She could have checked on her digital Toshiba, but she did not want to reveal to Cormier that she had the camera with her. "There were three sets, the victim and the other two."

"Go on," Grissom said.

"Probably pretty close to the route we took to get back. As if they came straight up from this rear entrance."

"So what should we be doing now?" Grissom asked.

"Looking for boot or shoe prints."

Moving carefully, Grissom and Sara started toward the edge of the lot that bordered the incline. Sara had gone barely ten feet across the lot when Grissom said, "Whoa, Sara . . . don't step down."

She froze (not hard in this weather), with her foot hovering just above the snow.

"There's an indentation just under your boot," Grissom said, making his way toward her, watching his own steps carefully. "These prints have almost filled in—hard to spot."

"I'm gonna lose my balance here!"

"Just put your foot down to the left—a good six or seven inches, please."

Sara did so. Grissom, at her side now, pointed to a series of the indentations—they were so nearly filled in, she had missed them; the snow coming down— and the accumulation the occasional wind gust was blowing around—had been no help, either.

Sara nodded that she saw the prints, then said, "We need to mark these!"

"And fast," Grissom said.

"What can we use?"

Cormier said, "I'll be right back! You two wait here."

When Cormier had disappeared inside the hotel, Grissom said, "Quick—snap photos."

Sara understood immediately—Gil wanted the photos but didn't want the hotel manager, who was still a suspect, to know that she had a camera. She was having trouble seeing the indentations but Grissom would guide her; and once he had, she'd see the print immediately. Her flash did well by her and, despite the darkness and snowfall, she got decent shots. Idly she wondered if digital photos were admissible as evidence in New York State.

For a guy in a coat too light for the heavy weather, Grissom hardly seemed to be feeling the effects of the cold. To Sara, the man seemed like he always did when he was working—content.

Finally, Grissom said softly, furtively, "Put it away."

Cormier—who'd been gone less than five minutes—stood at the edge of the parking lot, brandishing a handful of metal rods.

"My tomato stakes!" the old boy called, clearly proud of himself. "Got them from the toolshed!"

Grissom directed Cormier on a route to join them without disturbing the footprints. He handed over the tomato stakes and helped them plant one near each footprint, though the tracks were barely visible now.

When that task was complete, Grissom pointed to a blue Pontiac Grand Prix, perhaps a decade old, in the far corner of the lot. "That vehicle's got less snow on top, and more snow underneath, than the others."

"Nice catch," Sara said.

"That's our last arrival. You know who owns that car, Mr. Cormier?"

"Amy Barlow's ride—she's a waitress, here." He checked his watch. "She came in a little early—probably wanted to beat the weather. She's never missed a day. Hard worker."

Grissom led the way over to the car. The vehicles on either side were top-heavy with snow; the Grand Prix wore only a shallow hat of snow. A path of divots led from the driver's door to . . . nowhere, really. Grissom couldn't find any tracks—they'd all filled in.

"Maybe she's the last to arrive," Sara said, finding a few indentations near the rear entrance. "But she's been here long enough for her footprints to fill almost completely in."

"Could have seen something interesting," Grissom said.

Sara tilted her head. "Like somebody leaving in a car, maybe?"

"Or a person or persons, trudging up that slope, perhaps."

Picking up the thread, Sara said, "Or down it."

Grissom beamed at Cormier. "Name was Amy Barlow, was it? Now Amy is someone we do need to talk to."

"Not a problem," the hotel manager said. "But, uh . . . we're not going to just barge in and announce there's been a murder, are we?"

Grissom and Sara exchanged glances—admissions on both their parts that neither had considered this, as yet. Again, that was Jim Brass's bailiwick.

Grissom seemed gridlocked; Sara decided to carry the ball.

She said, "If we don't inform the guests and staff, and someone else dies, aren't we at least partially responsible?"

"Legally, you mean," the hotel manager said, keenly interested, "or morally?"

Suddenly the old man didn't sound like Pa Kettle; she was starting to think his cornpone patter was strictly color for the rubes.

"Possibly both," Sara said.

Grissom was nodding. "On the other hand, the killer or killers don't know that we know a murder's been committed . . . and we might be able to do a little investigating on the QT without tipping our hand."

"You mean, if the perps aren't aware that someone's investigating them, that puts the guests and staff in less jeopardy."

"And us in a better position to uncover evidence. The only exception would be if we're talking about a murderer poised to strike again . . . a serial killer or a multiple murderer with an agenda. Revenge murders against jury members, for instance."

Grissom was sounding like he was the one who'd been reading Agatha Christie.

"That strikes me as statistically unlikely," Sara said.

"I'd have to agree, Sara."

"Excuse me," the hotel manager said, "but don't I get a vote?"

They both looked at him.

"I don't think any good comes from scaring the be-jesus out of the people in there." He yanked a thumb toward the looming hotel. "I mean, they're stuck here, no matter what. And we don't even know for sure that the killer's in there. Or killers."

"Good point," Grissom said.

"And as for any litigation that might arise," Cormier said, a city savvy showing through the country-speak again, "I'd have more exposure if I panicked these folks, and if they went running off in the storm . . ."

Grissom flicked half a smirk. "A different kind of exposure would become an issue."

"What are we going to do?" asked Sara.

Glancing down at his watch, Grissom said, "It's almost dinnertime. Let's go inside and get warmed up."

"And we say nothing about the murder," Sara said.

"Not just yet." He turned to the hotel man. "Mr. Cormier, can you make sure that Amy Barlow is our waitress tonight?"

Cormier, whose relief at Grissom's decision was obvious, said, "That shouldn't be hard. None of the other waitresses probably made it in."

Grissom shot hard looks at both Sara and the hotel owner. "Right now, we need to just keep our wits about us . . . and process the evidence as soon as we can."

"That evidence is all ruined," Sara said glumly. "That crime scene's a joke . . . an unfunny one."

Grissom bestowed her a quiet smile. "Don't be so sure, Sara. Constable Maher's been working winter crime scenes a long time. There's tricks to this weather . . . just like we work our own magic in the desert."

Working a desert crime scene was, after all, one of the topics they would have been discussing at the conference. So Grissom made a valid point—as usual. For the first time since they'd stumbled onto that murder scene, Sara felt hopeful.

"Now," Grissom said, turning his attention to the hotel man, "what can we do about getting the authorities here?"

Cormier shook his head. "Lived here all my life, and this is all too familiar. . . . By now the roads are closed, phones are probably dead, and we'll be lucky if our power lasts through the night."

Sara got out her cell phone. "What's the state police number?"

Cormier told her, and she punched it in.

All she got was a robotic voice informing her that her call could not be completed; she reported as much to Grissom.

"When God decides to give technology the night off," Cormier said, "ain't a thing a man can do about it."

Grissom frowned, curiously. "Who said that?"

"Well, hell, man," Cormier said. "I did! Just now."

Sara said, "I'll keep trying."

Grissom said, "Good—in the meantime, we're agreed on how to proceed?"

Sara and Cormier both nodded. Sara didn't like the hotel owner knowing what they were up to; he was, after all, still a suspect. But she felt sure Grissom was keeping that in mind, lulling the man into a false sense of security.

Sara said to Grissom, "Let's get you inside, already. You look like the frostbite poster boy."

Snow clung to his hair, his eyebrows, and both his cheeks and ears were tinged red. "All right," he said, obviously oblivious to how he felt, much less looked.

Twenty-five minutes later, Sara—having treated herself to a quick hot shower and a mug of hot chocolate, courtesy of the coffee machine in her room—felt like a new woman (or anyway, a thawed one) and ready to begin their investigation anew. She pulled on a brown long-sleeved crewneck tee shirt and tugged on tan chinos. Over the tee, she climbed into a tan-and-brown wool sweater. Then she bopped down to Grissom's room and knocked on the door.

Again she waited, but nothing happened. She knocked harder, and this time Grissom opened the door and stepped into the hall, his gloves in one hand and a stocking cap in the other.

"Cormier donated this to me," he said, by way of greeting, holding up the cap.

"You'll need it," she said. "You smell good—what cologne is that?"

His eyes tightened as he processed the question.

Then he said, "Thanks . . . it's aftershave," and pulled the door shut.

In the elevator, Grissom said, "Cormier seems fine, but be discreet around him."

"Sure. If the victim turns out to be local, that makes him a prime suspect."

"Constable Maher's on the suspect list, too."

Sara studied Grissom's profile, but nothing was to be learned there. She said, "But what motive would a CSI from Canada have to kill somebody in upper New York State?"

He turned and gave her that maddening smile. "We discover two sets of tracks, Sara, moving away from the murder victim . . . and we hear shots. Soon after, we find a burned body with a fatal bullet wound . . . and shortly after that, two men walk out of the woods . . . one with a firearm."

"I still don't see what possible motive a Canadian constable would—"

"Everything we know about Maher, either Cormier or Maher himself told us. That his name is Maher, that he's a constable, that he's from Canada and so on. They could be in this together."

For a moment, it was as if Grissom had punched her in the stomach. Then she managed, "Where does that leave us?"

His smile turned angelic. "Well, for one thing, we're left with photos of the crime scene that neither suspect knows about."

A high-ceilinged chamber of dark carved wood in the Victorian manner, the lobby had an elegant old world feeling with the expected lodge ambience. The far wall was mostly a picture window that looked out at the snow falling on the frozen lake, beyond which rose rocky ledges and towering evergreens, surreally semivisible in the blend of blizzard and night; it was partly blocked by a tall, narrow, well-trimmed Christmas tree. Five people—Herb Cormier and four individuals Sara assumed to be among the guests—stood before the picture-postcard-like vista, watching the lovely, terrible storm.

To Sara's left stretched the front desk, attended by Jenny, the busty, redheaded female clerk who'd assured her the snow would let up soon. The desk clerk smiled and waved. Clearly perplexed by this gesture, Grissom raised a hand waist-high in response, much the way a Roman emperor might reluctantly acknowledge a subject; Sara, who would like to have throttled the woman, forced a smile.

The wall at right was dominated by a massive wood-and-brick roaring fireplace; above a mantel decorated with pine tree boughs hung a large framed oil painting of Mumford Mountain House in the summer season. Spread out before the fire on an oriental carpet were various velvet-covered settees, overstuffed couches and leather chairs, crouching between tables covered with well-thumbed magazines and vintage books. Three more guests sat reading by the soft yellowish light of tabletop lamps.

Herm Cormier—in a rust-colored corduroy jacket over a buttoned-to-the-neck white shirt, blue jeans and boots—caught their reflection in the picture window, turned and came quickly over to them, meeting them at the edge of the chairs and sofas.

In a voice barely above a whisper, he said, "Lookin' out that window, the world's so peaceful, so pretty—can't hardly believe what happened."

Not interested in such ruminations, Grissom asked, "Who else is here from the forensics conference?"

"Just you two and the constable. . . . Everybody else couldn't get into the airport in Newburgh, and of course some folks weren't comin' in till tomorrow, anyway. The phones've been out for a good hour, now, so we're not sure exactly what's what, in a lot of cases."

"Have you arranged for that waitress, Amy Barlow, to wait on us?"

"I've told my wife Pearl, she's the hostess. Amy's the only waitress made it in, though we do have a waiter workin'." Cormier looked Grissom over. "You're dressed warmer, I see—you look like you can survive a few hours out there. . . . I'll get my things and meet you in five or ten minutes. Here in the lobby?"

"No," Grissom said. "I'll be with Sara in the dining room."

"Fine with me," Cormier said, and took off toward the check-in counter, disappearing behind it, through a door marked HOTEL MANAGER—PRIVATE.

Sara and Grissom followed the arrowed DINING ROOM signs past the lobby down a hallway lined with framed photos of Mumford Mountain Hotel staff and management dating to roughly the beginning of time. At the end of the hall, to the left, was a wide stairway to the dining room.

The Victorian theme continued in the expansive restaurant, with its open-beamed two-story ceiling and scores of tables with white linen cloths and hardwood chairs, the quiet elegance of a bygone era reflected in the "M"-engraved sterling flatware and green monogrammed china. With only a handful of diners, the hall seemed absurdly large, the chandeliers bathing the all-but-empty chamber in soft yellow light, as if Sara and Grissom had wandered into an abandoned movie set on some vast soundstage.

They waited as the hostess showed another couple to a table. Heavyset, in her early sixties, her gray hair in a short shag, the hostess wore a midcalf gray knit dress dressed up by a white-and-red corsage, and sensible black shoes.

She trundled their way, greeting them with a big, wide smile, bifocals on a cord draped around her neck. "Good evening, folks," she said, hands folded before her; she looked like a fifth-grade schoolteacher scrutinizing her new pupils.

Grissom just stood there, as if the woman had been speaking esperanto.

"I think you should have a reservation for us," Sara said. "Either under Grissom or Sidle."

The woman's only jewelry, Sara noted, was a watch and a wedding ring with a good-size diamond.

"You must be the folks Herm told me about," she said, extending her hand. "I'm Pearl Cormier—Herm's wife."

Grissom shook the woman's hand and said, "I won't be dining with you this evening, but I will have a cup of coffee with Ms. Sidle."

"Right this way," she said. She steered them to a table not too close to the other couple (the only other diners at the moment), and they sat down.

"We serve family-style," Pearl told Sara. "Your choice of meats tonight is fried chicken or medium-rare roast beef." With a knowing nod and a wink, she added, "Amy will be right with you."

They had expected Mrs. Cormier to know they wanted to talk to Amy; nonetheless, Sara glanced at Grissom, who also seemed to be wondering what else Herm had told the missus.

Sara sat with her back to the kitchen, Grissom on her right, the varsity jacket slung over his chair, the CSI windbreaker exposed. Sara had barely gotten her menu open before a cheerful voice chimed, "Hi, I'm Amy. I'll be your server tonight."

They smiled up at her.

Amy smiled back and said, "Frankly, I'm just about everybody's server tonight."

Sara laughed politely and, after a beat, so did Grissom.

Their prospective witness was tall and thin, in her late twenties, her dark hair tied into a loose ponytail that ran halfway down her back. Amy Barlow's smile revealed wide teeth stained yellow, probably by cigarettes. She wore black slacks and a black bow tie over a white blouse whose buttons were tested by an ample bosom. A gauze bandage encircled her left hand.

"Start you folks off with a drink?" she asked.

Pleasantly, Grissom asked, "What happened to your hand, Amy?"

She shook the hand like it still hurt. "Cut myself cutting up an onion—they're short in the kitchen tonight."

"You all right?"

She nodded. "It don't need stitches—but boy,

it . . . Listen, you're sweet to ask, only there are better subjects to whet your appetites. Take your drink orders?"

"Coffee, black," Grissom said.

"Hot chocolate," Sara said.

When Amy returned with their beverages, Grissom said, "I heard you were one of the last to get here tonight, before the storm closed the roads. Or was it still afternoon?"

As she gave Sara the steaming mug, Amy said, "Afternoon. Two-thirty or three, I guess. But it was getting pretty slick out even then."

"Lucky you made it in at all," Sara said, over the rim of her mug.

"Yeah, I wanted to beat the storm in; don't like missin' a night's work . . . I can use the money."

"I hear that," Sara said. "You were lucky nobody hit you, rushing home, when you were coming in."

"I did see a couple cars, and it made me nervous—didn't want any slidin' into me, that's for sure. Some of these guests, with rental cars, if they're from some part of the country where it doesn't snow, well!"

"We're from Vegas," Grissom said.

"You're dangerous, then!" the waitress said, with a good-natured chuckle. "You people who aren't used to winter driving, you're lethal weapons on wheels."

"Sounds like you almost got hit," Sara said.

"Not really. It wasn't on the mountain drive, anyway, it was down on the road between here and New Paltz. Anyway, you decided on choice of meat?"

Grissom explained he was only having the coffee, and Sara asked for just the vegetable dishes.

And off Amy went.

"We need to talk to Amy in depth," Grissom said. "One of those cars may have been driven by the killer."

"If so, then our perp is off the premises, and even if that waitress has a photographic memory and gives us a license plate number, what are we going to do about it? With the phone lines down and cells dead and . . ."

Grissom shrugged. "How did detectives solve cases before all the technology came along?"

Sara paused. "By observing. By asking questions."

"That's what we need to be doing."

"That and guarding our snowbound crime scene, you mean."

"My turn now," Grissom said. "Yours will come soon enough. . . . Remember, Sara, Sherlock Holmes was a scientist too."

"Grissom—Sherlock Holmes was a fictional character."

"Based on Joseph Bell—a scientist."

Amy brought a basket of rolls and breads and butter, and Herm Cormier seemed to materialize next to them, an apparition in a heavy parka, bearing two thermoses of coffee.

With a thin smile, the hotel manager asked, "Ready to rough it, Dr. Grissom?"

Grissom nodded, got up, slipped on his varsity jacket.

A few other guests had found their way into the dining room and Cormier kept his voice low, trying not to alarm the customers starting to fill the restaurant. "I'm on record that this all-night vigil with the . . . the thing . . . is a bad idea."

"Duly noted," Grissom said. Then to Sara, he said, "See you in two hours. In the lobby."

"If I'm not there," she said, "call my room—case I fall asleep."

Grissom nodded and the two men headed for the door, Cormier's voice far too loud as he said, "And if there's anything else we can do to make your stay more comfortable, you just let us know!"

Sara finished her veggie dinner—mixed vegetables and parsley potatoes (she figured she'd ingested a stick and a half of butter)—and chatted some more with Amy, but got no real information out of the waitress. Pushing any harder would've been too obvious—she and Grissom would eventually have to interrogate the woman, Sara knew.

As she indulged in a sliver of pecan pie, Sara watched Amy and a tall, thin waiter handle what little there was of a dinner rush. Amy worked the cluster of tables around where Sara was seated, and the thin, dark-haired waiter worked some tables toward the entrance. He too wore a white shirt, black bow tie and black slacks, and seemed to possess the same energy to please that inhabited Amy Barlow.

Back in her room, seeking a little privacy and maybe even some rest, Sara pulled out her cell phone—it paid to keep trying. She flipped through the local White Pages, and tried the county sheriff, the New Paltz P.D., the state patrol, and even the phone company, all with the same lack of success.

On a whim, she punched in Catherine's cell phone number. Surprisingly, the phone rang! . . . and Sara felt a little jolt shoot through her.

"Catherine Willows," the familiar voice said, a nice clear, strong signal.

"Catherine! It's Sara."

"Well, hi, stranger. I see on the Weather Channel you're getting some snow."

"Are we. And you're not going to believe what happened, here . . ."

"Yeah, well you're not going to believe the case you missed out on. You may be the one hip deep in snow, but we've got the frozen—"

And the line went dead.

Sara quickly hit redial and another familiar voice— the robotic one—returned with the news that her call could not be completed and to please try again later.

Though Grissom and Constable Maher were, technically at least, nearby . . . just up that slope . . . Sara suddenly felt very alone.

Usually a person who didn't mind a little seclusion, Sara Sidle found herself wishing she could speak to just one person beyond the world of Mumford Mountain Hotel. But, for now at least, that appeared impossible.

Heaving a sigh, Sara returned the phone to her purse, placed it on the nightstand and took a nap with the light on. In part this was because she didn't want to fall too deeply asleep, with the two-hour stint of crime-scene duty ahead of her. But it was also because, for some inexpressible reason, she didn't feel like being in the dark, right now.

Before they'd left the hotel, Cormier loaned Grissom a muffler, but as the two men trudged up the rocky slope through the snow—the hotel man again leading the way—the CSI kept the woolen scarf off his face. Cold or no cold, he had questions to ask.

Grissom had to work his voice up over the wind. "Mr. Cormier . . ."

"Call me Herm!"

"Herm, now that you've had some time—any idea who the victim was?"

"Be a long time," Cormier said, " 'fore I forget that sight."

They were taking the same circuitous route up the slope as they'd used getting down. Trodding behind the man, in the howling storm, Grissom had to strain to hear; but even without Mother Nature's wintry distractions, he'd have had trouble catching the man's words.

"The truth is," Cormier went on, "that poor bastard's body was just too badly burned for me to recognize! If that was my own brother, I don't know that I could tell you."

"I understand!" said Grissom, practically yelling to be heard over the wind. He picked up his pace and fell in alongside Cormier, but the old man was far more at ease with the weather and terrain, and Grissom really had to work to keep up. "How many of the staff are actually here?"

"Those I already told you about—Amy, Mrs. Duncan, the head cook, Jenny at the desk, Pearl and me."

"Didn't I see a waiter in the dining room?"

"Oh, Tony! Tony Dominguez. He's one of our best workers, even if he is a little . . ." He bent his wrist.

"Gay?"

The hotel manager smirked humorlessly. "Let's just

say Tony ain't the macho-est guy around. But he does a helluva good job for us."

"Any other staffer you might've overlooked?"

They plodded along and the wind picked up in intensity for about a minute and a half. Just when Grissom was wondering if Cormier had either forgotten or ignored the question, the hotel man said, "Bobby! Bobby Chester made it in. . . . Lunchtime fry cook! He's also Mrs. Duncan's dinner-hour helper."

Grissom did the tally: Cormier, his wife, Pearl, and five others. Seven.

The wind kicked back in and shrieked at them until Grissom was forced to cover his face and fall back behind Cormier and let any other questions wait. And he had plenty more, but the pitch of the path had turned more steeply upward and every lungful of air now came with some effort. For now, Grissom would concentrate on just getting up the hill again and reaching that snow-blanketed crime scene.

Finally, Cormier said, "This is it," though Grissom would never have known it. Between the drifted snow and the darkness, they might well have been on the moon. Nor could the CSI see the constable, anywhere. . . .

Cormier called out to the man, who yelled back: "Over here!"

They followed the Canadian's voice and soon saw what he'd been up to while they'd been gone. Maher had carved himself a nook out of the snow at the base of a tree and hunkered down for the wait. The constable had apparently anticipated that even with Cormier guiding Grissom, it would take the Vegas CSI longer than two hours to get back up here; in fact, they were pushing three.

Not that that seemed to have bothered the Canadian. He had the bearing of a man who enjoyed the solitude of the woods and winter, and, of course, he'd had Cormier's .30-06 if anything had tried to disturb his serenity.

"You kept busy!" Cormier said.

"Got to work just after you left," the Canadian said. "Thought I better, eh, before the light faded too much!"

Cormier poured Maher a cup of steaming coffee from one of the thermoses while Grissom played a flashlight over the area. He immediately noticed changes that Maher had made at the crime scene. The tips of four sticks poked up out of the whiteness, indicating that impromptu stakes had been driven into the snow, forming a ten-by-twenty-foot square.

"You want to explain the sticks?" Grissom asked.

Maher grinned as he sipped the coffee. "Happy to! Thanks for the coffee, Mr. Cormier—I was starting to think you fellas forgot about me!"

"Sorry we took so long," Grissom said, almost hollering over the wind. "The sticks?"

As Grissom pointed his flashlight at one of the stakes, now nearly buried in the snow, Maher explained, "I found two tiny tracks in the snow on either side of the body. Did you two see them?"

Grissom nodded. "Sara and I saw them, but I have no idea what they were." He did not mention that Sara had taken photographs. "Misses, maybe."

"That's exactly what they were," Maher said. "Missed shots."

"And now they're buried under all this snow."

Maher smiled. "You pick things up fast, Dr. Grissom."

Pursing his lips, Grissom said, "And somehow you're going to use these sticks to find those bullets?"

The constable nodded. "Yes, sir. Soon as the snow stops."

"How?"

"I'll explain it when I do it. I was going to give a demonstration on that very thing this weekend . . . but I guess you and Ms. Sidle will be the only ones to see it."

Grissom filled him in on the parking lot shoeprints.

"I'll take a look at 'em after I get warm," Maher said. "Ms. Sidle going to be all right, pulling her shift, or should I come up early to relieve her?"

"Don't come up here a minute early," Grissom said, "or you'll just be insulting her."

"She's a good man?"

"As tough and smart as any CSI anywhere. You try to baby her, she'll only resent it."

"Take your word for it."

"She'll probably deal with the cold better than me."

Maher nodded. "I'll relieve her after her full shift. In the meantime, here's the rifle." Maher handed the .30-06 over to Grissom.

"Any advice?"

"Yeah," Maher said. "Don't move around much. The more you move around, the more chance you'll disturb evidence. I don't mean to be insulting, Dr. Grissom, but snow is fragile. Right now, it's our friend."

"Preserving our evidence," Grissom said.

"Exactly. But it won't take much to turn it into a liability."

Cormier handed Grissom the second thermos of coffee. "You'll probably be wanting this."

Grissom nodded his thanks.

"Be my guest," Maher said and pointed. Grissom's flash followed, swinging around, and found the dugout next to the tree. "That'll keep you out of the wind. Keep your face covered."

"Got it."

Cormier said, "I'll be back in a couple of hours with Ms. Sidle. I'll give you plenty of warning, now . . . so don't you go pluggin' us!"

"Just yell good and loud," Grissom said. "Get your voice up over this wind!"

"No problem. But don't you be trigger-happy."

"Don't worry, Mr. Cormier, if I can't see it, I won't shoot at it." He gave them a rueful smile that they probably couldn't make out in the pitch darkness of the woods.

Several minutes later, Grissom was straining to see the departing pair; but they'd already disappeared into the snow. Depositing himself in Maher's hideaway against the tree, Grissom eased down, his back against the bark, and did his best to relax.

Two hours wasn't such a long span, a mere 120 minutes; still, Grissom knew that out here—where darkness meant black, and the neon-bright night of Vegas was almost a continent away—two hours could be a relative eternity. As snow continued to fall, Grissom, clutching both the rifle and the thermos of coffee, settled in.

If the snow would just stop around daybreak, they could get to work at this crime scene, and let Constable Maher demonstrate his bag of tricks. Grissom was always willing to learn something.

On the other hand, if Maher was a fraud, a killer in disguise, Grissom was more than willing to teach a lesson himself.

6

THE ONE THING LAS VEGAS DIDN'T NEED WAS MORE FLASHING lights. This town trying to dress itself up for Christmas, in the opinion of Captain Jim Brass, was an exercise in overkill. How did you decorate a city already adorned with millions of lightbulbs, a desert oasis that glowed like a three-billion ka-gigawatt Christmas tree all year round?

And yet they still tried. As he rolled by the Romanov Hotel and Casino in his police department Taurus, an elaborate flashing display spelled out Merry Christmas and Happy Hanukkah over flickering Nutcracker Suite images; and Santas and elves and reindeer, it seemed, danced Rockette-style on every casino's electric marquee. Brass shuddered to think what Glitter Gulch would be like—neon Santa hats on the towering cowboy and cowgirl? The nightly overhead laser display with Sinatra singing "Luck Be a Lady" shifted to "Jingle Bells," rolling dice traded in for mistletoe and holly?

The Taurus cut confidently through heavy evening traffic, Brass weaving in and out between rental cars with the gawking tourists and various vehicles bearing blasé locals headed to dinner or a movie, or homeward bound. Darkness had settled over Las Vegas, with the temperature once again falling precipitously toward the freezing mark. The cars with their headlights only added to the light show.

In the passenger seat, Nick Stokes lounged in his dark-brown sport shirt and lighter-brown chinos, looking dreamily out at the Strip. "Don't you just love Christmastime in Vegas?"

"Yeah," Brass said, "it's nice to have the place livened up a little. You clock in early? If so, end of shift, you better clock out the same way—Mobley hasn't approved this case for OT."

"I know that. I didn't clock in yet." Nick beamed at Brass. "I'm your 'Ride Along' buddy."

"You're my *what?*"

A tiny smile traced the CSI's square-jawed countenance. "You know how the sheriff has been encouraging citizens and police to have better interaction—through the Ride Along program?"

"Oh, please."

"Now, Captain Brass—like any other interested citizen, I'm entitled to a police 'Ride Along,' long as I meet the criteria and sign the waiver."

Brass just stared at his passenger, who finally pointed toward the windshield and said, "Jim—the road?"

The detective returned his attention to his driving and barely avoided clipping a minivan.

"And as a citizen," Nick added, "I must say I expected the police to observe better highway safety procedures."

"You're pushing your luck," Brass said, meaning with Sheriff Mobley.

"I've signed my waiver," Nick said, plucking a folded-up piece of paper from the breast pocket of his sport shirt. "And I've met the criteria by being duly interviewed by a member of the LVMPD."

"What member was that—Warrick Brown?"

"Your detective instincts never fail to impress, Captain. Yeah, Warrick interviewed me for the Ride Along program, and signed off. And I duly interviewed and approved him, too."

The detective shook his head again, and couldn't keep the smile from forming. "You guys are pushing it, I tell you."

"Like you wouldn't try this, if you had a case that needed the extra hours."

Brass grinned over at Nick. "Maybe I'm disappointed I didn't think of this scam first. But my guess is, before long, Mobley'll clear the Missy Sherman case for overtime."

Nick nodded. "Media attention."

Brass nodded back. The missing housewife finally turning up had won Missy Sherman another fifteen minutes of headlines and TV news. That the body had been frozen, Brass and company had thus far managed to withhold—once that got out, the tabloid sensibilities of the media would really swing into high gear.

The detective got off Interstate 215 at Eastern Avenue and drove south to Hardin. After taking a left, Brass drove until he could turn back north on Goldhill Road. The house he eased to the curb in front of was a near mirror image of the Sherman place—similar stucco two-story mission-style but with the two-car garage on the right, and the roof tile more a dark brown. A black Lincoln Navigator and a pewter Toyota Camry sat in the driveway.

As they got out and Brass strolled around the Taurus, Nick asked, "You ever run into the likes of this before? Ice-cold trail, no evidence . . ."

At Nick's side now, Brass said, "In the days before all the high-tech stuff kicked in, yeah. You'd catch a case that you just knew you'd never crack, 'cause there was jack squat to go on."

"But you'd hang in there, right?"

"Right. Months devoted to dead ends, and the end result—another folder for the cold case file. You guys and your toys . . . you find a hair on a gnat's ass and match it to a pimple on a perp in Southeast Bumfuck, Idaho."

Nick chuckled and admitted, "Sometimes it's that easy. Only, this one doesn't feel that way. I'm afraid I've got that nagging feeling that we'll never crack this thing."

They were at the porch, now.

Brass shook his head, placed a hand on the young CSI's shoulder. "You'll crack this one, Nick. It's just . . . they can't all be easy."

Nick nodded, and smiled. "But it would be nice. . . ."

The front door resembled the Shermans' too, except not hunter green, rather a rich, dark brown. Brass used the horseshoe-shaped knocker, waited and then waited some more. The detective glanced at Nick, who glanced back and shrugged. Brass rang the bell, waited a few seconds and rang it again.

The door opened and the doorway filled with a large man, like a frame that could barely encompass a picture. Six-five easy, Brass thought, the guy was a muscular two-fifty; his head, just a little small for the massive build, like his growth had gone as far as it could when it got past his bull neck. His eyes were dark brown, his hair a close-cropped light brown with matching close-trimmed goatee. He wore black running shorts and an expensive black-and-white pullover sweater with the sleeves pushed halfway up his formidable forearms. His sandals cost more than Brass's house payment.

Brass tapped the star-shaped badge on his breast sport-coat pocket and said, "Captain Brass, Las Vegas police. Mr. Mortenson? Brian Mortenson?"

The big man nodded, his expression somber. "This must be about Missy." He shook his head. "How can I help?"

"We'd like to talk to you and your wife. Is she here?"

"Well, she's here, but this has got her very upset. Could we do this another time?"

"If you do want to help, sir, now is better. With you both home. . . ."

"Do I need an attorney?" he asked.

Brass shrugged. "Do you?"

The big man in the doorway thought that over. Then he said, "You know, Regan and I already told that Detective Varga everything we know. It's all on the record."

Brass's tone grew more businesslike. "It's Detective Vega, and you were questioned in the context of a missing person case. This is a murder."

He sighed heavily. "Don't misunderstand, I want to

help. We want to help. It's just, I don't want Regan any more upset than she already is."

"I do understand that, Mr. Mortenson. May we come in?"

Mortenson stepped out of the way and let them into the foyer. "I talked to Alex today. . . . He's shattered by this. It's terrible. Awful."

Like the Shermans' foyer, this one had a Mexican tile floor, albeit in a lighter shade. A cherry table next to the stairway to the second floor was home to a large glass vase filled with fresh-cut yellow roses, the pale yellow plaster walls contrasting with the brightness of the flowers. An open archway led into a cozy living room decorated with a floral sofa and overstuffed chairs and two maple end tables. In front of the sofa sat a matching coffee table littered with several remotes and a few fashion, sports and fitness magazines.

"Make yourself comfortable," Mortenson said, nodding toward the living room, his tone much less defensive now, "and I'll fetch Regan. She's upstairs in her office."

Mortenson went up the stairs two at a time; he had the easy grace of a natural athlete, which not all brutes possessed. Brass led Nick through the archway into the living room, where they claimed the two chairs that framed the sofa, leaving it open for the Mortensons.

After only a minute or so, the couple entered the living room, the small woman leaning against her husband, one of his big arms around her. Regan Mortenson seemed frail beside her husband, her mane of long blonde hair hanging loose, partly obscuring her heart-shaped face. Tanned and fit, with long legs,

Regan no doubt played a lot of tennis or golf. She wore denim shorts and a white tee shirt bearing a transfer that looked familiar to Brass (Nick recognized it as Picasso's lithograph of Don Quixote), the words "Las Vegas Arts" in loose script below the transfer. Though she was in her mid-thirties, Regan had a college coed, California-girl air.

Brass and Nick rose as the couple walked to the sofa, the husband saying, "Dear, these are the police officers who want to talk to us."

Brass made the introductions, then said, "We know you and Mrs. Sherman were very close, ma'am, and we're sorry for your loss. We will try to make this as brief and painless as possible."

"You're very kind," she said with a nod, brushing the blonde hair out of her face.

The couple sat, Mortenson making the couch whimper in protest; in contrast, Regan perched on the edge, poised to fly at the slightest provocation.

"What is there I can tell you?" she said, her voice tiny. Both Brass and Nick had to strain to hear. "Last year, we told that nice Hispanic detective everything we could remember."

"As you already know," Brass said, his tone official yet solicitous, "Missy Sherman's body has been found."

Brian said, "It was all over the news."

"And Alex called us, too," Regan said.

"The coverage was vague," the husband said, "about where she was found. Something about Lake Mead."

"Yes," Brass said. "Off the road that runs through the park."

"How terrible," Regan said, shuddering. "She did

love that area. We used to swim there, sometimes, Missy and I—sometimes we took midnight swims."

"Is that right?"

"Under the stars. We'd even been known to, uh . . . this is embarrassing."

"Go on."

"We used to swim on impulse. Which means, you know . . . skinny-dipping?"

Brian gave her a look. "Really?"

She nodded, even mustered a little smile. "We didn't invite you guys along for that."

Brian's expression was distant; probably, Brass was thinking, the husband was contemplating missed opportunities.

Now Regan appeared thoughtful. "Only . . . this seems like a little late in the year for that. You know . . . too cold?"

"Yes it is," Brass said. "I do need to go over some old ground."

"Please."

He took out his minicassette recorder. "And it's best I record it."

"No problem."

"But you will need to speak up a little." He clicked it on and asked, "How long have you known Missy?"

She sighed, shook her head, the blonde hair shimmering; she was a lovely woman—ex-jock Brian appeared to be a lucky man.

"Since Michigan State," Regan said. "We were both Tri Delts. Then, it turned out that our hometowns weren't that far apart—she grew up in Kalamazoo and I was from Battle Creek. We'd both been cheerleaders in high school and our towns played each other and . . . well, we were kindred spirits. So, anyway, we started riding home together for holidays and stuff. She was a year older than me, and helped me adjust to college and sorority life. We became best friends and . . . and have been ever since."

Her lower lip was trembling, her eyes moist. Nick handed her a small packet of tissues and she thanked him; but she remained composed.

Brass asked, "You moved out here because of Missy?"

"In part. I was looking for a new start, and Missy and Alex made it sound like such a great place to live. She'd keep talking about fun and sun, and me stuck in Michigan—anything to get the hell out of there!"

"Not much for winter?" Nick put in, with a friendly little smile.

She shook her head. "I just hate winter, I despise snow. Plus, I was having sinus headaches and my doctor recommended I go somewhere warm, with a more steady climate. And my best friend and her husband were here."

She was speaking louder now, more animated.

Brass asked, "What can you tell us about the last time you saw her?"

The upbeat attitude faded, her eyes clouding over. After a while she said, "It was such a typical day for us girls. Nothing special about it, but if you had to pick a representative day for what our friendship was all about, and what we did together, that day would've served just fine. Shopping, lunch, then . . ."

Her voice broke.

Brass paused in his questioning while Brian

Mortenson put a comforting hand on his wife's shoulder. Regan choked back a sob, digging into the tissues. She dabbed at her eyes. Her makeup did not run, however—studying her, Brass realized Regan's eyeliner was tattooed on.

"I . . . I'm . . . I'm sorry," she finally managed.

They gave her a long moment to compose herself, then Brass went at it again. "I do need more detail, Mrs. Mortenson," he said. "Let's start with what time you and Missy got together that day."

Regan thought back. "We were in separate cars. We usually didn't pick each other up or anything, we'd meet someplace. That morning . . . We met at Barnes and Noble, the one out on Maryland Parkway . . . by the Boulevard Mall?"

Brass and Nick both nodded.

"Anyway," she went on, "that was around ten. We had coffee and a scone, then browsed for a while. Alex had a birthday coming and he's such a movie freak that Missy wanted to get him this special movie book."

"And did she?" Brass asked.

Nick remembered that although the Chinese food had been found in Missy's Lexus, no other packages remained.

"She did," Regan said. "Missy found just the right book for Alex—this biography of Red Skeleton."

Nick smiled a little; but neither he nor Brass corrected her: Skelton.

She was saying, "Alex is into the old movie stars—but, actually . . . I wound up giving it to him."

"You gave it to him," Brass repeated, not following.

Twisting the tissue in her hands, she said, "We were

planning to have Alex's birthday at our house—we've done that before."

Brian nodded.

She went on: "The store wrapped it for her and she just gave it to me to keep, till the party." Regan's voice shrank even more. "Of course, we never had that party, not after Missy disappeared."

"And you gave him the book."

She nodded.

"When?"

For a second she seemed to not understand the question, then said, "On his birthday," as if that should have been obvious. "I stopped over and gave him the package, and told Alex it was from her."

"This was a month after she disappeared."

Another nod. "I thought he'd appreciate that. That it would seem . . . special."

"And how did he react?"

She smirked sourly. "I guess it wasn't the smartest thing I ever did—he really broke up. He cried and cried."

And then she began to cry too, muttering, "Stupid . . . stupid . . . stupid . . ."

Mortenson rubbed his wife's neck. "Don't beat yourself up, baby. You were just trying to be nice."

Picking the momentum back up, Brass asked, "Okay, where to after the bookstore?"

"Caesar's—the Forum shops for a couple hours. It's expensive but there's lots of fun stuff to see."

"So you were just window shopping?"

"Mostly, but Missy did buy a nice sweater at . . . I don't remember which store, for sure. It was a year ago. . . ."

"Think, for a moment."

". . . Saks, maybe? Only, we pretty much made the rounds that day and hit almost every store. She could have bought that anywhere. And maybe something else . . . But anyway, I'm positive she was carrying some bags when we went back to our cars."

"Okay. You get through shopping at Caesar's. Then what?"

"Lunch. It was after one by then and we decided to go to the China Grill at Mandalay Bay."

Nick, in his friendly way, asked, "That's kind of a tourist trap, isn't it?"

"Yeah, sort of, but the food is really good. And Missy and me, we're people watchers. We both get a kick out of watching the tourists and guessing who they are and where they're from. It's better than the zoo."

"Do you remember what you had for lunch?"

"Grilled mahimahi. That's what I always have there. It's great." Her grief over Missy appeared momentarily displaced by her enthusiasm for her lunch. "They grill it with pea pods, yellow squash, carrots, leeks, and shitaki mushrooms."

"What about Missy? Wouldn't happen to remember what she ordered?"

"She had a fave, too—Mongolian beef. Without fail, that's what she'd order. Great girl, but no sense of adventure when it came to food."

"What did you two talk about over lunch?"

Regan shrugged, her mood upbeat again. "Missy and I decided to get the boys to take us to see the Harry Potter movie."

Brian Mortenson rolled his eyes just outside his wife's line of vision.

"You girls talk about anything else?" Brass asked. "Was Missy having trouble at home?"

Regan shook her head. "Not really—she thought the world of Alex, and he's been crazy about her since college."

"When you say, 'not really,' that implies . . ."

"Well . . . she was a little miffed about him getting on her, for spending too much on clothes. She said sometimes Alex treated her like he was the breadwinner and she was the little woman."

"Missy didn't work outside of the home?"

"No, but she managed their apartments. She had a finance degree, y'know. So I think she resented, just a little, being treated like a stay-at-home housewife. But I don't want to give you the wrong impression. Missy wasn't bent out of shape or anything. Every marriage has its little bumps. . . . Right, dear?"

Brian nodded.

Brass asked, "How long did lunch last?"

"An hour, maybe two."

"And all the two of you talked about was going to see a movie? And that Alex had been on her lately about her shopping?"

Shrugging, Regan said, "The rest was the same stuff we always talked about—just girl talk."

"Girl talk."

"What we're reading, who's getting divorced, who's fooling around on who—the usual gossip."

"What was she reading?"

"Nick Hornby."

"Any of the divorce or 'fooling around' talk have to do with Missy herself?"

Regan's face hardened. "Now, I'm willing to help you, but Missy wasn't like that. She loved her husband and he loved her—a storybook marriage, the kind most people can only dream about."

Brian Mortenson sat forward now. "These are our friends you're talking about, Detective. Like Regan says, we'll help, but have a little common decency, would you?"

"Sir, you don't have to like the questions I ask," Brass said. "I don't even like them . . . but these are the things that have to be asked in every homicide case."

Fuming but saying nothing, Mortenson sat back.

His wife put a hand on his leg just above the knee. "It's all right, Brian."

Nick said, "You're mourning the loss of a friend. But Missy didn't just pass away—she was murdered. We don't have the luxury of common decency, in the face of indecency like this. . . . Not if we want to do right by Missy."

Brian was still scowling, but his wife looked up at him sweetly and said, "They're right, honey. We have to help. We have to do whatever it takes to find out who took Missy away from us."

Mortenson sighed heavily, then nodded. "I don't know, baby. This is getting a little . . . weird."

Nick rose and, seemingly embarrassed, said, "My timing is lousy, I know . . . but I wonder if I could use your bathroom?"

"Sure," Regan said.

"Down the hall, off the kitchen," Brian said, with a dismissive gesture.

Nick offered a chagrined smile, and said, "I'm afraid department policy requires I be accompanied by the homeowner. You know how it is—things turn up missing, lawsuits. . . . Could you show me there, Mr. Mortenson?"

"Oh for Christ's sake," Mortenson said. "What next?"

But he got up, reluctantly, and escorted Nick out of the room.

Suddenly Brass felt very glad he'd allowed Nick Stokes to be his "Ride Along"—there was no such department policy as the one Nick referred to. Nick had clearly sensed Brass's desire to speak to the wife without the husband around, and had made it happen.

"When you were shopping, Mrs. Mortenson, did you see anyone suspicious, maybe someone following you?"

"No! No one."

"What about at the restaurant?"

"Of course not."

"Please think back, Mrs. Mortenson. If someone was stalking Missy, you might have noticed."

She chewed her lip in thought, big ice-blue eyes wide, gently filigreed with red.

Brass tried again. "Nobody talked to you or hit on you? A couple of attractive women out shopping, could be a guy might take a run at one or both of you."

She smiled, almost blushing. "Well, in a town full of showgirls, a woman my age can only thank you for a compliment like that . . . but no. No one talked to us, other than the workers in the stores and our waiter at lunch."

"Did any of the clerks get overly friendly? How about the waiter? More interested in you two than usual?"

"If so, Detective, it flew over my head. You think a stalker was watching us?"

This was getting nowhere. "Did you actually see Missy get into her car? In the restaurant parking lot?"

"Well, I walked Missy to her Lexus, then went on to my own car. It was parked farther out."

"Then you did see her get into the SUV?"

Regan nodded, and a pearl-like tear rolled down her tanned cheek, glistening like a jewel. "She already had the door open. She set her doggy bag inside, then ducked back out and . . . we hugged. How was I to know we were saying good-bye, forever?"

"You couldn't have known."

Regan swallowed. "I said we'd see her and Alex on Saturday, then she got in, and I walked away."

"That was the last thing you saw? You didn't see her drive out?"

"No."

"Did she start the engine?"

"I don't . . . don't remember."

"Could there have been someone hiding in the car? In the back, maybe?"

"She put the doggy bag in front, side and rear windows are tinted. . . . Maybe. But I really don't think so."

"Where did you go from the restaurant?"

"I had another appointment."

"With whom?"

The onslaught of questions was clearly getting to her. "Really, Detective, is that important?"

Brass shrugged. "Probably not. But I have to check everything."

Nodding, Regan said, "I serve as a fund raiser for Las Vegas Arts."

Alex Sherman had mentioned that.

"Sometimes," she was saying, "I meet with artists. I met with one that day."

"Which artist? What's his name?"

"Her name," she corrected. "Don't be sexist, Detective."

"Sorry."

"Sharon Pope."

"Where can I contact her?"

"She's in the book."

Brass was reflecting, trying to think if he had any other questions for the woman, when he heard Brian Mortenson yelling from the back of the house.

The detective and the blonde exchanged looks, then got up and quickly followed the sound of the voice down the hall, the hostess leading the way.

Even if it wasn't really department policy.

Five minutes before, when Nick had requested a guide to the bathroom, Mortenson had led the CSI past a formal dining room dominated by a huge oak table and through a hall-of-mirrors kitchen with its stainless-steel appliances. Off the kitchen to the left, Mortenson pointed toward the bathroom.

"Knock yourself out," the man said sourly.

Nick had used the bathroom and took his time

washing up. Joining his host in the hallway again, Nick pointed past Mortenson toward an open door that led into the empty garage.

"You might want to shut that," Nick said. "Letting in the cold."

"Hell," Mortenson said, looking around. "Thanks . . . I was getting ready to put the cars into the garage when you and your partner knocked out front."

Mortenson moved toward the door, but before he could close it, Nick—at the man's side—was pointing into the garage at a white appliance against the back wall. "That a chest freezer?"

"Yeah."

Boldly, Nick stepped through the door out into the garage. Voice pinging off cement, he said, "I've been thinking about getting one. . . . This baby expensive?"

Mortenson followed the CSI. "Not that much—less than $500."

Nick whistled. "Hey, that's not bad at all." He gave Mortenson the look you give a used-car dealer. "Has it been good to you?"

Mortenson nodded, shrugged, then glanced back in the direction of the living room, mildly imposed upon, but not knowing what to do about it. "Had it three years," he said. "Not a lick of trouble."

Nick stood studying the freezer, admiringly. "Doesn't hurt it any, to be out in the garage?"

"Naw," Mortenson said, getting sucked into the seemingly mindless conversation. "Runs a little more, but there's nowhere in the house for it. This works fine." He opened the lid so Nick could peer inside.

While proud homeowner Mortenson droned on,

Nick checked out the freezer, though not for the reason the other man likely thought. Three-quarters filled with white-butcher-paper-wrapped packages with very clear dates printed in Magic Marker, the Mortensons' freezer was better organized than Nick's office. Beef on one side, chicken and fish to the back, pork to the right and vegetables in the front. Though only about eight or nine cubic feet—and stacked with enough food to keep a homeless shelter going for weeks—the freezer did appear big enough to hold Missy Sherman's body. A small layer of frost coated the walls, but Nick could still see every seam and the smoothness of the surface along the back.

What he did not see was something that could have made the round mark on Missy Sherman's cheek.

Nick asked, "How often do you have to defrost one of these?"

Mortenson shrugged. "Once a year, maybe. Not so bad—there's a drain plug in the bottom. Some of the more expensive ones coming out now are frost-free."

"Sounds good. Looks like you defrosted yours, recently?"

"Yeah—maybe three weeks ago."

Nick looked from the bottom of the freezer to a floor drain in the center of the garage floor. Pulling a plastic bag from his pocket, he asked, "Would you mind if I lifted a sample from your drain?"

Mortenson looked at him like he was crazy, then slowly, the man's eyes narrowed. "Why?"

The best Nick could come up with was, "It might be helpful. You said you wanted to help."

"In Missy's murder investigation."

"Right."

"In my garage."

"Uh . . . yeah."

"Which, means . . . what?" The eyes on the little face over the big body tightened; the goatee was like dirt smudged on his chin. "You suspect me of Missy's murder?"

Shaking his head, Nick said, "I don't suspect anybody yet. . . . I'm just doing my job."

"And here I thought you were just this nice guy interested in buying a freezer."

Risking Brass's ire, Nick revealed: "Missy Sherman was frozen."

Mortenson frowned. Trying to make sense of it, he said, "She was frozen to death? In Las Vegas? How the fuck cold was Lake Mead that—"

"No. Frozen. As in a freezer."

"What, now you suspect us? Are you high?"

"No. I'm just a crime lab investigator who needs to check that freezer." And Nick pointed to the appliance.

His voice rising and bouncing off the enclosed space, Mortenson yelled, "Alex told me you took his place apart, too! You really don't have any goddamn decency, do you?"

Nick glanced toward the house, afraid that the man's voice would carry and bring out the wife and Brass.

"Sir," Nick said tightly, one ex-jock getting into the face of another. "You said you wanted to help. I need to have a look at that freezer."

Looking down at Nick, noses almost touching, Mortenson blared, "There's some murdering lunatic out there, and you people come around and bother us! The people who knew and loved Missy! Isn't it enough that we lost our friend, that Alex lost his wife?"

Regan and Brass appeared in the doorway off the kitchen.

"Brian, what's wrong?" Regan asked, her voice rising, ringing off the cement, making her sound a little like Minnie Mouse in an old movie house. She rushed to her husband's side.

Brass trailed after, shooting a look at Nick, who could only shrug and nod toward the freezer.

The detective got the significance at once, and turned to Mortenson, who seemed just ready to launch into the next wave of his tirade.

Cutting him off, Brass said, "You're right, Mr. Mortenson, there is a lunatic out there, a murderer, and we don't have any idea who it is . . . so we have to suspect everyone, if only to start ruling people out."

Trembling, the big man said, "You have no right, no right at all . . ."

"We can do this now," Brass said, "and you can co-operate . . . or we can get a warrant and do it later. Either way, whatever evidence my criminalist wants, he's going to get. The question is, do you want to slow us down, or not? You choose."

Mortenson seemed to shrink a little, from King Kong to the son of Kong, his wife slipping an arm around his waist.

She said, "Just let them do what they want to do, Brian, and get them out of our house."

He gave her a sick look. "This guy says Missy was frozen, that somebody stuffed her in a damn freezer or something. They think . . ." And he looked toward the appliance.

Regan paled, horror-struck, but nonetheless said, "Don't make them come back here—I don't ever want to see these terrible people again. Please, Brian, I'm begging you—just let them do what they want, take what they want and leave us alone."

"All right, baby," he said with a sigh. Then he looked from Nick to Brass. "Do what you have to . . . then get the hell out of my house."

Brass stood in the garage with the Mortensons, trying to make peace with them, while Nick went to the car, got his camera and his silver toolkit. When he returned, the husband and wife stood watch accusingly, near the door to the kitchen. Brass had parked himself close by, but no further words were exchanged with the couple.

Nick snapped off several shots of the freezer from both a distance and up close, concentrating particularly on the seams and side surfaces on the inside. When he was done, Nick set the camera aside, pulled on latex gloves, bent down to the floor drain, removed the cover and fished out whatever he could from the shallow trap; then he placed his findings in the bag. The tense silence in the room and the eyes of the Mortensons boring into his back as he worked weighed on him and he wished Brass would say something to break the hush, but the detective seemed content to stand by without comment.

Nick sealed the bag, replaced the cover on the drain, rose and nodded to Brass. He ended by taking another half-dozen photos, this time of the drain. Without a word, Mortenson pushed the button on the wall that activated the garage door opener. As the double door whirred upward, the detective and CSI took the hint and walked out into the evening and down the driveway to the Taurus at the curb.

Nick glanced back and saw Regan Mortenson silhouetted in the corner of the doorway, while Brian walked out of the garage onto the driveway, stopping next to his wife's Camry. Mortenson stared at them until the car pulled away.

"That went well," Nick said.

Brass said, "You know, outside of Grissom and Ecklie, I don't know anyone who pisses people off like you do. At least they have an excuse, they're supervisors, they're supposed to piss people off. But you . . ."

"Some people like me," Nick said, mildly amused by this rant. "Some people love me."

"Probably not the Mortensons."

Nick hefted the bag of slime and grinned. "But I did win their door prize."

Nodding toward the bag, Brass asked, "And if that turns out to be nothing?"

Nick shrugged. "Ruling out innocent people is just as important as finding guilty ones, right?"

"I guess," Brass said, obviously not convinced.

Back in the lab, Nick went to work processing the goop from the Mortensons' drain. The glass-walled DNA lab was one of the most elaborate in the CSI facility. Closed off by two sets of double glass doors, one on the north and another on the west, the room comprised five workstations, not counting the microwave oven. One station was for the thermocycler, one for each of the two polarized light microscopes, another for the gas chromatograph and mass spectrometer, plus the one where Nick was hard at work.

He was almost finished when Catherine came in and dropped onto the chair at the station immediately behind and to the left of him at the stereo microscope. Hunching over the tool, he used reflected light to study in three dimensions the grime from the drain.

"Hey," she said.

Looking up, he said, "Hey." Tonight, she wore brown slacks, a burnt-orange turtleneck sweater, and a look of either exhaustion or frustration, Nick couldn't tell which.

"Where've you been?" he asked.

"Best Buy."

He grinned. "Consumer heaven." He looked at his watch. "They're not open this late."

She tapped her ID. "I had a special get-in-after-hours card."

"Looking for the perfect DVD player, huh?"

Catherine closed her eyes and rubbed her forehead. "Is that all men think about?"

"No," Nick said, carefully considering the question. "There's sex and sports, too. Then comes toys like DVD players."

She finally gave in and grinned.

"What were you up to, after closing at Best Buy?"

Sighing, stretching, she said, "I was going over every freezer in the place, trying to find one that matched the mark on Missy Sherman's face."

"Any luck?"

She shook her head. "I'll try another store tomorrow." Frowning, she asked, "Where's Warrick, anyway?"

"Still working the tires, I think. Haven't seen him for a while."

"What are you up to?"

"Went with Brass to interview the Mortensons—the Shermans' best friends?"

She nodded, interested.

He filled her in, building to the chest-freezer punch line and the slime he was currently processing.

Catherine perked up. "What did you get?"

"Just what you did."

"Shit."

Nick grunted a laugh. "I don't know where Missy Sherman's been for the last year, but it sure wasn't in that freezer."

A throat cleared, and they turned to see Warrick draped in the doorway. "FBI computer is taking its own sweet time with that tire mark."

Nick said, "With no more of a casting than you got, it's not going to help us much, anyway. We find a car to match it to, groovy . . . but for now . . ."

"I know," Warrick said. "Coldest case ever . . . You guys catch any luck?"

"Same kind as you," Catherine said.

Nick leaned on the counter and turned to Catherine. "What have we got so far, besides no overtime?"

Catherine flinched a little nonsmile. "A dead woman who has been frozen for the last year."

"A few tire tracks," Warrick added. "An indentation in the victim's cheek. Another longer, narrower indentation on her arm. Some Chinese food in her stomach . . ."

"And no fortune cookie," Nick said. "But I have ruled out one of the many chest freezers in Las Vegas. How many more d'you suppose there are to check?"

Warrick just looked at Nick, while Catherine sat there, apparently wondering whether to laugh or cry.

7

SARA SIDLE'S NOSTALGIA FOR THE BRACING WEATHER OF HER Harvard days had long since blown away with one of the many gusts of winter wind. Ensconced in the shelter Constable Maher had made in the snow, huddled against a tree, rifle gripped in fingers going numb despite Thinsulate gloves, Sara now clearly recalled why she'd gone west after graduation.

Guarding a snow-covered crime scene in the midst of a blizzard was a duty that neither training nor experience had prepared her for. Thank God the two hours were almost up. She wondered if, on her return, she should round up Amy Barlow—not that the woman would likely go anywhere, in the middle of this snowbound night. But the waitress remained the closest thing to a witness they had.

Prior to taking her first crime-scene shift, Sara had returned to the dining room, where she spoke briefly to Pearl Cormier. The half-hearted dinner rush was already over, and Amy was nowhere in sight.

Pearl, holding down the hostess station, explained:

"Amy's helping in the kitchen—short-handed back there. Short-handed everywhere in the hotel."

"You'll provide her with a room tonight?"

"Can't hardly make Amy sleep in her car, honey."

"Could you let me know the room number?"

And Sara had gone up to catch a little sleep, which the phone interrupted in what seemed like a few seconds, with Pearl informing the CSI that Amy Barlow had room 307; but right now the waitress was still working, helping waiter Tony Dominguez set the massive dining room for breakfast—a big task for two people.

Which meant that before Sara could follow up with the waitress, she had her outdoor duty to do. And so she'd followed Herm Cormier over the hill and through the woods to babysit a snowbound corpse who had not been content just to be shot, he had to be half-burned to a crisp, too.

When she'd thought about this duty, she had, frankly, pictured a winter wonderland, despite the dead body—sparkling crystal on white rolling drifts, reflecting the moon and stars. The reality? Clouds covered the stars and what little moon there was, and she was miles away from the nearest streetlight, and even the hotel wasn't in view. This was a darkness like she'd never known, an all-encompassing inside-of-a-closed-fist nothingness that embraced her in its frigid fingers—and also disconcerted the hell out of her, despite her hardheaded, scientific bent.

She had her flashlight, but was loath to turn it on for fear of taxing the batteries, which would really put her in hot water . . . well, cold water, anyway. Nestled there in her pocket, the flashlight provided a small reassurance, a promise of light more important to her, at the moment, than the light itself.

Pushing the button on her watch, illuminating the dial, Sara noted that another fifteen minutes remained before Maher was due to relieve her. Leaning the rifle against her shoulder, she pulled off one glove, reached carefully into her pocket and withdrew her flash.

Going left to right, she made her arc of the crime scene with the beam. The sticks that Maher had planted in the snow were all but buried. Grissom had told her that several inches had been exposed, when he'd noticed them. Now, the stakes would soon be memories under the white blanket. She continued the arc past where the body should be, the other set of sticks and on around to her right.

She saw nothing—no animal, no person. That was comforting. Also creepy.

Switching off the light and tucking it away again, a sudden sense of loneliness descended on Sara, heavier even than the falling snow. It was as if extinguishing the light had somehow shut off the lights on the entire world and every soul in it, and Sara—who normally didn't mind a little quiet time to herself—felt like the only person left. That was when she heard something crunch in the snow.

She held her breath and strained to hear over the wind as her fingers clawed for the flashlight in her pocket; what she heard, first, was her own heart pounding.

Then, another crunch—this one to her right.

She fumbled with the MagLite, then the beam

came to life and she thrust it out like a sword toward the sound.

She saw nothing.

Then, panning left, the light caught a flash of . . . fur!

Whatever-it-was had outrun her beam, and she whipped the shaft of light in pursuit, catching a glimpse of a furry form, going past it, then coming back to settle on the cold brown beautiful eyes of a big cat.

Not a house cat: a bobcat or a lynx.

Poised to leap, the beast bared its teeth and snarled— the sound was brittle in the night, yet it echoed. With each fang as long as one of Sara's fingers, the cat seemed torn between its desire to get at the corpse and being almost as afraid of Sara as she was of it.

Trying to raise the rifle with one hand, in a steady motion—not wanting to make a swift move that might inspire an attack—and yet keeping the beam on the growling animal, Sara knew that the cat could cover the ground between them in mere seconds. Carefully she traded hands, shifting the flashlight to her left, the rifle to her right, propping the rifle against her shoulder—all with no sudden moves. Once she had the rifle more or less in place, her right index finger settled on the trigger. . . .

Sighting down the barrel as she'd been taught, she kept the light trained on the growling cat, muscles rippling under its fur, and exerted pressure on the trigger. Don't jerk it, she thought, just squeeze . . . nice and easy. . . . When the trigger was about halfway down, she heard a loud pop!

But she had not fired.

A bullet thwacked into a tree behind the cat, and the animal jumped to one side—beautiful, graceful—and sprinted off, a brownish blur dissolving into the night.

Sara swiveled toward where the shot had originated—just behind her, and to her left, her ears still ringing from the rifle report—and captured Maher and Cormier in the MagLite's beam.

The Canadian handed a rifle over to the hotel owner. Both men looked like Eskimos, wrapped up in those parkas, hoods up, only the centers of their faces truly visible in the beam of the flashlight, perhaps ten yards from her.

"You scared the shit out of me!" Sara screamed, the adrenaline of the moment somehow combining to ratchet the volume of her voice in these woods, where the only other sound was the dying echo of Maher's gunshot.

Maher looked stunned for a moment, then smiled and said, "You're welcome."

"I mean . . . thank you. . . . But I did have the situation in hand."

"I know you had that cat in your sights, and I know I missed. I wasn't trying to save you."

"What?"

"I was saving the cat."

". . . The cat?"

Walking toward her, Cormier at his side, Maher said, "The cat's a North American lynx. Endangered species."

"Lynx?"

"*Lynx canadenis* to be precise," Maher explained, a

few yards away now. "You seldom see them this far south. . . ."

Cormier butted in. "Not unheard of either. Seen my share of 'em in my day. You can get in trouble shootin' 'em, Ms. Sidle."

Sara swung the MagLite to Cormier and said, "Maybe I should've let him chow down on our corpse—or offer him one of my legs to chew on."

"I just wanted to scare it off before anything happened," Maher said, squinting at the light.

Finally realizing she was blinding the men, she pointed the flash at a more downward angle. "Sorry, guys . . . didn't mean to lose it."

"No problem, eh?" Maher said.

"If I'd been any more scared," she admitted, "I don't mind telling you, I'da wet myself."

"Wouldn't worry none," Cormier said. "It woulda froze up right quick."

Sara arched a half-frozen eyebrow at the hotel manager. "You know, if you get any folksier, the next time I aim, it might not be at a lynx."

Cormier grinned, and so did Maher. "Let's get you back down to the hotel, little lady."

She looked at Maher. "Did he just call me 'little lady'?"

"I believe he did," an amused Maher said.

"Herm," she said to the hotel man, "I'm taller than you are, okay?"

"You are at that . . . but you don't mind if I lead the way?"

Every bone in her body felt leaden and every muscle ached, even burned, and now that the adrenaline rush had subsided, she thought her legs might betray her. Taking a deep breath, she moved around a little, hoping to encourage some blood flow to her extremities.

"Ready?" Cormier asked.

"Ready," she said. Then turning to Maher, she asked, "Anything I can do down at the hotel? It's only what . . . ten-thirty?"

Maher shook his head. "Just get some rest, 'cause we'll be keeping up the rotation. Snow seems to be letting up, some. Maybe by first light we'll finally be able to go to work."

Sara exhaled breath that hung there like a small cloud. "I am ready to do more than sit."

"Just sit and scare off bobcats, you mean?"

Sara grinned. "Constable, that was a lynx. I thought you knew your stuff out here, in the woods."

With tight smiles and nods, they bid their goodbyes. Maher returned to the cubbyhole he'd dug, thermos of coffee and Remington rifle both handy, while Sara took off after Cormier. The movement, rather than wake her up, only made clear to Sara just how exhausted she was, and any thought of interviewing Amy Barlow, or anyone else for that matter, evaporated from her mind. Making their way slowly down the rocky slope in the darkness, aided by flashlight beams, they trudged down toward civilization.

Which right now Sara Sidle defined as a warm bed.

The rest of the night passed uneventfully.

On that cloud of a bed, Sara fell deeply asleep, and when the wake-up call came, she arose groggy, really dragging; she had slept in her clothes and bundled into her coat, stocking cap, muffler and all, she sleep-walked down to the lobby and fell in with Herm Cormier.

Once outside, the cold air snapped her back to bitter reality. And at the crime scene, she never once drifted off to sleep—it was if anything colder than before, though the snow was half-hearted and, by the end of her watch, all but stopped.

She returned to the hotel for three hours of deep, blissful sleep; this time she beat her wake-up call. She felt refreshed, and—after a shower—invigorated, ready to make her way up that mountain and relieve Grissom.

Just after seven-thirty, she stepped off the elevator into a lobby deserted but for Mrs. Cormier behind the front desk. The older woman gave her a wave and Sara waved back, and was about to ask where Pearl's husband was when Herm Cormier materialized at her side.

"Rarin' to get at it?" he asked.

"Actually, yes. Last night was so odd, it's almost like looking back on a dream, or maybe a nightmare."

Cormier pointed a mildly scolding finger. "I wish you folks woulda let me take a turn or two out there."

She shook her head. "Really needed to be one of us, at all times. That'll be much better when this case eventually gets to court."

He grunted a laugh. "No bad guy yet, and already you're thinking about court?"

She nodded, grinned. "That's really where all of the work we do ends up. Where is everybody?"

"Things usually are a little livelier around here," he

said, glancing around. "We're a big haunted house this weekend—they say Stephen King wrote that book about this place."

"The Shining?"

"I guess," he said, with a shrug. "What guests we have are probably takin' breakfast. Amy, Tony, Mrs. Duncan and Bobby Chester are working the kitchen, naturally."

"Where's Constable Maher?"

"He's in the dining room, too. That's why I was out here, on the lookout for you. Mr. Maher asked, when you come down, I request you join him. And me, too. He says we all need to eat—it's going to be a long day."

"Sounds like a plan."

Soon they were entering the vast dining room where ten people, mostly couples, were seated centrally, having breakfast. Stares and whispers followed Sara.

"I guess word's out," she said, as Cormier led her past gawking guests toward a table where Maher waited.

"Well, you know how it is—in an environment this small, news travels fast. Especially with the four of us running in and out every couple of hours."

She nodded. "In other words, you told your wife."

He nodded. "Told my wife."

Maher stood as Sara approached and they exchanged good mornings. He'd been smoking a cigarette—this was the smoking section—but he stabbed it out as Sara neared. His eyes were as red-rimmed as hers, but he too seemed energized.

"I think you're going to enjoy today much more than yesterday, Ms. Sidle."

"Call me Sara, please," she said, sitting.

"All right," Maher said, taking his seat, Cormier doing the same, "if you'll call me Gordon . . . or even Gordy."

"Gordon, if you can make that crime scene shake off the snow and talk to us, I'll call you a genius."

The other diners were slowly returning to their food, if occasionally glancing over at the detectives in their midst.

The menu was a small single page, with only a handful of items—basically, a choice of ham, bacon, or sausage and various combinations of eggs and cakes—and she was still studying it, as if looking for hidden meaning, when a loud crash made her—and everyone else in the dining room—jump half out of their chairs. She whirled to see the waiter, Tony Dominguez, kneeling over a tray on the floor, half a dozen plates upended, food scattered.

"First time that ballet dancer ever got clumsy," Cormier muttered, and hustled over to help the waiter clean up the mess.

The pair worked fast, starting with carefully piling the broken pieces of dishes and glasses onto the serving tray. Sara caught sight of a pink stain on the left arm of the waiter's white shirt—from juice maybe; the stain looked dry, so it hadn't come from nicking himself due to this spill. Cormier went off to the kitchen for more cleaning utensils.

Turning back to her table, Sara leaned forward resting an elbow, touching a hand to her face. So much for waking up refreshed—the crash and clatter of china and silverware had almost made her leap out of her skin, and she realized how frazzled she still felt. So much for a peaceful getaway with Gil Grissom. . . .

"Brace up, eh?" Maher said. "We'll be getting to work before you know it—and I have a hunch you're the kind who's never happier than at a crime scene."

He seemed to be describing Grissom more than her, but Sara nonetheless brightened at the prospect. "I guess you planned on having more than just two students."

"With 'students' like you and Dr. Grissom, it's a master's thesis class. Limited enrollment."

A haggard Amy Barlow trod up to their table, little of yesterday's spring in her step. Her hair, though tied back in a loose ponytail, looked haphazardly combed, dozens of stray strands seeking escape; and she wore no makeup. She had on the same black slacks and white shirt but no bow tie, the crisp pressed look of last night's uniform absent. The only thing she seemed to have changed was the bandage on her left hand.

"You're one of those crime lab people, aren't you?" Amy asked Sara. "In for the conference that got canceled."

"That's right," Sara said, rather startled by the question.

"Then maybe you'll know—I asked Herm but he just said stay about your business."

"Know what, Amy?"

"Is it true?" She glanced in the direction of the mountainside. "That there's a body out there somewhere?"

Sara glanced at Maher, who nodded.

"I'm afraid so," Sara said. "The police can't make it up here in the snow, so we're doing what we can."

"What can you do?" Amy frowned curiously. "What happened?"

"A man was killed," Sara said.

" 'Nother skiing accident? Exposure . . . ?"

"No. It was intentional. Homicide."

Amy frowned. ". . . Murder?"

"Yes."

Somehow Sara had wound up on the wrong end of the Amy Barlow interrogation. Taking back the initiative, the CSI asked, "Can you tell us anything about the cars you saw on the road yesterday?"

Amy frowned again, in thought this time. "Would that have something to do with this?"

"Might. What did you see? What do you remember seeing, on your way in to work?"

The waitress shook her head, as if her response would be negative, then said, "One was an SUV, that much I can tell you . . . a Bronco, or Blazer? They all kinda look alike to me."

"That's a good start, Amy," Maher said. "What about color?"

Amy's eyes tightened as she searched her memory. "Dark red, like a maroon?"

That had been more a question than an answer, but it was something, anyway. "You're doing fine," Sara said. "What about a license plate? If not the number, were they New York State plates? Out of state . . . ?"

Amy drew in a breath, exhaled through her nose, shook her head, ponytail flouncing. "Didn't notice."

"And there was another car?" Maher pressed.

That had been the waitress's implication.

"Yes," she said. Then, proud of herself, she gave the following detailed description: "Something big and black."

Sara hid her frustration, while Maher kept at it, asking, "New or old?"

"On the newer side," Amy said. "Like a Toyota or a Honda—I don't know cars very well. That's Jimmy's thing."

"Jimmy?"

"My guy," she said, with a shrug. "Can I give you a piece of advice, hon?"

"Sure," Sara said.

"Never date a guy younger than you. Young boyfriend, they'll drive you crazy. You feel like you're raisin' a kid, sometimes."

Sara had been in that position once or twice, and smiled in recognition.

Back from mopping the floor, Cormier was sitting down with them again, and had caught the tail end of that. "James Moss," he said, filling in information. "Jimmy. He's a waiter here too." He looked up at Amy. "Wasn't Jimmy supposed to work yesterday too?"

She nodded. "Didn't make it in, in time. With the phones down, I ain't even talked to him."

"You two usually ride in together," Cormier said.

Another nod. "Not yesterday—Jimmy said he had some errands to run. Somebody he had to see, he said."

"That new restaurant in New Paltz is hiring," Cormier said. "Kid asked for a raise last week and I turned him down."

Maher kept his attention on the hotel man. "Did Jimmy call in?"

"I'd have to ask Pearl, but I don't believe so. But lots of the help didn't call in, and of course it wasn't long before the phones were down. Listen, in this part of the world, with this kind of weather, we're used to the help not calling when they can't make it in."

Amy smirked. "Probably holed up playing with his damned Game Cube, praying for snow all weekend. . . . Folks ready to order?"

They did, and Amy went away.

"Well, the snow has stopped," Maher said. "Any word from the outside?"

"Phones're still down," said Cormier. "I do have a ham radio, though."

"And?"

"Guy I talked to in Mexico hears we had a hell of a storm."

Sara laughed; so, after a moment, did Maher.

Cormier was continuing, "The county guys were probably up all night, with that damned chain reaction accident out on the interstate. If they get out here today at all, it probably won't be till afternoon."

Maher turned to Sara. "Cell phone?"

"Oh, I haven't tried it yet this morning." She took it from her purse, punched in Catherine's work number—it was what, 3:30 A.M. back there? She got nothing, not even the robotic voice.

Sara shook her head glumly, returned the cell to her purse.

"Snow might have screwed up the tower," Cormier

said, with a twitch of a humorless half-smile. "Happened before."

The waitress returned with coffee for the men and tea for Sara. "Breakfast'll be up in a few shakes," she said.

"So," Maher said, sighing, "we're still on our own."

"Looks that way," said Cormier.

"If I'm not out of line," Sara said to the constable, "you don't seem horribly disappointed."

A smile flickered on the Canadian's lips. "I like a challenge."

"Me, too. So we're getting to work?"

Maher nodded curtly. "Mr. Cormier's going to help us gather some gear, and I've got some things in my room I brought for lecture purposes. Breakfast first."

Sara sipped her tea. "You're the boss. . . . Just don't tell Grissom I said that."

He chuckled. "We've got a lot to haul—any problem with that?"

She grinned. "The bellboys went home, so I'm ready. Bring it on."

He nodded to her. "That's what I like to hear."

Amy brought their food and, as they ate, Maher outlined the morning's plan, then turned to Cormier. "I'm going to need a medium-speed snow dispersal device."

Scratching his chin, Cormier gave the Canadian a cockeyed look. "I don't believe I've got one of those, much less heard of one, before."

"Are you sure, Herm?" Maher grinned. "Aka, a leaf blower?"

"Well, hell! Sure, I got a beauty—gas-powered too. Which is a good thing, 'cause I'm not sure there's enough extension cords in the whole hotel to reach up the side of that mountain."

After breakfast, they went off respectively for their outdoor apparel, collecting their various equipment, and reconvened outside the rear entrance, for one last check. Sara had both her case of equipment and Grissom's (Pearl at the desk had loaned her Gil's spare room key), her camera and tripod. Maher also had two cases, one of which held his metal detector. Cormier looked as though he'd cleaned out the tool-shed—scattered around the edge of the parking lot were a leaf blower, two shovels, a push broom, a kitchen broom, a whisk broom, a roll of garbage bags, and a toboggan.

"That's your wish list," the hotel manager said to Maher.

"Good job, Herm," Maher said. "Leaf blower gassed up?"

Cormier said, "You could disperse snow from here to New Paltz with that sucker."

"And the toboggan's a fine idea."

"Thanks."

Sara asked, "Too steep for snowmobiles?"

"Yeah, too steep and too many trees up there, too easy to wind up twisted around one of 'em. Rocky, too. Toboggan's safer."

They loaded their equipment aboard the sled, then Cormier and Maher lashed everything down. Though clouds still covered the sun, daylight filtered through, and the reflective shimmer of ice crystals on the snow was breathtaking. That the snow had stopped was a blessing. A good foot of white had fallen since Sara and Grissom had come upon the burning corpse, and despite the Canadian constable's confidence, she wondered if there would truly be any evidence left to collect.

"At least it was a wet snow," Maher said.

He and Cormier still looked like Eskimos to her, in their parkas.

"Is that good?" she asked.

"Real good, for us—limited drifting."

"Won't that make snow dispersal harder?"

"It'll be harder to blow; but as long as it doesn't go slushy on us, it'll hold together better, and give us good detail." Nodding to himself, he added, "If there's such a thing as an ideal winter crime scene, this should come close."

Then they marched up the hill, Maher and Cormier taking turns leading the way, and pulling the sled; Sara offered to take her turn dragging the heavy toboggan, but somehow it never happened. Instead, she wound up bringing up the rear, to one side of the thing, making sure nothing tumbled off, due to hitting a rocky patch.

The walk to the crime scene—which before had taken just short of half an hour, in the deep snow— took nearly an hour as the load constantly shifted, causing them to stop again and again, and check it and reset everything.

After the fourth time this happened, Sara said, "I thought this was the twenty-first century."

"Back at the lodge it is, just barely," Cormier said. "Out here, time isn't just relative, it's pret' near nonexistent."

They were already late and Sara started to worry

that maybe they'd get up there and find Grissom frozen to that tree. Or maybe that lynx would be standing there studying Grissom, with Grissom more than likely studying it back.

When they arrived at the site, however, Grissom was already pawing in the snow near the body, like a kid on Christmas morning who hadn't waited for his folks to get up before getting at his presents.

"Dr. Grissom!" Maher called.

The CSI supervisor continued on as if he hadn't heard. Leaving the toboggan with Cormier, Maher strode on ahead and called Grissom's name again. This time Grissom, looking comical in the stocking cap and muffler, turned.

"Plenty of time to do the body later," Maher said.

"All right," Grissom said, stepping away. "What's first?"

Maher was at Grissom's side now. "If this was a crime scene back in Vegas, what would you do first?"

"Take photos of everything—I presume Sara brought her camera today." Grissom was nicely ambiguous about that, Sara noted.

Maher was nodding, saying, "What else?"

"Look for footprints."

"Then let's do that." Maher gestured to the white landscape. "We don't want to risk trampling the killer's footprints, so let's find them."

Sara had joined them, by now, and asked, "How, exactly?"

Maher extended a hand, like a hypnotist before a subject. "Grid it out in your mind—like you would any other scene. Ignore the snow."

She stared at him, eyebrows arched. "Ignore the snow?"

Maher gave her a gentle smile. "Just for now."

She looked all around the buried crime scene. "All right, Gordy . . . I've got it."

Grissom said, "Gordy?"

Maher said, "That's my name. Feel free to use it, too, Dr. Grissom."

Grissom said nothing, just glanced at Sara, who shrugged.

"Mr. Cormier," Maher said.

"Yes, sir?"

"Would you unpack the leaf blower, please?"

"You got it."

Soon the hotel owner was bending over the toboggan, untying ropes.

"Now, Dr. Grissom," Maher said, "and Sara—you two remember about where the footprints were, correct?"

"Well," Sara said, pointing, "the victim ran a fairly straight line. So . . . from the body down the hill."

Grissom said, "The other four sets—the two up and the two back—were scattered sort of on either side of the victim's."

Maher nodded, breath pluming. "We're going to have to work these from the outside in. Where would you say the tracks were the furthest out?"

Pointing to a tree slightly downhill from their position, perhaps ten feet to their left, Grissom said, "Just this side of that tree."

"All right." Maher turned toward the old boy at the toboggan. "How you doing there, Mr. Cormier?"

"Comin' along!"

Maher turned back to the Vegas CSIs and said, "Okay, for a few minutes I'll be doing all the work . . . but it won't be long and there'll be plenty for everybody, eh?"

They nodded.

"For now, Sara, you better start finding a way to warm your camera."

"It's digital."

"Yes, and you won't want the lens fogged, and the batteries don't like the cold, either."

"How about inside my coat, Gordy?"

"That may be a little too warm, but it's better than any idea I've got."

Sara went back to the sled, carefully unpacked her camera and slipped half-out of the coat—God, it was bitter!—and withdrew an arm from one sleeve, slung the strap over her shoulder and put the camera against her side. Then she tugged the coat back on and zipped up. Maher's concern wasn't misplaced—the camera already felt cold, even though it had made the journey up here in its leather case. She hugged it close and hoped it would warm up quickly.

Grissom followed Maher as the constable circled down to the point the CSI had indicated, and they stood just on the wrong side of the tree from where the footprints had been before being buried under all that snow.

"This is the tree?"

"Yes," Grissom said, pointing toward the area on the other side. "The prints were right over there."

With a Cheshire cat grin, Maher asked, "Do you get a kick out of experiments?"

Grissom said simply, "Yes," which was the understatement of the new century.

"This isn't exactly an experiment, Doctor, but I think you're going to like it."

Before very long, Maher fired up the leaf blower, yanking the cord, and aimed it at the new-fallen snow. Wet though it was, the white powder still flew in every direction as the leaf blower eased over it. Despite the use of forced air, the Canadian worked carefully.

Moving down to join them, careful to take the same path they had taken, Sara and Cormier came down to watch the show. The camera felt warm against her now and Sara decided to snap off a couple of preliminary shots, getting photos of Maher at work. She looked over at Grissom, who studied Maher in rapt fascination and even admiration.

Quiet and still, Grissom seemed mesmerized as the leaf blower cleared layer after layer. Within a few minutes Maher shut down the leaf blower and signaled them to join him. He had blown open a circle about fifteen by fifteen inches and—in the bottom, dug into the five inches of snow already packed there when they'd arrived yesterday—Sara saw a pristine boot impression.

She turned to Grissom. "No way."

Shaking his head, Grissom said, "I just saw him do it."

They had a little sunshine now, but Maher's smile was brighter. "Medium-velocity snow dispersal device. Pretty cool, eh?"

"Pretty cool, indeed," Grissom said. "I trust the term is designed to sound impressive in court?"

"That, and 'leaf blower' just has no charm."

Looking like an overgrown demented kid in that stocking cap, eyes gleaming, Grissom asked, "May I?"

"Sure," Maher said. "You saw how I did it—just be careful and don't hit the area too directly."

"I'm all over it."

"Just be all over it—carefully." The Canadian refired the leaf blower and handed the business end to Grissom. "Take her for a spin."

Grissom moved just under a yard downhill and a little to the left. The impression Maher had unearthed— or more accurately, unsnowed—was of a right footprint. That meant the next one should be a left, which was the reason for Grissom moving just a few inches off line.

While Grissom worked with the blower, Sara put a ruled scale next to the footprint and snapped a couple of photos.

"Wait," Maher said. "You need the scale, you're exactly right . . . but for it to be accurate in a photo, it should be at the same depth as the impression." He dug out beneath the scale and set it down. Sara took two more photos, then slipped the camera back inside her coat to keep it warmed up.

"You'll see the difference once you get those up on a computer screen," Maher continued. "Use your tripod too—that and some oblique lighting should raise the detail."

"Thanks. I will."

Maher moved to where Grissom was blowing away more snow. With a small amount of guidance from the Canadian, Grissom eventually uncovered another footprint.

"Got a left foot," Grissom said, his smile almost feral.

"You comfortable doing this?" Maher asked.

"I'm always at my most comfortable," Grissom said, "at a crime scene."

Maher said, "All right, then—you keep moving. Do one more set from this row, then try to find the other three and we'll do two molds each from each row."

"Sounds good."

"And while you're doing that, Sara's going to take more pictures, while I'm melting the sulfur."

Grissom just nodded and went back to work.

"Sulfur?" Sara asked.

"Never made sulfur casts?" Maher asked her, as he led her back up the hill.

"Can't say I have."

"Just dental stone, huh?"

"That's what works best in our climate."

Opening one of his cases on the toboggan, Maher withdrew a Sterno burner and handed it to Sara.

"Take this," he said, then pulled out a small saucepan and handed it to her. "And this."

Finally, he brought out a yellow block slightly smaller than a brick and a cooling rack with extended legs.

"Come on, Sara," Maher said, "and I'll show you how this alchemy works."

Clearing a spot in the snow, he lit the Sterno burner and—while it got going—he dumped the yellow brick into the saucepan. As Sara watched, Maher put the saucepan on top of the cooling rack he'd opened up and set over the flame.

"Okay, Sara—this is going to start stinking to high heaven before long, so why don't you set your tripod up, and take your pictures, before I pour the sulfur in. We're only going to have a small window before our sulfur smells real ugly."

"Anything you say, Merlin," she said, and grabbed her tripod off the toboggan.

"And while you're there," Maher said, half-turning, "could you bring me that can of gray primer?"

She looked in the nearest bag and found the paint. "Got it."

As she set up the tripod, so that the camera would be directly over the footprint, Maher shook the paint, then sprayed a light layer of primer over the print.

Alarmed, Sara said, "Hey—you're disturbing evidence!"

He shook his head. "I'm enhancing the visibility. And besides, you already have pictures of it, au naturel."

Grissom turned off the leaf blower and, watching where he was going, walked over to them.

"Look what the Mountie did," she said, pointing at the print.

Maher was taking out his own mini-MagLite; he set it in the hole he'd cleared, so that it shone at an oblique angle across the impression.

"The visibility is a lot better," Grissom said. "I've read about this a couple of places."

"You have?" Sara asked.

"Kauffman's guide to winter crime scenes is pretty

much definitive; and there's a good paper, done by two Alaska CSIs, Hammer and Wolfe. Still, reading about it's one thing—working it out in the field . . . that's the ticket."

"But paint?" she said.

Her supervisor shrugged. "No different than us using hair spray on tire tracks."

Sara thought about that.

"That's a good one," Maher said, giving them a thumbs-up. "I love my Aqua Net."

With a quick nod, Grissom turned and moved back to the leaf blower.

Looking through the viewfinder, Sara had to admit, the prints seemed better-defined. She snapped off several shots from various heights. The rotten-egg smell of the sulfur floated down to her and she fought the urge to gag. It wasn't her way to give in, and she prided herself on her strong stomach, so she decided to risk her breakfast and get a closer look. Edging up, she saw Maher stirring the sulfur as it melted into a translucent amber liquid.

"You were right," she said. "That impression looks great, Gordy. Sorry I snapped at you . . ."

"It may smell like Daffy Duck's backside," he said, "but, damn—it works, eh?"

"You prefer it to dental stone?"

"Detail with sulfur is even higher. Cures faster too. The downside is, it's a lot more expensive, and a pain in the ass to work with, sometimes. You let it get too hot, it'll either ignite or get flaky. . . . Then you have to cool it down and start from jump."

Sara wondered if any of this would ever come in handy at home. Chances were, probably not; still, it never hurt to learn new techniques.

"The optimum temperature is about 119 degrees. But you've got to be careful because the flashpoint is 207 degrees and the self-ignition point is only 232. Once it's at the right temp, though, all we have to do is pour it in and wait. . . . You ready?"

She nodded.

Maher took the pot off the flame and carried the brew toward the print. Eyes wide, he said, "And, oh yeah—never use this stuff indoors!"

Grinning a little, she said, "Kinda guessed that. Noxious fumes aren't my favorite." She watched as he carefully filled the impression with the liquid sulfur. "That won't melt the impression?"

He shook his head. "Not enough to matter. The detail'll still be better than dental stone, and we don't have to take a week off, waiting for it to cure. Besides, if you use dental stone, you'll mix it with potassium sulfate and that reaction creates enough heat that if you don't put it in the snow while it mixes, it'll completely melt your impression."

A short while later, Grissom came over to them again. "I've uncovered two sets in each row."

"Good job," Maher said.

"Just looking with the naked eye," said Grissom, "I'd say all four sets were made by the same person."

"No kidding? Not two killers, then?"

"Looks like one. Smaller person, too—men's size eight or nine, woman's nine or ten."

"So—what happened?"

Grissom explained what he knew so far.

The killer chases the victim away from the hotel. The victim sprints up the slope and the killer is shooting at him, at least three shots fired.

So the killer fires and misses, fires and misses, then connects, putting one in the victim's back, the victim pitching forward. Then the killer rolls him over and sets the victim on fire. To disguise the body, perhaps, or even . . . to punish the corpse, disfigure it vengefully.

"But what about the other tracks?" Sara asked.

"That doesn't make sense," Grissom admitted, eyes tightening with thought, "unless . . ."

Still kneeling over the impression, Maher asked, "Unless what?"

"Unless the killer didn't have the gasoline along, and had to go back for it."

"Or," Maher offered, "the killer may have had the gas along, but left something behind here at the scene—in the heat of the moment, eh?—and had to come back for it."

"Possible," Grissom granted.

Pulling the first cast up, Maher said, "One other thing."

"Yeah?"

He held the casting of the impression where they both could see it. "Our killer has new boots. I couldn't get a better casting in the parking lot of a shoe store with boots right out of the box."

"So," Grissom said, "we've finally got some real evidence."

Rising, Maher said, "Sara, take your photos of the

rest while I bring Grissom up to speed, with the sulfur process."

Pulling her camera out again, Sara asked Maher, "And what are you going to be doing?"

"Well, we've got the killer's feet. Be nice to know his weapon too, eh?"

She just looked at him.

"When I've got both of you working the footprints, I'll go to find our missing bullets."

The sun was hiding and the air was growing colder. Was it going to start snowing again? No wonder Maher was trying to work fast.

Cormier, who'd been a spectator on the sideline for some while, came up to them then. "You folks gonna be much longer?"

"Some time, yes," Grissom said.

"Then I'm goin' back down to the hotel and see if anybody's tryin' to dig us out or anything . . . and find out if the phones are workin' yet. Be back in an hour, okay?"

"Should be fine," Maher said. "And bring up some more coffee, eh?"

Sara whispered to Grissom, "Good day, eh?"

But the reference was lost on him.

Cormier waved and started down the trail.

"Smallish feet for a man," Sara pointed out as the hotel manager disappeared in the trees.

"He doesn't have new boots, though," Grissom said.

"At least, not that he's wearing."

"Then," Grissom said, "we can't eliminate him—or anybody else—as a suspect, yet. So let's get back to work and dig up some more evidence."

Grissom rejoined Maher over by the Sterno burner. Sara went back to work taking pictures, using the tripod and digging down with the scale. She even sprayed the gray primer in a couple of the prints. Sneaking a look at Grissom, she noticed that again he seemed utterly content in his work. Sara wondered idly if she looked that happy as she was spray-painting snow.

Somehow, she doubted it.

8

CATHERINE WILLOWS COULD THINK OF ONLY ONE PLACE TO go, on a case this cold: back to the beginning. Under her direction, the CSIs watched old security video-tapes from Mandalay Bay, the Chinese restaurant; they read original reports of the detectives and the day-shift crime lab, combing them for any lead that might have been missed thus far. Nothing promising had yet emerged.

Catherine refused to be intimidated by the year they had lost. Nor would she accept the option that they'd run into a killer smart enough to get away with murder. Some murderers did go unapprehended, of course—rare ones who really did outsmart the police; and others who were lucky enough to draw second-rate detectives and third-rate crime labs. Most killers—even the smart ones—made at least one mis-take, often many more than one, in the commission of their homicides.

Tonight, Catherine was playing Grissom's role, checking in with her people, cheering them on, exchanging ideas, priming pumps. Walking down the hall through the warren of labs under the cool aqua-tinged lighting, she ran into Greg Sanders, the young, spiky-haired lab rat who looked more like an outlaw skateboarder than the bright young scientist he was. Under his white lab coat, Sanders wore a black tee shirt with a WEEZER logo.

"Tell me you found something," she said.

"I have checked every result from the day-shift lab reports."

"Tell me," she repeated, "you found something."

"I have personally examined every bit of evidence collected by Ecklie's people: random hairs, fibers, even the Chinese food container from the Lexus."

"Tell me. You found something?"

He pursed his lips as he thought, carefully; then, abruptly, he said, "No."

She placed a hand on the young man's shoulder. "Tell me when you find something."

Catherine moved on.

She found Warrick Brown—still working on the tire marks—at a computer terminal, fingers flying on the keyboard. His manner was cool, deceptively low-key. Catherine considered Warrick an intense, even driven investigator—the sharp, alert eyes in the melancholy face were the tell.

"Anything?" she asked.

He looked up at her glumly. "The tire mark closest to where Missy got dumped is a General. It's an after-market tire that fits a lot of SUVs."

"Which tells us an SUV stopped along the stretch of road where Missy Sherman was found."

"Yes—an SUV that may or may not have been driven by the killer who dumped the body there. With a tire distinctive enough to say it belongs to an SUV, but not narrowing it down much."

"So," Catherine said, "nothing."

"Not nothing," he said. "It's a start."

"Some people say the glass is half-full."

"Grissom says, dust the glass for prints and see who drank the water."

Catherine chuckled softly. "What about the other marks you casted?"

"Two motorcycles."

"Probably not significant."

"Probably not," he agreed. "One tire from an ATV, which is a possibility, but a stretch; the others still unknown."

Catherine nodded. "Keep working it."

"You know I will."

As she moved down the hall, Catherine savored the sweet thought of solving a case day shift had dropped the ball on. That was hardly the top priority, of course—finding the truth and making it possible for justice to be meted out remained much higher on her list; but she'd be lying to herself if she didn't admit the appeal of outshining Sheriff Mobley's lapdog, Conrad Ecklie.

First-shift supervisor Ecklie, after all, gloated over each perceived victory, and had a ready excuse for every loss. He'd made his bones badgering the other two shifts at any opportunity. It would be nice, Catherine thought, if they could find a way to shut him up, if only for a little while.

In the morgue, Dr. Robbins was doing only marginally better than the others.

"Definitely, suffocation," he said. "And it was a plastic bag."

"We know this because . . . ?"

The bearded coroner showed her a sheet of paper. "Read for yourself—tox screen came back, heightened CO_2 level."

"All right," she said, "at least that's something."

"Yeah, but that's all I can tell you on the subject. If you're waiting for me to identify the type and brand of the plastic bag, you'll be disappointed."

Catherine shook her head, patted his shoulder. "You're never a disappointment to me, Doc. . . . Just keep looking."

That left Nick and the videotapes. She found him in the break room with an open bag of microwave popcorn, a Diet Coke, and the remote. His three-button gray shirt had flecks of popcorn salt on the front, his black jeans, too.

Draped in the doorway, she said, "Midnight movies, huh? What's playing—*Rocky Horror?*"

"Well, it's the time warp, all right," he said, and his grin had a little pride in it, which encouraged Catherine.

"Meaning?" she said, at his side now.

"These year-old tapes gave up something. I think. You tell me. . . ."

She pulled up a chair and said, "Pass the popcorn."

He did, and she nibbled, while he went on: "First, you have to understand that there are no cameras on any of the exits at the Mandalay Bay . . . so we have nothing of cars leaving the premises."

"Well, we wouldn't want it to be too easy, right?"

"That's a sentiment I've never quite grasped." He backed up the tape a ways and hit PLAY. "This is at just about 1:35 P.M."

The tape rolled and Catherine, munching the popcorn but glued to the screen, watched the grainy black-and-white image of cars turning into the Mandalay Bay parking lot from the Strip. The camera looked down at the cars and made it impossible to see inside the vehicles. Three or four cars rolled by before she saw what Nick wanted her to see, a Lexus RX300, pulling into the lot.

"That's Missy?" Catherine asked.

"Yeah. Their Lexus had a Michigan State sticker in the rear window, and it's tough to see at this angle, but, if you know it's there . . ."

He showed her what he meant, and Catherine was able to catch the sticker with its helmeted Spartan head, despite the high angle, or enough of it anyway to sell her on this being Missy's Lexus.

"Now the next car . . ." Nick backed the tape up again, and let the tape play again until the Lexus pulled through the camera shot once more, and was replaced by a dark, boxy car. ". . . is Regan Mortenson's gray Camry."

"All right. Both women were at the Chinese restaurant. Any security tapes available from inside the place?"

He nodded. "The two of them walking through to the restaurant and again when they're leaving. One on one camera, other on another."

"They arrived together," Catherine said, no big deal, "they left together."

"The tape doesn't lie. It's just like Regan told Brass and me, only . . . look at this."

Nick fast-forwarded the tape, the clock in the corner rolling over in high speed. Just after 11:45 P.M., he slowed the tape and brought it to normal speed.

As the grainy images flickered across the monitor screen, Nick said, "I was going through the rest of the tape at high speed . . . probably the same way Ecklie's guys did it . . . but my soda took a tumble and as I reached out to catch it, I stopped the machine right about here."

Cued up properly, the tape revealed several cars rolling past the entrance without pulling in. A few made the turn into the lot, then at 11:49—according to the timer in the corner—an SUV slowed as it approached the entrance, rolled by, then sped up and disappeared.

Catherine froze, a half-handful of popcorn paused in midair. "Holy . . . That looks like . . ."

"It sure does," Nick said, and he backed the tape up until the SUV was once again in front of the entrance, then still-framed the image and—using a nearby computer keyboard—punched keys, zooming in on the side of the vehicle, a Lexus RX300, same color as the Shermans'. It wasn't terribly clear, but in the rear window was the white-and-green Michigan State sticker, Spartan head and all.

Catherine returned the handful of popcorn to the bag. Quietly, as if in church, she said, "And Ecklie's people never noticed this?"

"Apparently not—no record of it." Nick shrugged. "I might've missed it, too, if I hadn't almost knocked over my Coke. We were all looking for cars coming in the entrance, not passing it by. . . . Let me tweak this a little. . . ."

He zoomed in even closer and tried to clear the picture. It remained a little pixilated, but the sticker was unmistakably the Michigan State sticker on the passenger rear window of a Lexus RX300.

"What," Nick asked, "are the odds that this is someone else's Lexus with exactly the same Spartan sticker, in the same position on the same window?"

"Grissom would give you a figure," Catherine said. "I'll just say, slim and none. But, Nick—that car was found in the parking lot!"

He nodded. "That's a fact." Gesturing at the still frame again, he added, "Another fact: this is the main entrance. There are other ways into that lot, and not all are covered by security cams."

Catherine, amazed, said, "Can we ever see the driver?"

"I don't think so. We'll try some image enhancement, but with the angle, and reflections . . . Probably not gonna be lucky on that one."

"Nick, what about talking to the people inside the hotel, when the SUV drove by?"

"Even assuming the driver came inside at some point, there'd be thousands of people in that casino alone. And that was over a year ago. How are we going to track them down?"

"You're right," she admitted. "If this crime had gone down yesterday, we'd be facing tough odds—a year later. . . . So Missy was abducted in her own car, and driven off, and after her murder, the Lexus was returned to the lot?"

"Looking that way."

She thought for a moment. "If the Chinese food in Missy's stomach is undigested, then by the time her car comes back to the hotel . . ."

"She's dead," Nick said.

Perplexed, Catherine pointed at the screen. "Then who the hell is driving that Lexus?"

"Maybe somebody who owns a chest freezer."

"May," Catherine said, "be." She pushed a button on the intercom. "Warrick?"

His voice crackled back over the line. "Cath?"

"Head over to the video lab, would you?"

Soon they were showing Warrick the tape; then they shared with him what they'd surmised.

"If you're thinkin' I need to put my proctology tool up that Lexus," Warrick said, shaking his head, "I gotta tell ya—that baby wasn't that spotless at the dealership. Anything I find could've been easily displaced when Sherman had the interior professionally cleaned."

Catherine asked innocently, "You ID those other tires yet?"

Warrick twitched half a smirk. "That's a work-in-progress."

"Which is the better lead?"

"The Lexus."

"Well, then," she said. "Round up a detective and head back to the Sherman place."

Warrick stood and gave her a grumpy look. "You know, if Gris was here—"

"He'd send your ass out to the Shermans to pick up that Lexus."

Warrick considered that for a second. "Yeah, he would," he admitted, and was gone.

Jim Brass drove Warrick back to the quiet upper-middle-class housing development; calling on people so late at night—it was approaching midnight—was something Warrick could never get used to, rolling into slumbering neighborhoods, delivering nightmares.

Again, one light was on upstairs, and another in the living room of the mission-style house on Sky Hollow Drive. No loud TV emanated, however, and Alex Sherman answered on the first knock. For a change, they were expected: Brass had called ahead, though the detective had given the man no details.

His white sweatshirt (with green Michigan State logo) and green sweatpants rumpled, Sherman greeted them with the hollow look of a man who was either sleeping way too much or hardly at all.

"Do you know something?" he asked, his tone at once urgent and resigned. He had lost his wife and even the best news could not bring her back.

"We do have a lead," Brass said. "You remember Warrick Brown, from the crime lab?"

"Of course."

Warrick picked up the ball. "Could we step inside? We need to talk again."

"Sure . . . come on in. I made coffee."

They did not refuse the offer. This time it was Warrick who sat beside Sherman on the couch, while

Brass perched on the edge of a nearby chair. Sherman's dark razor-cut hair stuck out here and there at odd angles, and the man's glasses rode low on his nose. He hadn't shaved in a while.

"I'm a little out of it," he admitted. "I'm getting calls from Missy's relatives, and . . . I haven't even made the funeral arrangements yet."

Brass said, "It's hard getting used to the idea of your wife being gone."

Sherman looked sharply at the detective. "I was used to her being gone. What I'm not used to is her being back . . . and murdered . . . and . . ."

Warrick thought the man might weep, but it was clear he was way beyond that. Nothing to do but get into it. . . .

"Mr. Sherman," Warrick said, "did you ever wonder why it was that you couldn't find your wife's SUV that night?"

Sherman shrugged—not just his shoulders, his whole body seemed to capitulate. "I assumed I was just . . . too screwed up. Too worried and anxious to tell my ass from a hole in the ground."

"It never occurred to you that the car actually may not have been there."

Frowning, Sherman said, "What are you talking about? It was found right there in the lot."

Warrick nodded. "What did you say at the time, when you were questioned?"

"I said, I know my own car, and it wasn't there or I would have seen it."

"You were right."

Sherman didn't grasp Warrick's meaning yet. "But

like I said, I've come to realize I must've been so out of it . . ." Sherman's features had a hard, almost sinister look as he turned a burning gaze on the CSI. "Or . . . are you saying something else?"

"I'm saying something else, sir. Tonight, we finally figured out why you didn't see the Lexus."

"My God," Sherman said, jumping ahead a step, sitting up; it was almost as if he'd been woken with a splash of water. "You mean it really wasn't there?" Sherman finished for him, his eyes widening a little behind his glasses.

Warrick nodded slowly.

"Well, where the hell was it, when I was looking for it?"

"That's just it—we don't know."

"Then how do you know it wasn't there?"

Warrick explained, in some detail, what had been discovered by Nick, going over the surveillance videos.

Sherman's voice rose, and possessed a tremble that might have been sorrow or anger or perhaps both, as he said, "Why, after more than a goddamn year, are you people just now figuring that out?"

Warrick searched for words. Should he tell the grieving husband that the reason was because Nick spilled a pop can? Or maybe share with him the superiority of Grissom's graveyard crew over Ecklie's day shift?

Brass, who'd been quietly sitting drinking the coffee, now sat forward and bailed Warrick out. "A year ago," he said, "a whole different set of investigators, assigned to a missing person case, were looking for cars coming into the hotel. Now, one of our crime lab investigators, new to the case . . . the murder case, Mr. Sherman . . . caught a glimpse of what looked like your car driving past the entrance."

This seemed to placate Sherman, who said, "Well, you told me fresh eyes would be a good thing for the investigation. And I appreciate the validation of my original statement . . . but what good does it do?"

"Plenty," Warrick said. "We think Missy was abducted in her own car, driven away and the car brought back to the Mandalay Bay and parked again."

"To confuse the issue," Brass said.

"All right." Sherman seemed more alert now. "What can I do to help?"

Warrick said, "Allow us to take your van into custody and search for evidence again."

This seemed to disappoint him. "The police didn't find anything a year ago. And the van has been cleaned since then. Stem to stern."

"We know. But with this new information, we need to take another look. We hope you won't ask us to go to the trouble of a warrant, because that will slow us down."

Sherman said, "Whatever it takes. It means a lot to me that you people are doing something."

As Brass went back to the Taurus to call for a tow truck, Warrick said, "We appreciate this, sir. And we'll stay at it until we find whoever did this."

Sherman's expression seemed doubtful. "No offense, but you hear a lot about unsolved cases, and even about people who get caught and then walk . . ."

"We have high arrest and conviction rates, Mr. Sherman. We're ranked the number two crime lab in the country."

Sherman found a smile somewhere. "Well, I guess I know what that means."

"Sir?"

"You try harder."

Warrick returned the man's smile.

"I'll get you the keys," he said, and went off.

The tow truck showed up quickly and, within an hour, Warrick had the SUV in the CSI garage, ready to do his own search of Missy Sherman's Lexus.

The exterior was clean and he checked for prints, but came up with only a few, probably mostly Sherman's, and maybe those of employees at the car wash. Warrick had already asked Brass to contact Premium Car Wash and take employees' prints. Any employees who'd quit in the meantime would have to be tracked down; once again, Warrick was glad not to have Brass's job.

He compared the prints from the Lexus with Sherman's prints on file; one of two sets of prints on the driver's door and the hood belonged to Sherman. The other set belonged to some John Doe—a car wash employee, maybe . . . but almost certainly not Missy's killer.

Being essentially a liquid, fingerprints on the exterior of the vehicle would have long since evaporated in the dry Vegas heat. A fingerprint found in, say, Florida, where the humidity was much higher, would evaporate more slowly. The only way that fingerprint belonged to the killer was if the killer had touched the van a hell of a lot more recently than when murdering Missy.

Warrick also got prints, some full, some only partials, from the other door handles on the vehicle and also from the hood; but all proved to be Sherman's. Getting trace from the tires—to see where the vehicle had been during its missing time—would be useless after the car wash, and Ecklie's people had neglected to do it at the time of discovery because they'd assumed they knew where the SUV had been the whole time.

And when we assume, as Grissom was wont to say, *we make an ass of you and me.*

Warrick opened the rear hatch and combed the carpeting for clues. As he expected, Alex Sherman's cleaning up after Ecklie's people had left little evidence behind: a scuff mark here, a stray hair there.

The scuff mark on the plastic seemed to have come from something black and rubber, but probably not from Missy Sherman's shoe. Chances were that if she had been thrown back there and scuffed the plastic with the heel of her shoe, more than one such mark would've been left.

As for the hair, it was black and short, more likely from Alex Sherman than from his wife or her killer.

Still, Warrick took a scraping from the scuff mark and bagged the hair. He just didn't expect them to pan out.

More of the same awaited him in the backseat, where he bagged a fiber or two and another hair, the latter looking like it was indeed from Missy—black, but much longer than a stray from Alex's razor-cut, where it might have fallen from the driver's seat. He drew a blank on the front passenger seat, then finally made his way to the driver's side.

Using his mini-MagLite, Warrick went over every square inch of the seat and the back. He was about to give up when he glimpsed something pressed between the headrest and the top of the seat. He moved in closer: a blonde hair. Missy's hair was black; also, this hair was longer than Missy's hairstyle would have given up. He plucked it carefully with his tweezers, then bagged it.

As Warrick closed the last door, Brass strolled in, looking bored; but then the detective always appeared bored, even at his most interested. "Anything?"

"Few hairs and a couple of fibers, but this wagon's been cleaned so thoroughly, I was lucky to find 'em."

Warrick stood looking at the SUV for a long moment, as if this were a showroom and he was seriously considering buying. What had he missed? His gut . . . which he listened to religiously, despite Grissom's warnings . . . told him there must be something.

But if there was, why hadn't Ecklie's people found it?

Then he said to Brass, "Is Ecklie a dick?"

"Does a bear shit in the woods?"

"Is graveyard crime lab better than day shift?"

"You're better than just about any CSI shift in the country."

Warrick, surprised by this admission from Brass, said, "Yeah, I know. Thanks. I don't think I'm done here. . . ."

The criminalist went to the driver's side door, bending, looking hard . . . the top ridge, the window, the handle, the . . .

Hooooold it, he thought.

The handle.

Just like the guys on Ecklie's crew, he'd dusted the outside, but what about the underside? Getting out his mini-MagLite, he knelt next to the door and shone the beam up at the underside of the door handle.

"Something?" asked Brass.

"Another brilliant idea . . . nets another nothing."

Warrick stood, stepped back, surveyed the vehicle again. Then he opened the door, glanced around the interior. Looked at the steering wheel, the dash, the windshield and, finally, looked up at . . .

. . . the visor.

"Jim, get me a forceps out of my bag, would ya?"

Brass withdrew the instrument from the silver case and brought it to Warrick. "Got something?"

"Don't know yet."

Using the forceps, Warrick slowly pulled down the visor. Next to the airbag warning label lay a small plastic lid. He used the forceps to raise the plastic and a tiny light came on next to a business-card-sized mirror. Warrick looked at himself in the mirror, and also at a small bit of fingerprint on the corner of the glass.

"There you are," he said, as if to his own image.

Brass was alongside the vehicle now. "Like what you see?"

"It's more than just my handsome face—it's a fingerprint that Ecklie's people missed."

"How'd they manage that?"

"Didn't pull down the visor. And I bet once I dust the plastic lid, we may have more."

"I thought you didn't bet anymore," Brass said.

"Not often," he said, climbing out of the car to go after his fingerprint kit. "And I couldn't tell you what the odds are, here . . . other than that they've just improved."

A white plastic Sears bag in hand, Catherine Willows walked briskly down the corridor, like a shopper at a mall heading for a really great sale.

Catherine, however, had already made her purchases. After making the rounds of just about every appliance store in Clark County, Catherine had finally ended up "where America shops," to quote a slogan from bygone years. The Sears bag held—potentially—two of the most elusive answers in the Missy Sherman inquiry.

She barged right in, startling Dr. Robbins, who was at his desk taking care of paperwork.

"Need a look at one of your customers, Doc," she said, striding over to the vault where Missy Sherman still resided.

"Catherine—what are you doing?"

Setting her bag on a nearby worktable, Catherine opened the vault, slid out the tray bearing Missy's body, then turned and grabbed something from the shopping bag. As she did, Robbins came hustling over, barely letting his metal crutch touch the floor.

"You're pulling a Grissom, aren't you?" Robbins asked.

"I prefer to think of it as a Willows." She held up a

small blue piece of rubber that looked a little like a pudgy bullet, rounded at one end, flat on the other end, barely an inch long.

"What do you have there, Catherine?"

Carefully brushing the hair away from the face of the victim, Catherine placed the rounded tip of the rubber nipple against the dead woman's cheek.

The indentation matched perfectly.

Smiling triumphantly and holding up the blue rubber object between thumb and forefinger, Catherine said, "Doctor, you are looking at a frost warning device found in Kenmore chest freezers sold at Sears."

"So," Robbins said, "she was kept in a Kenmore freezer."

"That's the theory. Give us girls a hand, would you?"

"My pleasure."

Grunting, Catherine said, "Here—let's sit her up . . ."

"Okay . . ."

They lifted Missy's corpse so that she . . . it . . . was now sitting on the slab, leaning a little left toward Robbins, almost as if Missy were trying to lay her head on Robbins' shoulder, restfully.

Then, while Robbins held Missy more or less upright, Catherine removed the other item from the bag, a metal rack covered with white plastic, designed to sit across the opening of the freezer and hold smaller items.

Catherine held the tray to the hash mark on the back of Missy's arm.

"Shit," Catherine said.

It didn't match.

Perplexed, she stepped back. "Why didn't that work?" she said.

Robbins looked at the corpse's arm, then at the rack and finally back at the arm. "Flip the rack," he suggested.

She did, then placed it against Missy's arm—perfect!

"That's more like it," she said with some satisfaction. "Now we know what kind of freezer we're looking for."

She helped Doc Robbins lower Missy back down. As the coroner covered his charge carefully, and eased the slab back inside the vault, he asked, "How are you going to track down the specific unit?"

She shrugged. "Frankly, Doc, I have no idea. I'm just happy to put a couple of the pieces together, and start making out a picture. What do you think? Should I go door to door?"

He closed the vault, consigning Missy Sherman's remains to cold storage—again. "How many Kenmore chest freezers with racks and little blue plugs are there in Vegas?"

"Haven't the foggiest. No database I know of would be any help at all."

"What about sales records?"

"Possibly," she said, "but if we go back to when Kenmore started using the blue plug and the rack, that might be a year ago or it could be twenty. Haven't checked, yet."

"If it's twenty," Robbins said, "I would imagine Sears has sold its share here in Vegas."

"And who's to say the freezer was sold in Vegas? Hundreds of people move here every month, bringing their freezers and other things along in the back of their covered wagons."

Robbins nodded. "No offense, Catherine, but I'm glad I don't have your job."

Catherine glanced toward the vault where Missy resided. "You may find this hard to believe, Doc, but I don't spend much time envying you, either."

He smiled at her. "Nice work, Catherine."

"Thanks. Later, Doc."

For almost five minutes, Catherine raced around CSI HQ looking for Warrick and Nick, going room to room with no luck. Finally she found Warrick in the fingerprint lab.

"You wouldn't be in here," she said hopefully, "if you hadn't found something in that Lexus."

Warrick reported his findings, concluding, "The hair and fibers are at Trace, and I'm doing the print off the mirror."

"And?"

"And it doesn't belong to either Alex or Missy Sherman."

"Dare I hope . . . ? But it could be someone from the car wash."

"Could be," Warrick admitted. "And we won't be able to print and eliminate any of them until the car wash opens in the morning."

"You don't have to wait till morning to run it through AFIS, though."

"That's my next step. . . . You've got that look, Catherine."

"What look?"

"Cat? Canary? What have you come up with?"

She told him what she'd learned about the freezer.

"Sweet," Warrick said. "Forward movement. Gotta love it."

Nodding, she said, "Stay on those prints."

"Try and stop me."

She was barely out the fingerprint lab door when her cell phone chirped; she answered it.

"It's Nick." In the background, she could hear the familiar howl of the Tahoe's siren.

Talking and walking, she said, "Where are you rolling to?"

"Murder scene! I think you need to be in on this."

"We're focused on the Sherman woman. You've gone solo before, Nick—what's the problem?"

Nick worked his voice up over the siren: "Radio chatter I been listening to, street cops think it's a strangulation. But no ligature marks!"

Like Missy Sherman.

"Who's the vic?"

"As-yet-unidentified woman about Missy Sherman's age. If she's a thawed-out corpse-sickle, too, we could have a whole 'nother deal, here."

Just what they needed: another serial killer.

"Where's the crime scene?" Catherine said, almost yelling into the phone, which leached siren noise.

Nick was almost yelling, too. "Charleston Boulevard—all the way out at the east end."

"Nick—there's nothing out there."

"Just our crime scene . . . and some houses, up the hill."

"I'll grab Warrick and we'll meet you there." She clicked off without waiting for his response.

In the Tahoe's front passenger seat, Warrick said, "This damn case didn't make any sense when it was just a missing person turned murder. Now you're telling me it might be a double homicide?"

Deciding not to get him stirred up with her serial-killer notion, Catherine—behind the wheel—shook her head. "We don't know the murders are connected."

"Then why are we heading out to the crime scene?"

She shrugged. "Back Nick up."

After that, the pair drove mostly in silence, Warrick unsuccessfully fiddling with the radio trying to scrounge up the same kind of chatter Nick had overheard. They surely would have arrived at the scene a minute or two sooner if Warrick had been driving, but his race-car tendencies made Catherine nervous, so she'd slid behind the wheel. She had enough stress right now.

Soon, she was easing to a stop near Nick's Tahoe. They exited their Tahoe into the chilly night with field kits in latex-gloved hands, their breath visible. Streetlights didn't reach this far past the end of the paved road and halogen work lamps had been set up near the body.

Charleston Boulevard dead-ended at the foot of a mountain, near where several half-million-dollar homes nestled on a ridge, modern near-mansions with a view on rocky, scrubby desolation. Little more than a hundred yards to the south from the houses, near the entrance to a construction road that led off

around the mountain, a ditch on the very edge of the
desert had become a dumping ground for trash—
bulky waste items like carpeting and old sinks, and—
tonight—the nude body of a slender white woman
around thirty years old.

Just off the side of the construction road, on her
back, arms splayed, legs together, the corpse rested
amid the garbage, alabaster skin glowing under the
brightness of the halogen beams. The glow intensified
every time the strobe on Nick's camera went off.

Catherine and Warrick came closer. The uniformed officers were divided into three pairs, their
cars blocking the eastbound lane of Charleston
Boulevard and a gravel area to the left of the CSI
Tahoes. The first pair of officers stood guard near the
body, the second pair were assigned to keep any cars
coming up Charleston from stopping and gawking
and the last pair stood between the dead woman and
a handful of concerned, confused residents who'd
wandered down from the expensive homes in the
mountain's shadow.

"She frozen?" Warrick asked.

Nick snapped off two more quick pictures. "You'd
have to ask Doc Robbins, but I'd say no—none of that
moisture under the body found at the Lake Mead
scene."

"Strangled, you think," Catherine said.

"Suffocation, anyway," Nick said.

The woman's eyes were open, staring skyward at
nothing—with the distinctive petechial hemorrhaging
of asphyxia.

"Want me to check for tire marks?" Warrick asked.

"Please," Catherine said.

Moments later, Catherine glanced over to see Warrick slowly looking over the gravel area at the end of the road, in search of tire tracks from the vehicle that had dumped the body. Catherine walked up to the detective who'd caught this case, Lieutenant Lockwood, a tall, athletically built African-American. He gave her a grim smile as she approached.

"Lieutenant," she said.

"Catherine," he said.

"Any witnesses?"

"None we know of."

"Who called it in?"

He nodded toward one of the squad cars, where an Hispanic woman sat quietly in the back, a tissue to her face. Catherine watched until the lady dropped the tissue and Catherine could get a better look at the woman's profile. About all Catherine could tell from here was that the woman's black hair was tied back in a bun. "Who is she?"

"Lupita Castillo," Lockwood said. "Domestic." He turned and pointed toward a rambling two-story stucco.

"Who lives there?"

Tilting his notebook toward the halogen work lights, Lockwood checked. "Jim and Catherine Dietz. He's a honcho with the Democratic party, she's a high-powered attorney. Ms. Castillo, off work, was making her way to the bus stop, couple blocks from here. Stumbles on our dead naked woman."

Looking at the rocky ground, Catherine said, "And Mr. Democrat and Mrs. Mouthpiece can't drive their maid home, or at least to the bus stop?"

"I had the same thought," Lockwood said. "Ms. Castillo says her employers usually drive her to and from work, but they're out of town. Comes by the house every other day just to make sure everything's okay."

"The Dietzes are where?"

"Disney World with their six-year-old daughter."

"Where'd Ms. Castillo call from?"

"She went back up to the Dietz house."

"What was she doing there so late on a Saturday night?"

Lockwood chuckled. "Jeez, Catherine, we think alike."

"Great minds."

"I asked her and she said that she came over after Mass, made herself dinner and watched a cable movie. She said the family lets her do that, when they're away—makes it look like someone's home."

"Sounds credible," she said. She gave Lockwood a tight, businesslike smile. "Time to go to work."

With Nick taking photos, Catherine was free to do a detailed study of the body.

The woman's blonde hair spiked a little on the top and, on the back and sides, was no longer than Nick's. Tiny, junkie-thin, with nearly translucent skin, the woman reminded Catherine of the dancers she used to work with who were locked in clubs all night and their apartments all day. They never saw the sun and their skin took on a ghostly pallor. This woman shared that unhealthy skin tone, but for the crimson slashes of lipstick.

With her eyes open, the dead woman seemed to

float above the garbage pile; she might have been on her back in a swimming pool, looking up at the piece of moon and the scattering of stars.

Catherine sensed someone at her side.

Nick.

"Just threw her away," he said, his expression grave. "Like another piece of trash." He shook his head.

"Oh yeah," Catherine said. "We have to nail this monster, Nick . . ." She gave him her loveliest smile. ". . . for leaving us a garbage dump to process as a crime scene, if nothing else."

He nodded, eyebrows high, a smile beginning to dig a dimple in one cheek, and said, "You got that right."

And they went to work.

9

THE CRIME SCENE WAS STILL AND LOVELY, SUNLIGHT DANCING off the white expanse, with almost no wind. Sara was taking photos when the hotel manager trudged back up into the crime-scene area, a thermos under either arm. His expression was grave, but he sounded cheerful enough as he called, "Hot coffee!"

Grissom and Maher immediately slogged over to where Cormier had set up shop at the tree that served as their watch post. Maher in his parka might have been reuniting with his Eskimo brother, when he approached the similarly attired Cormier. The hotel manager poured the brew into Styrofoam cups he'd withdrawn from a coat pocket. Sara finished her latest series of photos, then joined the group. Cormier handed her a steaming cup, which she blew on before taking a hesitant sip.

"I was just telling your partners here," Cormier said, "the sky's plannin' to dump more snow on us."

She looked from Grissom to Maher, their faces as grim as Cormier's. "More snow," she said.

Cormier nodded. "Weather report is not encouraging. Could be as many as ten more inches."

"So much for the forensics conference," Grissom said.

"Officially canceled," Cormier said. "Got an e-mail from two of the state board members who set it up."

Maher sighed over his cup, and the cold steam of his breath mingled with the hot steam of the coffee. "Is anybody getting in?"

With a quick head shake, Cormier said, "No one gettin' out, either. I don't look for the State Police to even try, till later."

"Define 'later,' " Grissom said.

"Not right now," Cormier said, ambiguously.

Sara sighed a cloud, and in exasperation said, "What next?"

Grissom turned to her and spoke over the ridge of his muffler. "Finish our coffee and go back to working the crime scene. Just because it snows doesn't change the job, Sara."

Yes, out here in the beautiful snowy woods, Sara was experiencing a true Grissom moment. Only her boss would provide a literal answer to what a billy goat would have easily perceived as a rhetorical question.

Grissom was asking the Canadian, "What's the story with the sticks over there?"

Sara had been wondering that herself.

"It's a technique developed by two Saskatchewan game wardens," Maher said. "Buddies of mine—Les Oystryk and D. J. McGill. Come on, I'll show you."

Maher led the CSIs to the stick he'd planted at the downhill end of his line. "It's a pretty simple theory, really," he said, gesturing with a gloved hand, as if passing a benediction. "I placed a stake where the bullet entered the snow."

Eyes tight, Grissom asked, "Denoted by the beginning of the streak you saw yesterday?"

"Exactly. Normally, we'd run a string or flagging tape twenty feet to a second stake, aligning it with the streak in the snow that showed the bullet's path. But with snow this deep, I simply ran the second stake as straight as I could, and planted it without the string."

Sara asked, "And the bullet never deviates from the path in the snow?"

" 'Never' isn't in my lexicon," Maher said. "If the slug hit a rock or something, deviation is possible, even probable—but with snow like this to slow the bullet, the path won't be altered much."

Grissom gestured back toward the toboggan. "Which is where your metal detector comes in."

"Yes," the constable said. "Lucky I brought it along for my presentation, eh? . . . I think we'll find the bullet within three feet of that line, on either side."

"This technique," Grissom said. "How often is it successful?"

"Most of the time . . . 'Always' isn't in my lexicon, either." He turned toward the hotel manager, who was still under the tree, and called, "Mr. Cormier!"

"Yes, sir?"

"Need a favor!"

Cormier came over. "What can I do you for, Mr. Maher?"

Pointing just beyond and to the left of the body,

Maher said, "Take the shovel and clear me a space in the snow, oh, three by three feet."

Nodding, Cormier asked, "How deep?"

"Down to the dirt, please. We're creating a control area."

"Shovel's just about my level of high tech," Cormier said, and marched off to the toboggan, where he fetched the shovel and went over to start digging.

While Grissom worked on casting footprints, Sara helped Maher get his metal detector assembled and running. Giving him room, she accompanied the Canadian as he and it traveled back and forth over the track the bullet had taken. Every time he pointed at a spot, she placed a smaller stick.

She'd marked only two spots when he stopped, stared at the ground in confusion, and said, "Well, that's weird, eh?"

"What is?"

"Gettin' a beep here, on something a whole lot bigger than a bullet."

"Any idea what?"

Maher shook his head. She inserted a stick at the spot and he kept moving. When he finished, four different places had been marked by Sara in that fashion.

Sara asked, "Now what?"

"We run the metal detector over our control area," Maher said.

She watched as he ran the detector over the bare spot Cormier had created.

"All right," Maher said. "It's clear—no metal in the dirt. Sara, get a garbage bag from the sled, would you?"

Sara trotted over, grabbed one of the black bags, came back and handed it to Maher.

As he ripped out the seams, Maher said, "Now we'll cover the bare spot Mr. Cormier made for us."

"Oh," Sara said, understanding. "We're going to put the snow we marked onto the plastic, and sift through it."

Maher nodded. "But first we dig. You take those two," he said, pointing at the two marked spots nearest the downhill end of the line. Then he went over and knelt in the snow, next to two spots further up the line. "And I'll take these two."

Sara had hardly begun to dig down when she saw something pink, and froze. "Constable! Grissom! . . . I think you both better see this."

They came over.

Grissom crouched over her find. "Blood . . ."

Maher, hovering, asked, "What the hell's that doing here?"

Reflexively, they all glanced back toward the snowy hump of the body almost ten yards uphill; but the victim wasn't talking.

Maher looked from Grissom to Sara. "Didn't you say the only blood was near the body?"

"That's right," Sara said. "We didn't see any this far down."

Grissom asked, "Could this patch of blood have already been covered by snow?"

"I don't think so," Sara said. "Not in the time between our hearing those shots and coming onto this crime scene."

Maher's expression, in the fuzzy cameo created by

the parka, was thoughtful. "Could be someone covered it on purpose, hastily kicked snow over it. . . . Besides those footprints, you see any other disturbed snow?"

Grissom said, "No," and Sara shook her head.

Then she asked her boss, "Do you have one of those bug specimen bottles on you?"

A small bottle materialized in Grissom's gloved palm; he handed the container over to her.

Using the cap, she shooed the pink snow into the bottle, then closed it. She handed the little bottle to Grissom and went back to her digging, only now she was more careful, much slower, searching every inch to make sure she didn't miss any evidence. Maher went to work on his spots, and Grissom returned to footprint duty.

Stripping off her gloves, she started digging with her fingers, not trusting the shovel or even her gloves to keep her from contaminating any more evidence. The cold and wet of the snow was kind of refreshing at first, but it only took a couple of minutes before her fingers turned red and the tips started to numb up.

She was just starting to think taking off the gloves was a really dumb idea when she touched something hard.

Her hand jumped out of the hole as if she'd been bitten by a snake.

"Are you all right?" Grissom asked, running over to her. He sounded genuinely concerned.

"Something metallic," she said. "Not small . . ."

They both looked toward Maher, working at his

own spot; but his eyes were on them, as well. The constable came over and drew a forceps from a pocket. "Can you get it with this?"

"Should be able to." She accepted the tool, inserted her bare hand and the forceps down into the hole. Maneuvering carefully, she worked the ridged jaws around the object. Squeezing, she dragged the object out of the snow, like pulling a tooth. It felt heavy and came out slowly. When the object finally appeared from the snow, they all froze, as if the cold had finally caught up with them.

Only it was not cold, rather shock.

"A knife?" Maher asked, as if he wanted confirmation of what his eyes had shown him. "You said our vic was shot."

"He was," Grissom said.

Sara held up the knife in the jaws of the forceps, squinting at it. The thing wasn't that big—blade no more than four inches long.

"Our victim was shot, all right," she said. "And so . . . how do we explain this?"

"More blood," Grissom said, almost admiringly.

A pink sheen covered much of the blade.

They all traded looks.

"There's no knife wounds in the body, right?" asked Maher.

"None plainly visible," Grissom said. "Does this mean our killer took defensive wounds away from this scene?"

All three looked up the hill to where the body lay, almost thirty feet away. *Still not talking* . . .

"Blood," Maher said. "How is that possible?"

"There's not much blood here," Sara said, meaning both the knife blade and the snowy stuff she'd gathered.

"Which means?"

It doesn't start out as a chase. The victim-to-be and a companion come partway up the hill together. They're talking, arguing even, and a verbal confrontation turns ugly and physical . . . and the vic-to-be stabs the companion, who pulls a gun in self-defense . . .

. . . and now it's a chase, beginning somewhere down the slope. The companion is running and shooting, and by the time the two reach this point, the killer's missed twice, two wide shots. The vic drops the knife, in the process of trying to escape, running for his life; but he only makes it another ten yards, before he catches a bullet in the back and goes down. Then the companion goes to the fallen victim, dead now, and decides to disfigure or disguise the body. The killer goes back to the hotel, collects the gas can, and returns for the impromptu funeral pyre.

"It plays out similarly with three participants," Sara said with a shrug.

Grissom and Maher were both nodding.

"It's a scenario that suits the evidence we have," Grissom said. "Let's keep working and get some more data, and see what we can build from that. . . . Sara, put your gloves back on. We don't want to have to amputate your fingers."

Ruefully, Maher said, "Looks like our vic was one of those poor bastards who brought a knife to a gunfight."

"Not much of a knife, at that," Sara said.

"Still," Grissom said. "Pretty big for a pocket knife."

"But not big enough," Maher said, "to go up against bullets."

Moving in from the sidelines, Cormier asked, "Is . . . is that blood the killer's?"

Maher said, "Good chance of it."

"Don't mean to tell you experts how to do your job," the hotel man said. "But can't you just get the killer's blood type from that, and identify him?"

"In a lab we could," Grissom said. "Not out here." He spread his gloved hands, indicating the forest. "Anyway, the blood on that blade froze overnight, and the red cells will all have ruptured. If we had the lab, we could type it through the plasma, but not under these conditions."

Going back to work, they carefully emptied the snow from the other holes one shovelful at a time. When they had emptied twelve-inch circles around each of the markers and placed the snow on the spread-out garbage bag, Maher went over the smaller pile again with the metal detector as Sara and Cormier watched.

When Maher got a hit, Sara dropped to her knees, and slowly sifted through the area. After a moment, she found it. Holding it up, she stared at the tiny ice ball with the dark, lead center. "What happened?"

With a little grin, Maher said, "Snow happened. The hot bullet melted it, then the condensation froze around the cartridge as it slowed the bullet down."

They repeated the process with all the snow from the places they'd marked, but they found only one more bullet and a coin, a quarter.

"Here ya go, Gordy," she said, flipping the quarter to the Canadian.

"Not that much less than I usually get," Maher said, catching it.

"Yeah," Sara said, with a grin, "but that's American."

"Good point, eh?"

Moving over to Grissom, Sara said, "Two bullets. When I get the ice off 'em, we'll have a better idea what we've got."

"Good work," he said. Then, rising from the print he was working on, he picked two different left-foot castings from the line he'd done. "What do you think of this?"

She studied the castings. "They're the same boot."

He nodded. "Two different sets of tracks made by the same boots. One killer, two trips out and back."

"That confirms my reconstruction."

"Far as it goes . . . We need more evidence."

Maher joined them. "How are the castings coming, Dr. Grissom?"

"Finished. Just getting ready to pack up."

"All right. I've got the bullets. Don't think there's anything else we can do here."

Sara asked, "What about the body?"

Maher gave Grissom a hard look. "What do you think, Dr. Grissom? Are we done with the scene?"

Grissom glanced around, eyes tight with thought; then, slowly, he nodded.

"I agree," Maher said. "I suggest we take the body with us . . . which is part of why we brought the toboggan."

"Hold on!" Cormier called from the sidelines,

where he'd been listening. "How come you can take the body now, when you couldn't before?"

"Before," said Grissom, "it was part of an active crime scene. Now that we've worked the scene, we can remove the body."

Shaking his hooded head, the old man walked away.

Maher glanced toward the sky, saying, "If we can pack up quick enough . . ."

"We have a shot at the parking lot," Grissom finished.

"Let's go sledding, then," Sara said.

Grissom and Maher carefully dug out the body, wrapping it tightly in the space blanket and binding it to the toboggan. As they worked with the remains, Sara gathered up the tools and added them to the load. Within fifteen minutes, they were starting back down the slope.

Again, Cormier was in the lead, Maher dragging the toboggan, Grissom and Sara bringing up the rear, making sure their package stayed wrapped up. As they trudged along, they discussed what to do with the body.

When they reached the edge of the parking lot, its scattering of vehicles so topheavy with snow they resembled big white mushrooms, the CSIs were still hashing over the subject.

Maher said, "Maybe we should just bury it in the snow again."

Sara made a face. "We just dug it out!"

The Canadian nodded, saying, "Yes, but the killer set it on fire for a reason . . ."

Grissom said, "And you're worried that by bringing

it into the hotel, we're giving the killer a chance to finish the job."

The constable shrugged. "It is a consideration."

"If we bury it outside again, we'll have to set up another rotating shift," Maher said, "to guard it from predators."

"Please God," Sara said, the hotel and its promised warmth so nearby, "let there be another way."

They had reached the shoveled area near the rear door of the hotel, parking the toboggan alongside.

Grissom looked toward the manager. "Mr. Cormier, do you have a walk-in cooler?"

Cormier snorted a laugh. "Can't run a hotel this big without one. . . . You're not . . . ?"

Cormier's eyes followed Grissom's to the blanketed body strapped to the toboggan.

Grissom asked, "Does the cooler have a lock?"

"Well, padlock, yeah, but—"

"Who has keys?"

"Me, the Missus, and Mrs. Duncan, she's the head cook. But you can't seriously—"

"What about the fry cook?" Maher asked. "What's his name?"

Cormier said, "Bobby Chester. He doesn't have a key. Usually, he only works during the day, and the Missus or me is always around. But gentlemen, you can't honestly be considering . . ."

Grissom and Maher were trading looks.

Then Maher said, "Mr. Cormier, we're going to have to ask you to collect the keys and give them to us."

The hotel man was shaking his head. "You can't really be suggesting we stow that . . . corpse, in the walk-in cooler?"

Grissom and Maher just looked at him. Sara, astounded herself, was enjoying watching this play out.

"There are sanitary issues," Cormier was saying, "there are laws we'd be breaking . . ."

"Not more serious than murder," Grissom said. "We have to insist. We're commandeering your cooler."

"Tell me this is some sick joke," the hotel manager said. "What would I tell the health inspector?"

Maher said, "Mr. Cormier, it's really the only option that makes sense."

"But the guests, what will they say?"

"You're not to tell them," Grissom said. "The fewer people that know what we're doing, the better."

"Well, now," Cormier said, "finally we agree on somethin'!"

Maher smiled pleasantly, but in an entirely business-like way. "Would you get us that padlock key, please?" He turned to Grissom. "We really should start to hurry on the parking lot."

The hotel man sighed and it hung in the air. "Be back in a few minutes."

Cormier started away, and Sara called out: "Sir!"

He turned. "Yes, Ms. Sidle?"

"You might not want to mention this to Pearl."

The hotel man's eyebrows rose, then he nodded, saying, "Good thought, Ms. Sidle. Good thought."

They watched as the dejected-looking Cormier went inside.

Maher asked Sara, "What's this about Mrs. Cormier? We got another suspect?"

"If our host really wants to keep the news about a stiff in the cooler from the guests," Sara said, "he'll be wise to keep it from his wife. . . . She's one of the few communications systems around here not affected by the storm."

"Ah," Maher said.

"Now about the blood on that knife blade," Sara said.

Maher and Grissom faced her.

"What about it?" her boss asked.

"That waitress, Amy Barlow? She's got a bandage—cut on her hand."

Grissom nodded, remembering. "She said she got it slicing onions in the kitchen. Do we believe her?"

Sara shrugged. "She's the only person I've seen with a cut."

"There's the waiter," Maher said.

Sara frowned. "The one who dropped the tray?"

"Spot on his sleeve, eh?"

Sara smiled. "Oh, you noticed that. . . . I couldn't tell what it was. He's working with food and liquids, so that stain—"

"Might have been blood," Maher said. "Could explain why he dropped that tray. Weak arm, sore arm."

"Have we narrowed the list of suspects," Grissom asked, "or increased it?"

Maher shook his head. "We still don't really have any significant evidence pointing toward anyone."

Sara asked, "Is there any way to cross-match the blood on the knife?"

Grissom shook his head as well. "Doubtful the hotel has the tools for that."

Cormier emerged and trailing him—surprisingly enough—was Tony Dominguez, the tall, slender Hispanic waiter. Instead of his white-shirt-and-black-slacks uniform, the young man wore a loose-fitting white sweatshirt with an orange Syracuse logo on the front, and new black jeans. In white tennis shoes, Dominguez did not venture into the snow, rather stayed on the shoveled sidewalk near the rear door.

The investigators were trading what-the-hell expressions when Cormier strode over and said, "You said you all were in a hurry—I thought you might need some help carrying the . . . uh . . . package inside."

"Thanks," Grissom said tightly, "but we can probably manage."

Cormier gestured toward the building. "You sure? We'll be going in through the delivery entrance down there. It's a long haul."

Maher said to Grissom, "I know it's not exactly what we had in mind, but why don't you and Herm and . . . what's your name, son?"

"Tony," the young man said, hands dug in his pants pockets.

"You should have a jacket, son."

"Mr. Cormier said this wouldn't take long."

"It doesn't have to. If you three will escort the . . . package inside, Ms. Sidle and I will get started out here. Snow's coming and the sooner we're at it, the better our chances of finding something useful."

Grissom, clearly not liking this a bit, nonetheless said, "All right."

Then Maher, Sara, and Grissom stripped the lawn tools and CSI equipment off the toboggan, and Sara and Maher—weighed down by their load—went off across the parking lot to where the tomato stakes barely peeked out of the snow.

While Sara worked with the constable, Gil Grissom took command of the corpse-hauling detail.

He said to Dominguez and Cormier, "You'll have to lead the way, gentlemen."

Cormier, who'd already shown himself to be squeamish around the remains, didn't make a move. And the young man just stood there staring at the sled.

"Is that the . . . body?" he asked.

Grissom shot an irritated look at Cormier, who shrugged and shook his head, his expression saying, *I didn't tell him!*

"So much for discretion," Grissom said to the hotel man. Then, with a tight smile, he said to the waiter, "This is a body, yes. It needs refrigeration. We're preserving evidence."

"Ohmigod . . ." The young man swallowed. "I thought it was just a rumor."

Grissom, whose patience had run out already, said, "Are you up to helping with this? I can get Ms. Sidle back here, if you two aren't capable."

Dominguez, his eyes still riveted to the space blanket lashed to the toboggan, said, "I . . . I'm up to it. Do we . . . undo this, unwrap it, or . . . are we moving the toboggan, too?"

"Toboggan and all," Grissom said. "There's other perishable evidence here, and it's all going into the cooler until the police arrive."

Grissom hated having another of the suspects this close to the remains, but at this point there was nothing to be done. It was almost as if Cormier were trying to complicate matters.

He glanced over at the work going on in the parking lot, Maher with the leaf blower, again dispersing snow, clearing the footprints near the blue Grand Prix, Sara assisting. Already snowflakes were drifting to earth all around, the wind picking up too, and Grissom knew that the only way they had any chance of getting the prints from the parking lot was to get the body inside with the help of the waiter—suspect or not.

"Can we do this, please?" Grissom asked.

Intimidated, the waiter took the front end and Grissom the rear, facing each other as they lifted it between them.

"I'll get the doors and clear a path," Cormier said, moving out ahead; but Dominguez was already backing toward the little receiving dock at the far end of the parking lot.

They were off the shoveled area now, shuffling through high snow, taking care to keep their balance. The sled and its charred cargo seemed surprisingly heavy to Grissom. The victim hadn't been a particularly large man, but with the added weight of the toboggan, Grissom might have been helping haul anvils. Having the corpse buried in snow overnight, with the beginnings of the freezing process kicking in, had cut the foul odor of the roasted flesh, at least.

"Who is this?" Dominguez asked suddenly, eyes on the space-blanket-wrapped "package."

"No ID," Grissom said. "Don't look at it yet."

The two of them made eye contact then, the waiter backing toward the loading dock, Grissom with the corpse before him, the pair working together, Cormier slogging through the snow to get ahead of them.

"Stairs," Grissom said, for the waiter's benefit, and they halted for just a moment so Cormier could kick the snow off the four concrete steps that led up to the dock. When the man had finished, the waiter took a moment to get his bearings, then nodded at Grissom and backed up the first step.

Starting up the steps put even more of the weight on Grissom, and he let the young man set the pace—if Grissom pushed, they might lose their grip and wind up dumping their cargo. But Dominguez—slightly built though he was—was doing fine, taking the second and third steps with no trouble. Cormier was unlocking and opening a door on the loading dock when Dominguez reached the landing . . . and slipped.

The weight came forward, as if Grissom was on the down end of a seesaw, and Cormier—to his credit—quickly grabbed on to the waiter's abandoned end of the toboggan, bracing it.

In the meantime, Dominguez had sat down, rudely, on the loading dock, the baggy lefthand sleeve of his sweatshirt hiking up to reveal a white-gauze-bandaged arm. Quickly, obviously embarrassed, the young man got to his feet, tugging the sleeve down over his bandaged arm, and took his end of the sled back from the older man.

"You all right, Tony?" Grissom asked.

"Caught some ice—sorry."

Grissom, gritting his teeth and supporting most of the weight himself, asked, "Ready?"

"Sure."

Cormier had returned to his post, holding open the door, as they once again started moving.

"Just a littler further," Cormier said.

The complex arrangement of rope and bungee cords that bound the body to the toboggan had held tight all the way down the hill, but now—as Grissom and the waiter turned the sled on an angle, to fit it through the narrow door—a rigor-stiffened hand slipped free.

No one but Grissom had noticed this—yet—and the CSI wasn't about to call attention to it, not and risk winding up holding the heavy end of the load alone, again. Once they were through the door, the CSI and the waiter tipped the toboggan back upright, the hand sliding partway back under the space blanket.

The hall was concrete—floor, walls, ceiling. Light-bulbs encased above in wire cages, every fifteen feet or so, half-heartedly lit their passage down this damp, cold hallway, which had all the charm and ambience of a Tower of London dungeon. Slipping by on Grissom's right, on the side away from the exposed hand, Cormier moved on ahead of them, boots clomping like horse hooves.

Grissom heard the click as Cormier tripped the padlock, then the cooler door yawned open, the rubber seal at its base scraping along a floor already scoured to a high sheen.

"You almost expect the Crypt Keeper to step out," Dominquez said with a nervous laugh.

Grissom, having no idea what the kid was talking about, nodded noncommittally.

"All the way to the far wall, now," Cormier said from behind the open door. "I keep the meat on the left, and I don't want this thing near it. . . . Tony, you know where to stow it."

"You got it, Mr. C," Tony called.

The refrigerated room was about the size of a holding cell. Shelves on the left wall were stacked with boxes marked with the names of individual cuts and types of meat, fish, poultry and pork. The wall at right was lined with wire baskets, small bins brimming with bags of lettuce, stalks of celery, bunches of radishes, bags of carrots, sacks of onions and also some fruit—grapefruit, oranges, melons. Behind Grissom, on the wall the door opened from, were stacked cartons of ketchup and mustard bottles, jars of pickles and relish, gallon tubs of salad dressing and the like. The far wall was a blank metal slate, nothing even piled there, and that was where Cormier directed them to deposit this delivery.

Cormier was throwing together a basket of food—meat, vegetables, fruit, as if he'd been shopping. "I need to get tonight's food out of here—rest of this stuff is probably gonna be condemned."

"Fine," Grissom said.

The hotel manager was scurrying out as Grissom and the waiter set the sled down with great care on the concrete floor, parallel to the steel wall. They both stood and then Dominguez glanced down and saw the hand. Kneeling, he raised the edge of the blanket to tuck the hand back under.

"I'll get that," Grissom said.

But Dominguez had already seen more than any of them had bargained for; his expression was horror-struck.

Grissom said, "You know this man?"

Gasping, the waiter was backing away, then turned and ran, almost knocking Grissom down and bumping into Cormier, who was on his way back in.

The young man collapsed against the corridor wall, in a sprawled sitting position, heaving sobs, hugging himself.

Grissom exited the cooler. To Cormier he said, "Keep an eye on him."

"What the hell happened?"

"He recognized the victim."

While Cormier stayed with the waiter, Grissom went back inside and carefully repackaged the body under the blanket. When Grissom emerged, Dominguez was still sitting, leaning against the wall, his head in his hands, Cormier crouching next to him, a hand on the young man's shoulder.

"You have the keys?" Grissom asked Cormier.

The hotel man nodded.

Grissom snapped the padlock shut. At least the body was secure, now.

Still crouching by his employee, Cormier handed up a ring with three identical keys to Grissom. "This is all of them."

With a dismissive nod, pocketing the keys, Grissom turned his attention to the waiter. The CSI pulled off his stocking cap, stuffed it in a jacket pocket, removed the muffler, did the same with it; gloves came off, too. All the while he was watching Dominguez as he might an insect specimen, observing as the waiter seemed to implode there against the wall, his legs stretched out in front of him, face buried in his hands, sobs racking his body.

"If you can get ahold of yourself, " Grissom said to the waiter, as gently as he could, "we should talk. All right?"

Dominguez didn't acknowledge Grissom's presence, much less his question.

Cormier remained at Dominguez' side, that supportive hand still on the boy's shoulder. Taking the other side, Grissom sat beside the boy, too.

"How did you recognize the victim?" Grissom asked. "Without seeing his face?"

Dominguez looked up at Grissom, finally; tears pearled the handsome boy's long eyelashes. The waiter's voice was a pitiful rasp. "I knew . . . know . . . the coat. I gave it to him. To James."

"James? Jim Moss?" Cormier interrupted.

Dominguez nodded.

"He's a waiter here," Cormier explained.

Grissom nodded, his attention on the boy.

"You gave that coat to James. You must have been good friends."

Dominguez shrugged. "We were lovers."

Cormier's eyes widened and he blew out breath, like Old Man Winter; but whatever Old Man Cormier might have thought about such a relationship, his hand never left Dominguez' shoulder.

"He really loved that coat," Dominguez was saying.

A coat, Grissom knew, wasn't near good enough for an ID. "Does James have any distinguishing marks?"

"Well . . . a tattoo."

"Where? Could you describe it?"

"On his back." Dominguez touched a spot just over his own shoulder. "A rose. A tiny rose . . . for his mom. Her name was Rose. She died when he was in high school."

Suddenly Dominguez grabbed the front of Grissom's varsity jacket, startling the CSI. "That's the kind of person James was! Remember that! You tell people that! Be sure to!"

"I will," Grissom assured the boy, who released the CSI's jacket and sat back again, deflated after the outburst.

Cormier, whose hand had been jerked away when Dominguez sat forward, was sitting quietly, just watching his employee.

"Tony," Grissom said, each word emerging with care, "I'm going to need you to identify that tattoo."

The waiter's eyes went wide again and he shook his head rapidly. "Oh no, oh no! I can't go back in there!"

"You can," Grissom said. "You have to."

"I do not have to!"

"If you want to help James—"

"He can't be helped now!"

"We have to determine what happened to him. That's the only help we can give him, now. . . . All right?"

The boy thought about that.

Then he swallowed and nodded.

"Herm," Grissom said, "please sit here with Tony."

"No problem," Cormier said, and put his hand on the boy's shoulder again.

Grissom rose. "Now, Tony—just wait here. Stay calm. I have to go in and get things ready. Then all you have to do is identify the tattoo . . . if there is one."

Another swallow, another nod.

Grissom arched an eyebrow. "Remember, this could be someone wearing a coat like James's, or even wearing James's own coat. We have to be sure."

The boy's eyes brightened. "You mean, it might not be him!"

"That is possible."

"It could be someone else wearing his coat! Somebody he loaned it to, 'cause of the cold. He was always helping people . . ."

The CSI supervisor noticed that Dominguez had used the past tense. Did that mean anything, or was the boy's mind already accepting the inevitability that the corpse in the cooler was James?

Grissom unlocked the door. Inside the cooler, he uncovered the body, rolled it over to get at the victim's back, which hadn't been burned at all, and slowly peeled away layers until he got to the dead man's shoulder . . .

. . . where could be seen a small red-and-blue rose, a rather delicate tattoo.

After covering as much of the body as he could, leaving only the area with the tattoo exposed, Grissom called, "Mr. Cormier! Would you bring Tony in here, please."

Cormier's arm was around the boy, who entered on wobbly legs.

"Is this James?" Grissom asked. He was kneeling next to the body, gesturing to the red-and-blue rose. "Do you recognize the tattoo?"

Dominguez stepped away from Cormier's protective arm, staggered over and glanced down. Again he swallowed, nodded and tears immediately began to flow again, sobs shaking his chest. Grissom covered the victim up, nodded to Cormier to lead Dominguez back to the corridor, which he did, and then Grissom exited and relocked the cooler door.

Cormier was standing beside the boy, who again sat slumped against the wall, staring hollowly, breathing hard, but the tears and sobs had ceased, for now anyway.

"Give us a few moments, Mr. Cormier," Grissom said.

The hotel man nodded, said, "You'll be fine, Tony—Dr. Grissom here is a good man. . . . I left my basket of food out on the dock. I'll cart it up to the kitchen."

"Do that," Grissom said.

And then Cormier left them alone, the inquisitive CSI and the heartbroken waiter.

"What was your friend's full name?" Grissom asked.

The reply was sharp, angry; that was bound to come. "He wasn't my friend. He was my lover . . . okay?"

"What was your lover's full name?"

"James R. Moss. The 'r' stood for Rosemont. It was a family name. Maybe that's why his mother was named Rose. . . . You're a doctor?"

"Not a medical doctor, Tony. Tell me about James."

Dominguez answered with his own question. "How did he get burned like that?"

Grissom wondered if the question was serious or calculated to keep him from suspecting Dominguez. He had no reason to doubt that this boy had loved James Moss; but love, like hate, was among the most common murder motives.

Grissom gave it to him straight: "He was shot and killed."

"Oh my God . . ."

"And whoever did that, for some reason, set fire to the body afterward."

"What? Why?"

"That's part of what I'm trying to determine. That's the kind of a doctor I am, Tony. Forensics."

" . . . for the conference this weekend."

"Right. Tell me about him."

Dominguez wiped his eyes with the back of a sweatshirt sleeve, the one belonging to the arm without the bandage. "James was sweet and funny and kind. Honest, too, very honest. Nobody would ever want to hurt him."

"Did the two of you have any problems?"

"Oh, no! We were happy. Very compatible."

Grissom gestured toward the boy's sleeve. "When we almost dropped the sled out there, I noticed you have a kind of nasty cut, there."

Unconsciously, the waiter touched his wounded arm. "How could you see that?"

"Well, I mean . . . I saw the bandage."

Dominguez pushed up the loose sleeve and exposed gauze running from his elbow nearly to his wrist. "Looks bad, huh? Hurts worse."

"How did that happen, Tony?"

The boy took a moment, then said, casually, "Working on my car."

"I need you to be more specific."

He shrugged. "Cut myself putting on a new exhaust system."

"Really?" Grissom said, with an insincere smile. "People still do that themselves?"

Dominguez found a small grin somewhere, relieved by the apparent subject change. "Well, I do. I've got an old car. I do it to save money, but I'm into it, maybe 'cause it's so . . . so . . . ." He laughed a little. ". . . butch."

"Is your car in the hotel lot right now?"

His smile faded. "No. Why? Does that matter?"

"James was your lover."

"I told you that."

"The evidence indicates that James fought back. That his assailant was cut. That fact, along with your intimate relationship with the victim, makes you a suspect in James's murder."

Dominguez' eyes widened. "You think I killed James? That's bullshit, man, I loved the dude! He was the only thing that kept me going in this hellhole!"

"I said you're a suspect . . . and you are. And so is everyone else in this place. Even me, and my assistant, because we found James, and the first people to discover a body . . . they're always the first suspects."

"What are you trying to say?"

"Just don't get bent out of shape. Try not to give in to this grief. Help me find who did this to James."

Grissom paused, drew a breath, went on. "Tony, being a suspect doesn't make you guilty; but we should both recognize that the probability is . . . James was killed by someone he knows."

"Why? Everybody loved him!"

"Love can be a murder motive. And the statistics say that most murder victims know their murderers . . . often intimately. None of this makes you guilty or makes me believe that you're the killer . . . but, Tony, you're bright. You must see how this looks."

Calming down, Dominguez finally nodded. "I can see how it looks," he admitted. But then he bitterly added, "Two gay guys—one must be a homicidal maniac."

Grissom shook his head. "That's not the issue."

"The one you *should* be hounding is Amy."

"Amy Barlow? The waitress?"

"That's right," Dominguez said. "Amy Barlow, the waitress. She was with James before, you know . . . me."

Grissom's eyes tightened. "James was bisexual?"

"Whatever. I'm not into labels."

"What do you know about his relationship with Amy?"

Dominguez shrugged. "She latched on to him when he started here. Maybe a year and a half ago. They went together for, oh . . . six months, I guess. Then he and I got to be friends—we liked the same music, same movies. We were just made for each other. Really clicked."

"That's nice."

"It was nice, and Amy, she didn't like it at all. When

James started seeing me, she really flipped. She just would not let it go."

"Even though James told her it was over?"

Dominguez shrugged again. "Truth is . . . he never did really break it off with her, not entirely. His dad is this retired master sergeant from the marines—Born Again, superstraight. And James just didn't think the old man could've understood his lifestyle—he would've died if his dad ever called him a faggot."

Grissom winced at the word.

"Anyway, I don't know, I guess James just couldn't let it go. He kinda did keep stringing Amy along."

"How did you feel about James living this double life?"

The waiter's face turned to stone. "What do you think? I hated it."

"It had to make you angry, that he hid your relationship."

Dominguez said, "I hated it, but I could never be angry with James. I knew he loved me, and that's all that mattered. I was his real love—Amy was the sham."

"All right, Tony." Grissom stood. "I appreciate your frankness."

The boy got to his feet, too. "You need to talk to Amy. You really do."

"Oh, I will. But I'll be talking to a lot of people. By the way," Grissom added, glancing down at the waiter's tennis shoes, "those surely aren't the shoes you wore to work, yesterday."

"These are strictly for the dining room. You don't live up here and not have good boots. I got a kick-ass pair of Doc Martens. . . . James gave them to me."

"Generous of him," Grissom said.

"He was a wonderful guy," Dominguez said.

"Honest, too," Grissom said.

"As the day is long."

Grissom did not point out that the days were getting shorter. He merely walked the waiter out into the cold air of another gathering storm, anxious to report what he'd learned to Maher and Sara.

He knew who the murder victim was, now; and, he felt confident, soon would know who the murderer was, as well.

Honest.

10

After five grueling hours at the Charleston Boulevard garbage dump—wearing white Tyvek jumpsuits
over their clothes, painter's masks, multiple pairs of
latex gloves and fireman boots—the graveyard CSIs
dragged in to HQ for showers and to climb in their
spare clothes and finish out their shift.

Warrick caught up with Nick in the Trace lab, hunkered over the MP4 camera, enlarging prints. Nick
would feed these prints into the AFIS terminal on the
desk, over against a side wall keeping company with a
little family of filing cabinets.

The back wall was home to a refrigerator for
chemicals, a work counter and a paper-heating
oven. Racks of chemicals owned the other side wall,
and on a large central table sat the comparative microscope, which allowed the matching of parts of
two different slides—an invaluable tool for bullet
comparison.

"That was fun," Warrick said dryly, meaning their
garbage-dump duty.

Nick smirked. "Vegas is one glamorous town."

"Who's the AFIS candidate?" Warrick asked, at Nick's side now.

"Suffocated naked woman, number two."

Catherine wandered in with a newspaper folded under her arm and that devilish half-smile and single-arched eyebrow expression of hers that told Warrick she was onto something.

"Either of you guys into the local avant-garde scene?"

Nick gave her half a smile back. "I have a buddy in the National Guard."

She dropped the folded newspaper onto the desk next to Nick—the Arts section of the *Las Vegas Sun.* "Lavien Rose mean anything to you, boys?"

Warrick, trying, said, "Edith Piaf song, isn't it?"

Nick looked up at his friend. "Woah . . . Mr. Music. You can name that tune in how many notes?"

"Actually," Catherine said, "he missed that question—it's not 'La Vie En Rose' . . . it's Lavien Rose."

She tapped a red-nailed finger next to a photograph on the folded-over Arts section. "Look familiar, fellas?"

An article on local performance artists included a sullen photograph of the spiky-haired blonde woman they had not long ago seen in the dead altogether out on Charleston Boulevard.

"Is that what that was," Warrick asked, "back at that trash pile? Performance art?"

Nick's eyes were large as he picked up the paper and stared at the punky blonde. "If so, it must've been closing night."

Catherine was grinning almost ferally. "I knew I'd seen that face somewhere before!"

Doc Robbins' voice came over the intercom. "Catherine, you in there?"

She stepped over to the intercom and touched the talk button. "Yeah, Doc—Trace lab, a CSI's home away from home. What have you got for us?"

"Cause of death on your blonde Jane Doe."

"Great," Catherine said, "only she's not a Jane Doe anymore—we got her IDed."

"Well, come on down and fill out the form. But just so you know, she suffocated with the help of a plastic bag. Same heightened CO_2 count in her blood as Missy Sherman."

They all traded meaningful looks.

Catherine said, "Thanks, Doc! Be down in a few, to fill out the ID."

"Paperwork rules us all, Catherine."

Warrick stood with hands on hips. "Another naked woman killed with a plastic bag? Tell me this isn't a serial."

"The similarity of MO suggests serial," Nick said. "But the victim profile is out of whack."

"I don't know," Warrick said, shaking his head. "Two attractive women, about the same age . . . ?"

"True. But otherwise, what do a brunette middle-class housewife and a blonde starving artist have in common?"

"I don't know if she was a starving artist, exactly," Catherine said. "Bulimic, maybe."

"She was a skinny thing," Nick said.

"Easily overpowered," Warrick said.

The computer chirped and Nick turned to see a match on the woman's prints. He tapped the keys and was soon looking at an arrest report.

"Her name was Sharon Pope," Nick said.

Archly, Catherine said, "You don't suppose 'Lavien Rose' was a stage name, by any chance?"

"Ms. Pope was arrested two years ago September," Nick continued, reading from the screen. "Part of a group protesting at Nellis."

Nellis Air Force Base—northeast of the city, out Las Vegas Boulevard—frequently drew protesters of one kind or another, so a Federal record like that popping up was not a shock.

Still, someone had to ask; and it was Catherine: "Arrested for?"

"Trespassing," Nick said, "failure to disperse, interfering with an officer."

Catherine lifted her eyebrows. "Well, she hit the trifecta."

"Touched all the bases at the base, yes," Nick said. "A fine but no jail time."

"Address?"

Nick read it aloud, then added, "But we better check it—this arrest is a couple of years old. She could've moved by now." His forehead furrowed. "You know, I've heard that name somewhere before."

"Lavien Rose?" Catherine asked.

"No. Sharon Pope. . . ."

Nick mulled that over as his fingers danced on the keyboard, checking out the Pope woman's address—and another red flag came up.

"Well," Nick said, "and the hits just keep on comin'. . . ."

"What song is Lavien Rose singing now?" Warrick asked.

Frowning suspiciously, Nick turned toward Warrick and Catherine and gestured to the monitor screen. "See for yourself—her current address is the same as two years ago, but when I typed in her performance-artist alias, a different address came up."

Catherine and Warrick leaned in on either side of Nick and read over his shoulder.

Nick asked, "Why is our bulimic artist keeping two cribs under two names?"

"We need to check them both," Catherine said.

Warrick's expression was doubtful as he pointed out, "It's almost end of shift."

"This is a fresh murder case." Catherine's features were firmly set. "We need to stay on it."

Nick said, "Brass sent a memo around saying the Missy Sherman case is on the approved-for-OT list . . . and the two murders may be connected. MO indicates it."

Warrick shrugged. "Good enough for me."

"All right!" Catherine said, eyes bright. "We'll split up. . . . I'll see if I can round up Brass and check the Pope address. O'Riley's back on graveyard rotation—you guys grab him and head over to Edith Piaf's."

"Don't forget to give that ID to Robbins," Nick reminded her.

"On my way out," Catherine assured him.

Twenty minutes later, Warrick and Nick stood outside apartment 217H in The Palms, a vaguely seedy two-story apartment complex on heavily traveled Paradise Road. Six-thirty in the morning was a little early to be bothering the super, but Sergeant O'Riley was off doing just that.

The morning had a tentative quality, dawn not quite finished with the sky, and the temperature still hung around the freezing mark. Warrick had thrown his good leather jacket over his running togs; hands in his jacket pockets, he bounced foot to foot, staying warm while they waited on the second-floor concrete walkway.

Finally, O'Riley appeared, coming up the steps. A stubby Hispanic man, the super presumably, trailed behind him in flip-flops, cut-off denim shorts and a threadbare Santana tee shirt, and didn't seem to notice it was colder out than the inside of a Kenmore freezer.

As the detective and super drew closer, Warrick got a better look at the super—unruly black hair over a wide forehead, red-rimmed brown eyes, and a frequently broken nose that meant either an ex-boxer or street fighter.

"This couldn't wait till after my damn breakfast?" the man was saying.

"No," O'Riley said gruffly. "Just open the door, then we'll be out of your way in no time, and you can get back to your bacon and eggs."

"They're probably already cold," the super protested.

"Then it's a moot frickin' point," O'Riley said. To Warrick and Nick, he said, "Meet the super, Hector Ortiz."

Nods were exchanged as the super riffled through a ring of keys. "Miz Rose, she in trouble?"

Ignoring Ortiz' question, Warrick gestured toward the door with his chin. "What kind of tenant?"

"Best kind—quiet as a church mouse. Always pays the rent on time, pays in cash—what's not to like?"

"Pays in cash . . . Is that typical around here?"

Shrugging, the super asked, "Who knows what's typical these days. Who am I to argue with money? And hers is always on time."

"What's she pay?"

Ortiz gave Warrick a sideways look. "I'm not sure I have to answer that."

Warrick sighed. "You have any openings, here at the beautiful Palms?"

"Maybe. Why?"

"In case I wanna move. If I do, what kind of rent am I lookin' at?"

"One bedroom?"

"I guess. Something like Ms. Rose has."

"Five bills—five-fifty, you want a garage."

"Pretty reasonable, considering," Warrick admitted.

"I know, everybody else around here's twenty percent over that, easy. But the landlord's a nice guy, and 'cause of that, we tend to hang on to tenants."

"Ms. Rose have a garage?" asked Nick.

"No."

Finally the super opened the place up, and they peered in at an empty living room—not a stick of furniture, as if the renter had moved out in the night, or burglars had made a hell of a haul.

The super, astounded, blurted, "What the hell?"

As they stepped into the living room, O'Riley asked Ortiz, "When was the last time you were in here?"

"I guess, lemme think—not since Ms. Rose signed the lease. She never had any complaints, and nothin' went wrong, no plumbing trouble or nothing. She shows up at my door with the envelope of money. . . . What reason did I have to come in?"

Not even the impressions of furniture could be seen on the well-worn wall-to-wall carpet; no one had lived here for some time. Some cheap but heavy curtains blotted out the window. Warrick opened the front closet door—not even a wire hanger.

A doorless doorway at the right led to the kitchen, where several appliances waited—a stove, a refrigerator. Warrick followed Nick, who opened the fridge, checked the cupboards.

Nick looked back at Warrick, eyes tight. "Got a box of cinch-top bags and a roll of duct tape," he said.

Warrick grunted noncommittally, then wandered back into the living room, where the super stood in the middle, arms folded, rocking on his heels, bored to death. O'Riley was poised before two closed doors that faced each other in a tiny alcove at the rear of the living room.

Frowning in thought, Warrick said, "Why rent an empty apartment?"

Opening the alcove's right-hand door, O'Riley said, "Bathroom! . . . Not much, pretty stripped. Empty squirt bottle on the sink, is about all."

"What?" Warrick asked, coming over.

The big man shrugged. "You know—like to water plants."

"Shit," Warrick said.

O'Riley turned. "What?"

"I think I know why we're standin' in an empty apartment. . . . Do not touch anything else!"

O'Riley, eyes wide, held his hands up in surrender. "Okay, okay . . ."

"We're in a crime scene," Warrick said. "Nick!"

"What?" Nick asked, coming from the kitchen, a wary expression around his eyes.

Warrick said, "The only thing in this apartment is a squirt bottle, some duct tape and tie-bags. . . . You wanna guess what's behind door number two?"

Nick paled. Somber, businesslike, he said, "Detective O'Riley, you escort Mr. Ortiz out, now—don't touch anything." Nick got latex gloves out of his jacket pocket, and started snugging them on. "I'll get the door for you. . . ."

The burly cop took Ortiz by the arm and said, "We need to leave."

"Well, don't get rough about it! Are you arresting me or what? I didn't do nothin'!"

Nick was already at the door; he carefully opened it with a gloved hand. "Sir, we've stumbled into a probable crime scene. Just our presence potentially contaminates evidence. Please step outside and we'll explain."

Once the four of them were back on the concrete walkway, O'Riley asked, "What did you see that I didn't see?"

While Nick went off to gather their equipment from the Tahoe, Warrick filled the detective in. "Didn't you read Doc Robbins' report? He said Missy Sherman was frozen, and had to be wetted down in order to avoid freezer burn."

O'Riley's eyes widened and he nodded, getting it. "I remember—the doc said it could have been accomplished with somethin' as simple as a . . . squirt bottle."

Ortiz stepped closer to Warrick. "What does all this mean?"

"We're going to be investigating in there."

Ortiz frowned, shaking his head as if warding off flying insects. "Don't you people need a warrant or something?"

"Not for a probable crime scene, sir."

"But . . . how long you gonna be around?"

"Long as it takes."

Nick came up the stairs with their field kits in his hands, and started by unpacking his camera.

The super looked stricken. "The landlord might not like this."

"I thought you said he was a nice guy."

"Oh, he is . . . but this is private property, and—"

"Sir," Nick said, his camera out, "we're going back inside. If we don't find what we expect in there, we'll be out in fifteen minutes. If we do find what we expect, we're going to be here for . . . a while. Let us go in and find out—if we need to stay longer, you can call the landlord, and we'll talk to him, personally."

"Maybe I should call him now."

With a boyish grin, Nick said, "That's your choice, sir. But be sure to mention that you've already given us access, voluntarily."

Ortiz' face took on a sick look; he hung his head and leaned heavily against the wrought-iron rail of the walkway.

Warrick nodded to O'Riley, who nodded back—an exchange that meant, *Stay with this guy and keep an eye on him.*

Nick and Warrick went back inside.

While Nick snapped some pictures of the squirt bottle in the bathroom, Warrick faced the closed door that might lead to a bedroom. Touching as little of the knob as possible, he turned it and allowed the door to swing open, mostly under its own power.

Like the living room, this room was empty. It too had old carpeting, and cheap heavy curtains; but stretching from an outlet on the wall opposite him, a long orange extension cord snaked away to slip under the closet door at right. The closet was formidable—three sliding doors, each almost thirty inches wide.

"Nick!" Warrick called. "Looks like we were right!"

Nick joined him in the bedroom as Warrick slid the far door to the left. Filling most of the closet was a large white Kenmore chest freezer, a padlock joining lid to chassis.

Warrick said, "That's the model Catherine came up with."

"Oh yeah."

Warrick inspected the lock, and said, "We're going to need a cutter and goggles. I left the tool bag on the walkway. I'll go get the stuff; you're the man with the camera."

"Go," Nick said.

Outside, Warrick found O'Riley and the super leaning against the rail.

"What's the verdict?" the detective asked.

" 'Guilty,' eventually—we have what appears to be the murder site."

"Holy mother of shit," blurted the super. "Should I call the landlord now?"

"I wish you would," Warrick said. "We're going to be here a while."

Warrick bent down, sorting through his bag to get out the electric cutter.

O'Riley, taking notes, was asking Ortiz, "What's your landlord's name?"

"Sherman," the super said, who had calmed down. "Nice guy. He won't give you any trouble."

On his feet now, cutter in hand, Warrick froze. "Sherman? Alex Sherman?"

"Yeah! You know him? Him and his wife bought this place, couple of years ago. She's the lady that disappeared. Since she vanished, he hasn't been around much. Leaves most of the maintenance work for me to do. . . . It's a little much for me, really. We're gettin' kinda run-down."

Warrick said, "Well, he needs to come around now—in person."

O'Riley said, "Where's your office, Mr. Ortiz? I'll help you call him."

Warrick's cell phone trilled. He pulled it off his belt and punched the button. "Warrick Brown."

"Catherine," the familiar voice said. "At the Sharon Pope residence. Nothing to write home about here."

"Well, you might want to stop by over here," Warrick said. "There's plenty of subject matter at the Rose crib."

He quickly filled her in.

"Blink and I'm there," she said and hung up.

With the cutter and two pairs of goggles in hand, Warrick went back where Nick was snapping pictures of the plug snaking across the carpet.

"You ready for this?" Warrick asked, hands on hips. "You want to take a flyin' stab at who owns this lavish apartment complex?"

Nick shrugged. "Alex Sherman?"

Warrick frowned. "Now how the hell did you figure that?"

"Catherine mentioned that Sherman and his wife had real estate and you just made it clear somebody tied to the case owns this place. Had to be Alex Sherman."

"You been reading Gris's Sherlock Holmes books?"

"No. But I was raised on Encyclopedia Brown."

Warrick smirked. "I was a kid strictly into John Shaft."

"Shut your mouth . . . and pop that freezer. And don't pout, Richard Roundtree—you were the one who figured out the Kenmore'd be in here."

"I was, wasn't I?"

Warrick tossed Nick one pair of the goggles while he put on the other, then plugged the cutter in and turned it on, small blade whizzing back and forth at 20,000 rpm. Leaning in, he touched the tool to the hasp and sparks flew. He was through the cheese-ball lock in less than a minute, the smell of burning metal leaving its industrial bouquet hanging in the air.

With the lock out of the way, they each carefully took a corner of the lid and raised it—the best way not to disturb any fingerprints where people might typically lift the lid.

The freezer was about a quarter full of water, with a short, slotted metal shelf at one end and a little blue nipple on the back wall that—when ice-covered—was a manufacturer's signal for time to defrost.

"Killer's trying to clean up after himself," Nick said, "with this defrosting. Get the water out, get the evidence out."

"Trouble is, we got the water first . . . which means we have the evidence."

"See, we do like it to be easy," Nick said.

Warrick pointed at the blue tip on the freezer's back wall. "That look like a match to the mark on Missy's cheek?"

Nick studied it for a second. "Sure does. Slots on the shelf should match up to the marks on her arm, too."

"I'll work the freezer, and find O'Riley and give him the good news that he's gotta get us a truck to haul this bad boy back to the lab."

"Sounds good. Then I'll take another look around—never hurts to look twice."

"Never hurts to look three times."

Warrick was just finishing lifting fingerprints off the lid when Nick returned holding a clear oversize plastic bag with two large shopping bags inside. The bags within the evidence bag—one white and one red— were from boutiques in Caesar's Palace. One of them looked to be stuffed with clothes.

"Where'd you find those?" Warrick asked.

"Under the sink in the bathroom. Nobody'd got to that yet, when we shooed O'Riley and Ortiz out." Nick hefted the bag. "When Brass and I talked to the Mortensons, Missy's friend Regan Mortenson said

Missy bought some clothes at the Caesar's mall, day she disappeared."

Warrick shook his head, gave Nick a wry half-grin. "You may be right about this 'easy' theory."

Nick opened the evidence pouch and withdrew a pair of jeans from one of the shopping bags. Nick pointed to a silver stripe several inches wide, near the cuff. "Looks like the killer duct-taped the victim, while she was dressed."

"Which is why no duct tape residue was found on the body—Missy was stripped naked after the killing."

"And that's why there's no signs of struggle, even though the killer killed Missy by holding a plastic bag over her head."

Warrick sighed, sourly. "Trussed up like that, woman never had a chance. Killer ties a bag over the victim's head, sits back and just watches while she dies."

"Smoke 'em if you got him," Nick said.

"We have one cold killer here, Nick. We been up against our share of evil ones, but this . . ."

"Let's see if we can't hold this to two kills. I don't want to do any more crime scenes where women die like this."

"Good plan."

Catherine and Brass arrived at the Palms apartment complex after a ride during which the detective had continually pissed and moaned about not being able to use the siren because it wasn't an "emergency."

"What's the point of being a cop if you can't use the siren once in a while?" he griped.

"Life just isn't fair," Catherine said, and he looked

at her, searching for sarcasm, but apparently wasn't a good enough detective to find it.

Catherine, in latex gloves, her own silver field kit in hand, entered the apartment, took in the empty landscape, then went into the bedroom to help Nick and Warrick secure the freezer. They bagged and packed the squirt bottle, the cinch-top bags, the duct tape, the extension cord, the old padlock and the boutique bags with the clothes, all of which Nick hauled down to the Tahoe.

Catherine slapped a new combination padlock onto the freezer, saying to Warrick, "We don't want this popping open on the ride back to HQ."

Waiting for the truck to arrive and haul the freezer away, the CSIs and the two detectives stood outside in the early morning sunshine. Bone-tired from the extended shift, they were nonetheless basking in the overtime they were squeezing out of Sheriff Mobley, as well as enjoying the thought of the progress they'd made on what had been until now a stubborn, frustrating investigation.

They were still waiting for the PD truck when Alex Sherman rolled in, in his Jaguar. Dressed business-casual, the dark-haired Sherman looked as though he'd taken his time getting ready.

"Captain Brass," Sherman said. "I'm surprised to see you—I spoke to a Detective O'Riley, on the phone. He said we had some kind of crime scene here. . . ."

"Mr. Sherman," Brass said, "we believe we've found the place where your wife may have been murdered."

Understandably, Sherman paled at the mention of

his wife in those terms, but quickly he asked, "You did? Where?"

"Here." Brass pointed up toward the second-floor apartments.

"Oh, my God! Right in one of our own apartments?"

Brass nodded. "217H."

Sherman's eyes flicked to Ortiz, who shrugged. Then Sherman said, "I don't even know what to say. . . . Can I see . . . ?"

"No. It's a crime scene. I will tell you that the apartment was in the name of a woman named Lavien Rose."

"Never heard of her."

Brass arched an eyebrow. "She was your tenant."

"That's Mr. Ortiz' job. What does she have to say?"

"Nothing. The apartment is empty except for a chest freezer."

"Oh, Christ . . ."

"And as for Ms. Rose, she and your wife actually have something in common."

"What's that?"

"They're both murder victims."

"Oh . . . oh hell . . ."

"Both suffocated with a plastic bag over the head."

Sherman stumbled over to the cement steps and sat heavily. He looked dejected, haunted; but he did not cry.

"I didn't kill my wife," he said. "I didn't even know this . . . Rose person."

Brass went to him. "Mr. Sherman, we need to move this talk to the station."

" . . . police station?"

"Yes, sir."

Sherman took a long breath and let it out slowly. Then his face turned to stone, the color draining out of it. Was he going to throw up? Catherine wondered. Clearly the man was fighting hard to maintain control.

His voice hard, Sherman asked, "Do I need a lawyer?"

The detective shrugged. "That's your decision. You don't have to make it now. We'll provide you with a phone."

"Oh, is that right?" he asked bitterly. "My 'one phone call'?"

"You can make all the calls you want, Mr. Sherman. But you need to come with us."

"Should I . . . leave my car?"

"Why don't you? We'll give you a ride back."

Brass and Catherine accompanied Sherman, while Warrick and Nick piled their tools into the Tahoe. O'Riley and the super were left to wait for the truck that would carry the freezer back to CSI. O'Riley would bring Ortiz in, too, though the super was clearly not as strong a suspect as Sherman now seemed.

When they got back to HQ, the first thing the CSIs did was fingerprint Sherman. The computer-whiz-cum-landlord had been reluctant to allow them to do it, but once Catherine assured him it was the fastest way to prove his innocence, and get them back on the trail of the real killer, he'd complied. Ortiz, on the other hand, allowed his prints to be taken without question, with the air of a man accepting his role in a system vastly larger than himself.

In the Trace lab, as Warrick and Catherine tested the prints of the men—she through AFIS, he using the comparison microscope on prints lifted from the apartment—Warrick said, "That was smooth in there with Sherman, Cath."

"Thanks."

"You really think he's innocent?"

She shrugged, laughed humorlessly. "I can't seem to tell, anymore. I used to think I had good instincts with people, and you'd think that would only sharpen and improve, after years on the job . . . but the longer I stay at this, the less I feel I know anything about people. They are always a surprise."

"And so seldom a good surprise." Warrick got back to his work, then added, "Ortiz seems like a dead end."

"I agree. A harmless nobody. And next thing you know, we'll find a freezer in every Palms apartment with a dead plastic-bagged-suffocated girl in it and his fingerprints all over."

Warrick let out a nasty laugh. "Gacy the Chamber of Commerce guy, Ed Gein the shy, quiet farmer, Bundy the nice helpful dude wantin' to give you a lift . . ."

Catherine grunted a sigh. "There's only one thing that keeps me going."

"Which is?"

"The victims."

They kept at it.

Finally, Catherine said, "Nothing from AFIS. Far as it goes, Sherman's clean." A minute later, she said, "Ortiz is clean too."

She pitched in to help Warrick as he went through every print they'd gathered in the apartment, door-knobs, appliances, toilet handle and most significantly, the freezer. Not a single print matched Sherman and only the front doorknob had a print from Ortiz.

They were just sitting there, a long way away from the euphoria they'd felt a short time ago, and were just wondering if they should call it a shift, when Nick entered, bright-eyed as a puppy.

"Freezer's here," he said. "I'm going to work on it. Anybody want to give me a hand?"

"I'm in," Warrick said, sighing, standing. "Not doing any good in here, anyway."

Catherine rose. "I'm gonna go eavesdrop on Brass and Sherman."

And she did, watching through the two-way glass as the short detective managed to loom over a disheartened-looking Alex Sherman, his crisp business attire now looking as wilted as he did. Sherman sat at one of the four chairs at the table—the room's sole furnishings—feet flat on the floor, hands folded in front of him.

Brass was saying, "You told us before that you never owned a freezer."

"I don't. Didn't. Never have."

"What about the Kenmore in apartment 217H?"

"None of our apartments have freezers, unless you count the little built-in ones that come with the refrigerators."

"So, we just imagined that freezer in apartment 217H?"

"It must belong to the tenant."

"Lavien Rose."

"If you say so."

"A dead woman."

"Again, I only know that, Detective Brass, because you mentioned it."

"Your wife handled the business end of your real estate holdings."

"Mostly, yes."

"Would she have known Lavien Rose?"

"No. Hector dealt with all of that. The name may have been written down somewhere, but we don't deal directly with the tenants."

"Does the name Sharon Pope mean anything to you?"

Sherman shook his head. "Never heard of her, either."

Catherine was watching Sherman closely. Her gut told her the man was telling the truth; but then she recalled what she'd just told Warrick about trusting her instincts. . . . Maybe the guy was just a hell of an actor.

"Who is she?" Sherman asked, turning the tables on Brass. "I mean, who was she? My tenant?"

"Lavien Rose."

"No, I mean—who was she? That's an odd name. It sounds like . . . a stage name."

"It is," Brass said, obviously unnerved by the turnabout of the interrogation.

"Well, I never heard of her—what was she, an actress? A stripper?"

Catherine blinked.

"Performance artist," Brass said.

Sherman twitched a half-smirk. "I have to admit, that's a concept that eludes me . . . performance art. But Regan might know her."

Brass sat down. "Regan?"

"Missy's friend. She hangs out with half the artists in town, in her job. Particularly the pretentious ones."

Catherine felt an electric tingle.

Brass was saying to the suspect, "Remind me—what's Mrs. Mortenson do again?"

"She's a fund raiser for Las Vegas Arts—meets with not only patrons of the arts, but also the artists . . . the screwballs who apply for grants."

"Excuse me, Mr. Sherman," Brass said, getting up. "I'll be with you in a moment."

Sherman was giving him a quizzical look as Brass walked out. He instructed the uniformed officer on the door to stay put.

Catherine caught up with Brass in the next interview room, where he was gazing through the two-way glass at O'Riley interrogating Hector Ortiz. Nothing of import seemed to be going down.

"I caught most of that interrogation," Catherine said. "Come with me."

"You got something?"

"I will have."

They went to the break room, where Catherine had left that newspaper with the article on local performance art. Brass stood patiently while she quickly scanned it.

"Lavien Rose," she said, looking at the article, "has been awarded numerous grants by Las Vegas Arts. . . . Can you wait while I check something?"

"I can keep you company."

This time she led Brass to the computer terminal in the layout room. It took less than fifteen minutes to learn that Sharon Pope, aka Lavien Rose, had made about twelve thousand dollars last year as a performance artist.

"At least," Catherine said, Brass next to her as she gestured to the monitor, "those were the grants she got from Las Vegas Arts. And I can't find any other job for her. Now, we know her rent at The Palms was six thousand a year; we also know her real home across town cost her seventy-eight hundred a year. That's almost fourteen thousand in rent alone. How do you squeeze fourteen G's outa twelve thousand bucks?"

Brass said, "You don't."

"Exactly. But maybe the rent for The Palms wasn't coming out of her pocket."

Brass had a hollow-eyed look. "Oh, shit . . ."

"What?"

"I missed something."

"What?"

He was shaking his head, his expression self-recriminatory. "When I interviewed Regan Mortenson, and she said she worked for the Las Vegas Arts Council, she told me she'd had an appointment, a meeting with somebody, right after the lunch with Missy."

"And?"

"It was with an artist . . . a woman. I'd have to check the notes I made from the interview tape . . . but I'm almost positive Regan said the woman's name was Sharon Pope."

Catherine's eyes widened. "That's who Regan claims she was spending her time with, while Missy was getting murdered?"

"I think so. . . . Maybe 'Lavien Rose' was supposed

to be her alibi, and it went south on her? D'you think Regan ended up whacking her alibi?"

Catherine hadn't processed that fully when Greg Sanders knocked on the doorjamb. The DNA tech, working on a soul patch that was not making it, carried a sheaf of papers in one hand.

Rather irritably, she said, "What, Greg?"

"Woah! Chill—I'm just lookin' for Warrick and Nick. They brought me the hairs they found in that freezer. They told me it was a rush job, and now they're MIA."

"What did you find?"

"Hairs from Missy Sherman and an as-yet-unidentified person."

Sitting up, Brass asked, "What do you know about the other person?"

"Blonde, female," Sanders said. "All I know at this point is that her hair matches one Warrick brought me earlier."

Getting that electric tingle again, Catherine asked, "Where did he get it?"

"Not sure—if you can find Warrick, you can ask him."

Catherine looked at Brass, who said, "Regan Mortenson and Sharon Pope—both blonde."

Catherine nodded. "But only one of them is still alive. We have enough to call on Regan Mortenson, wouldn't you say?"

"Oh yeah," Brass said.

Nick appeared in the doorway next to Sanders, putting a hand on the lab rat's shoulder and smiling at him impatiently. "Tell me you have our results."

Jumpily, Sanders gave up the papers like a thief caught in the act.

"Thank you," Nick said.

"Don't go anywhere, Greg," Catherine said.

She convened the group in the layout room. Nick, Warrick and Sanders sat, while an edgy Brass paced by the door.

"What good things have you been up to?" she asked the two CSIs.

"We were in the Trace lab," Warrick said, "running prints and matching evidence."

"I thought we were past that," Catherine said.

"Yeah," Warrick said, "but when prints from Sherman and Ortiz didn't match anything, I decided to go back to try to match our freezer prints against the one I lifted from Missy's visor mirror."

"And?"

"Perfect match . . . I'm good, by the way."

"I noticed," Catherine said with a smile.

Nick said, "I may not be as good as John Shaft here, but I matched the duct tape adhesive we found in the apartment to the adhesive on Missy Sherman's clothes. That do anything for you?"

"Nice," Catherine said. "Greg—your turn."

Sanders filled Warrick and Nick in on what he'd found; then Brass told them what he and Catherine had been discussing, including the Sharon Pope detail, an oversight he copped to.

"I missed it, too," Nick said, through clenched teeth. "Damn—it was in your notes, Jim! . . . That's why that name seemed familiar."

"We need to go see Regan Mortenson," Warrick said.

"Actually," Catherine said, "Jim and I'll handle that. You and Nick'll gather the rest of the evidence we need. . . . Nick?"

"Yes?"

"Talk to the people at Las Vegas Arts and see if we can track the money."

Nick was on his feet. "On it."

"Warrick—run down that freezer. The Sears stores are open by now. Kenmore's the house brand."

"Shopping on overtime," Warrick said, getting up. "Fine by me."

Then they were in the hall, walking together, except for Sanders, who made his getaway back to his lab cubbyhole.

"In the meantime," Catherine told her fellow CSIs, "Captain Brass and I will discuss the fine art of murder with Regan Mortenson."

"Maybe you'll get a grant," Warrick said.

11

HAVING JUST EMERGED ONTO THE LOADING DOCK, IN SNOW driven by a stiff wind, Gil Grissom and Tony Dominguez stood with hotel manager Herm Cormier, as snug in his parka as the waiter in his sweatshirt was not. Though it was barely 5 P.M., night was already conspiring with the storm, ready to cast the Mumford Mountain Hotel into darkness.

Grissom looked toward the parking lot, where Constable Maher and Sara Sidle had been working, and saw nothing but the snow-covered vehicles. "Where did they go?" he demanded of Cormier, having to work his voice over the wind.

Cormier shook his head. "They went off that way," he said, pointing toward the far end of the parking lot. Grissom could barely hear the man, but could read his lips.

"I'm going to join my associates," Grissom told the hotel manager. "You two need to get back inside!"

"No argument!" Cormier said.

But Dominguez—so underdressed in this bitter

snowy weather—said nothing, his eyes staring but not seeing. The tears had stopped, but the grief was probably just starting. Grissom had no doubt this boy had loved James Moss; that just didn't mean Dominguez hadn't killed him.

And much as he hated losing custody of his best suspect, Grissom wanted to hook back up with Maher and Sara, and share what he'd learned, and see what they'd found. Anyway, where was there for Tony Dominguez to run?

The criminalist had nothing on the waiter, beyond the circumstantial evidence of a sexual relationship with the victim and a cut forearm. The most dangerous aspect of releasing the suspect—Grissom was half-forgetting his lack of authorization, here—was the possibility that Dominguez would get rid of his boots before Grissom could try to make a match. But he didn't think the boy knew that his Doc Martens were potential evidence.

Shouting over the wind, Grissom said to the pair, "You need to go in and act like you don't know anything about this!"

That riled the waiter out of his funk, momentarily anyway. "Don't know anything?" Dominguez exploded. "That's James in there! How can you expect me to—"

"Tony," Grissom said, cutting him off. "If you're as innocent as you say you are . . . there's likely a murderer in that hotel."

"Yeah, that bitch Amy!" he snarled.

"If that's so, I can't have you tipping her off that we suspect her." The wind howled. "Do . . . you . . . understand?"

The young man nodded. He was shivering now.

"Now get inside. You're freezing."

Through the haze of snow, Dominguez was studying Grissom. "You say you suspect Amy . . . but you really suspect me, don't you?"

"I told you, everyone here is a suspect, including Mr. Cormier and Constable Maher. The only people not on my list are Sara and myself."

"You suspect me?" Cormier blurted, eyes wild.

Calmly, Grissom said, "You and everyone at the hotel, Herm. But no innocent person need worry— the evidence doesn't lie. And remember—the fewer people who know what we know, the easier it'll be to catch the killer."

Cormier nodded.

Dominguez said, "I'll do what you want . . . for James's sake."

"Good. Now go in and warm up and dry off!"

Cormier locked up the loading dock door and he and Dominguez went down the stairs and trudged through the deepening snow to the hotel's rear door.

Grissom shuffled out onto the parking lot, going first to the blue Grand Prix. The tomato stakes were still visible, but Sara and the constable—and their equipment—were gone. Their tracks, however, weren't hard to follow.

The sky was a gunmetal gray, a darkening shroud over him, as Grissom slogged on past the parking lot to the end of the building, where he still saw nothing but drifted snow. He turned the corner and, as he plodded on, slowly scanned the horizon. In the distance, through the slanting white, he could—finally!—make out two dark figures.

They were standing on the lake.

He had a tiny jarring moment before he realized the lake would be frozen over and safe—relatively safe—for human footsteps.

Soon, moving as fast as he could, Grissom had made his way around and to the front of the hotel; he began to tramp down the hill, almost losing his balance. He could now plainly see Maher and Sara up ahead. Shouting would be useless, he knew, over the ghostly shriek of the growing blizzard; his voice just wouldn't carry to them.

And then he had an odd, dread-inducing thought—what if Maher was the killer? What if all the help in the snow, the forensics magic, had been deception and cover-up, not straightforward detection? What if Maher had lured Sara out there, to where the man knew the ice was weak, to throw her to an icy death?

The thought of Sara thrashing in the glacial waters, her screams in the storm unheard by a world gone deaf, gave Grissom a ghastly chill; Sara, another victim for him to process . . .

He had closed half the distance between himself and them when he glanced left and saw the dock. He knew instantly that he was running across the lake and that Sara and Maher were almost in the middle of the thing. The ice would get thin, the farther out they went—but as he neared, he realized that his imagination had run away with itself; and he felt foolish.

Maher, his metal detector still tucked under his left

arm, was leaning over and digging through the snow with his right hand. He seemed to be going very carefully. Nearby, in her parka, Sara—now a convert to the Canadian's ways—liberally sprayed gray primer into a footprint.

They both looked up at the sound of his approach.

"You're all right?" Grissom said to Sara.

Still kneeling, she gazed up at him curiously. "Of course . . . We're doing the best we can, in this snow."

"What happened to working the tomato stakes?" he asked the constable.

Maher said, "Somebody must have figured out what we were up to, and moved them to try to throw us off."

"But whoever moved the stakes left new prints," Sara said, "and they led down here."

Grissom smiled a little. "That confirms the presence of the murderer in the hotel."

"Yes it does," Maher said.

"And I know who the victim is," Grissom added.

Sara got to her feet, her eyes bright. "Who?"

"James Moss—a waiter."

Maher and Sara traded a look.

Grissom frowned. "What?"

"Amy Barlow's boyfriend, you mean?" Sara said.

"Well, yes and no," Grissom said, and he explained about the love triangle involving the two waiters and the one waitress.

"Amy told us that 'Jimmy' didn't make it in to work yesterday," Sara said. "They usually ride together, but he had an appointment with somebody."

Grissom shook his head. "She's lying."

Maher said, "Is she? What if that 'appointment' was with Dominguez?"

Sara arched an eyebrow. "Amy's got that cut on her hand, remember."

"And Dominguez has a cut on his forearm," Grissom said. "Claims it's from working on his car."

"We should go back and talk to Amy," Sara said.

Maher said, "Not just yet—I got a major hit on the metal detector. . . . Let me dig a minute."

And he was back on his hands and knees. Sara and Grissom exchanged shrugs and were about to join him, when Maher called, "Jackpot!"

The Canadian stood and displayed his find: a plastic ziplock bag that seemed to have some heft to it.

"It may not be Christmas yet," Grissom said, "but I'd go ahead and open that. . . ."

The Canadian did, carefully undoing the ziplock top, and they all looked in at the contents: a pair of bloody leather winter gloves, a rock about the size and shape of a softball and—peeking out from under the gloves—the silver barrel of a small gun.

"Are we looking at the murder weapon?" Maher asked.

Sara, snow-flecked eyebrows high, said, "That a .32? Looks about right."

"Obvious, isn't it?" Grissom asked.

Feeling the noose tightening, the killer decides to lose the murder weapon. He or she packs the gun and the incriminating gloves in the plastic bag, adds a rock for weight, and walks out and buries the package in the snow atop frozen Lake Mumford. In the spring, the snow and ice will melt, the package will sink and the evidence will be gone forever.

Using a pen down its barrel, Maher lifted the .32 Smith and Wesson revolver out of the ziplock bag. He carefully opened the cylinder and allowed five spent cartridges and one bullet to drop out, down into the bag, then he closed the cylinder and slid the pistol back into the bag as well.

"Okay," Grissom said. "Sara, you have pictures of the footprints out here?"

She nodded.

"Good—can we still cast it?"

"I've got one block of sulfur left," Maher said.

The snow was hammering them now, the wind whistling its carefree tuneless tune—the storm had plenty of time. The criminalists didn't. They worked fast and accurately and made a cast of the print Sara had shot . . .

. . . and the team was back inside the hotel in less than an hour. The newfound evidence was dry and safe, locked inside Sara's field kit. Soaked and freezing, they paused in the underpopulated lobby and stripped off their coats.

Cormier had been waiting for them, and he carried over an armload of towels. The trio of detectives sat down in front of the roaring fireplace and began to dry off. Grissom and Sara, both in black, shared a sofa facing the fireplace, Maher in a nearby overstuffed chair perpendicular to the fire.

The hotel manager went over to the desk, used the phone and came back and reported to Grissom, "Just called up to the restaurant—somebody'll bring some hot coffee right down for you folks."

Grissom glanced around the lobby—at the Christmas tree, the big picture window looking on a winter landscape that seemed far more picturesque from the indoors and the handful of guests seated reading and relaxing. Then he turned to the hotel man, who stood alongside the sofa, and said, "I don't see Tony Dominguez."

"He's locked himself in his room, Dr. Grissom."

"I was hoping you'd keep an eye on him."

"He's not going anywhere. He's a wreck."

Grissom curled a finger and the hotel man drew closer, as the CSI whispered, "Tony talk to anybody?"

Cormier shook his head. "No, sir. I took him up to his room, and neither one of us said not a damn word to nobody. . . . Just like you said. Listen, Dr. Grissom—you don't really consider me a suspect, do you?"

Grissom beamed at him. "Of course."

Cormier frowned, and moved off.

A moment later, Amy Barlow—in her white shirt, black bow tie and black slacks outfit—appeared with a pot of coffee and a tray of cups. The bandage on her hand appeared fresh and Grissom made a show of studying it as the waitress placed a steaming green mug of coffee on the low-slung table in front of him.

"Is that any better?" Grissom said, nodding toward her bandage.

"I'll live," she said.

"Cutting onions in the kitchen, wasn't it?"

"That's right. . . . Maybe I'll sue ol' Herm and wind up ownin' this place. . . . Any of you folks need anything else?"

They all said no, she gave them a quick smile, then

Grissom's eyes followed her as she walked back toward the stairs to the dining room.

When the waitress disappeared from his view, Grissom said to Sara, "Got a pen and notebook?"

"Sure." She scrounged them out of her coat pocket, on the floor, and handed them to him.

He turned to Maher and asked, "Don't suppose you brought any fingerprint powder along, for your demonstration?"

Shaking his head, the Canadian said, "Didn't bother—too basic. Sucks to travel with, eh? So easy to get that stuff all over everything."

Grissom nodded, having had similar experiences. He quickly scrawled a list and tore the page out of the notebook.

"What's that about?" Sara asked.

Grissom glanced over at the desk, behind which Cormier had retreated. "Herm! A moment?"

The hotel manager came right over and Grissom said, "I need a few things," and handed the man the paper.

Cormier took the list, read it over, and looked up in confusion. "What kind of scavenger hunt are you on, Dr. Grissom?"

"The best kind. Can you fill my grocery list?"

"Well, certainly."

"Good. And what room is Tony Dominguez in?"

Cormier told him.

"Thank you. Could you deliver those items to my room?"

"Sure—but I wouldn't mind knowin' what you have in mind with 'em."

"Show you when you get up there, Herm . . . but the quieter we keep this, the better."

"I know, I know. . . . You're kind of a Johnny One Note, ain't ya?"

Cormier wandered off, going over the list again as he went.

Then, turning to Sara, Grissom said, "Let's go up to my room."

She just looked at him.

He continued: "Or don't you want to solve this murder?"

"Am I invited, too?" Maher asked.

"Your attendance is required, Constable. I'm going to need your help. But, first, I need you and Sara to go up to Tony's room, to pick up a couple more items."

Maher frowned. "What items?"

Grissom told him.

"Will he cooperate?"

"I think so. But as he is still a suspect, I'd like both of you to go."

Sara's eyes tightened. "You think he's dangerous?"

"Whoever killed James Moss is definitely dangerous. And just because Tony seems devastated, that doesn't mean he isn't our man."

Sara nodded.

"You two be careful," he said. To Maher, he said, "Look after her."

"I can look . . ." Sara said, but then stopped. She was obviously going to say she could look after herself, but for some reason she didn't complete the thought. Instead, she smiled and said to Grissom, "Thanks."

What was that all about? he wondered.

Maher and Sara headed out of the lobby, while Grissom lagged. Gingerly, he picked up his coffee cup, careful to touch only the handle—the part Amy hadn't touched—and walked across the lobby. In the men's room, he dumped the coffee down the drain. Again carrying the cup by only the handle, he went to the elevator and waited for its return—Sara and Maher had already gone up.

Grissom's room was hardly designed to be a crime lab, but, this evening, it would just have to suffice.

The door and bathroom occupied the north wall; a window on the south wall overlooked the lake, in front of which squatted a round table and two chairs. The east wall was home to a fireplace, and to the left stood an armoire with three drawers and two doors that opened to reveal the small television. The single bed and a nightstand hugged the west wall.

He had just finished clearing the table of his books and hotel literature when a knock came at the door, which he opened to reveal a perplexed Herm Cormier, standing next to a galvanized steel garbage can.

"How'd you do, Herm?"

"Hope you been a good boy, Dr. Grissom, 'cause Santa brought you everything on your damn list . . . but I can't for the life of me figure why you wanted this bunch of stuff."

"You're welcome to stay, Herm—and see for yourself."

"I thought I was a damn suspect!"

"You are," Grissom said pleasantly. "This way I can keep an eye on you.

Shaking his head, Cormier picked up the garbage can and squeezed past Grissom into the room. "You know, Dr. Grissom, I can't tell when you're kiddin' or not."

"Good," Grissom said.

Before the CSI supervisor could close the door, Sara and Maher appeared as well, the constable holding a pair of stylishly clunky black boots, Sara holding a plastic bag with a drinking glass inside.

"Mr. Cormier, could you get me that pan now, please?"

"Sure."

"Make sure it's good and hot."

"Oh I will," he said, and stepped back out, pulling the door shut behind him.

"He'll be right back," Grissom assured his confused associates. Turning to Sara, he asked, "Any trouble with Dominguez?"

"No," Sara said, and her expression was compassionate. "He really is broken up. Just sitting there. Not even crying, just . . ."

Maher finished for her: "Kid says he'll help us any way he can, to catch James's killer."

Sara shrugged a little. "He seemed sincere."

"Well, let's see," Grissom said. "First, Sara, I want you to compare Tony's boots to the castings from both the crime scene and the lake. You can use the bed as a workstation."

She nodded and Maher handed her the boots.

"Set the glass on the table," Grissom said to her. "That's my fingerprinting station."

She placed the plastic bag next to the coffee cup

that Grissom had brought up from the lobby. "Amy's prints?" Sara asked, indicating the cup.

"That's right," Grissom said.

"What can I do to pitch in?" the constable asked.

"You can start with helping me unload that garbage can. Then we'll set you up in the bathroom."

Maher grinned. "That's my station, eh?"

They took the lid off the can and were greeted by a cornucopia of seemingly unrelated items. Grissom reached in for a battery-operated drill and handed it to Maher, who gave him a quizzical look. Next Grissom withdrew a five-pound sack of flour, a basting brush, a tube of Super Glue, two wire coat hangers, a magnifying glass and an inkpad for rubber stamps.

"Not exactly a cutting-edge lab," Maher said.

"No, but they like it rustic here at Mumford Mountain Hotel, right? . . . Let's start by getting you going. Cormier'll be back soon, and we need to be ready."

Sara, already hard at work, called out, "Size is way off on the boot—not even close. Soles have way different markings too."

"Appears the Doc Martens are innocent, anyway," Grissom said. "Now, Sara, see what you can get from the gloves."

She went back to work.

In the bathroom, Maher put the garbage can in the tub, then sat on the toilet, drilling holes in the can's lid, while Grissom pulled down hard on the bottom of one wire coat hanger, thinning and elongating the hanger until it was hotdog-shaped with a hook on one end; then he pulled the tail end up into a U, forming a small rack.

"How's the trashcan?" asked Grissom.

Maher said, "She's ready."

A knock at the door told Grissom that Cormier was ready, too. Putting the hangers in the sink, the CSI left the bathroom and answered the door.

Herm Cormier stared at the nearly red-hot pan he clutched in a pot-holder-protected hand.

"Hot comin' through," the hotel man said.

Grissom stood aside and allowed Cormier to pass by, holding the orange-bottomed frying pan away from him, as if he had a skunk by the tail.

"Bathroom, Herm," Grissom said. "Put 'er right in the bottom of the garbage can."

Cormier did as he was told, then backed out of the bathroom.

"Good job," Grissom said to him.

But Cormier had the dazed expression of a small child forced to attend a long ballet.

In the bathroom, Grissom found that Maher was ahead of him, having already bent the hooks of the hangers through the holes in the lid of the garbage can. Grissom dripped drops of Super Glue onto the red-hot pan, as Maher carefully draped the folded zip-lock bag from the lake over the normal hanger. On the bent hanger, the constable balanced the knife across the bars of the U, and said, "Ready."

After a dozen or so drops, Grissom stopped and waited; a few seconds crawled by and the glue began to smoke. "All right," Grissom said, timing it, "now."

Maher eased the lid down on top of the garbage can.

"Mind if I ask you boys what the hell you're up to?" Cormier asked.

Matter-of-factly, Grissom said, "Fingerprinting."

The old boy's eyebrows rose. "Fingerprinting . . . with Super Glue, coat hangers, and a garbage can?"

Grissom shrugged. "You use the tools at your disposal."

Rising from the toilet, Maher said, "If you don't mind, eh, I'll step out in the hall and have a smoke."

"It's a life choice," Grissom said.

Maher thought about that for just a moment, then went out.

It would be at least ten minutes, Grissom knew, before they could open the can. The process would have to be repeated with the gun, the casings, and the bullet. While he was waiting, he went in to check on Sara's progress.

Cormier was now leaning against the armoire, watching Sara work.

Sara smiled tightly at Grissom, holding up the gloves, and said, "Killer definitely wore these."

"The cut on the cloth mirrors the cut on Amy Barlow's hand."

Enthusiasm danced in the young woman's eyes, though her words were understated: "I would say so."

Grissom prized her love for the job.

The hotel manager stood away from the armoire; confronted with damning evidence regarding his waitress, he looked stricken. "I can't believe it—Amy? She's such a nice girl . . . such great people skills."

Sara arched an eyebrow. "You may wish to revise that opinion."

Grissom moved to the table by the window on the lake, and sat down with the flour and the basting brush. Carefully, he applied a little flour to the coffee mug that Amy had served him downstairs—that it was a dark green cup was a nice little break. Brushing away the excess flour, he saw a surprisingly well-defined partial.

Flour was maybe five percent as good as commercial fingerprint powder, but in a spot like this, five percent was a good number. When he finished, Grissom had three partials and a pretty good thumbprint. He dusted the glass from Tony's room and discovered a workable set of prints there as well. Of course, Sara had asked the waiter to pick up the glass specifically to provide his fingerprints—no trickery, as with the waitress—so Grissom wasn't terribly impressed.

Maher strolled back in and they opened the garbage can to reveal several smudged fingerprints, a couple of good ones and what appeared to be a partial off the glove. And they got three more prints from the ziplock.

Grissom called out for Cormier.

A few moments later, the hotel manager peeked into the bathroom; he still had a shell-shocked look, no doubt due to learning his waitress, a good and valued employee, was likely a murderer.

Without looking at the man, Grissom asked, "Could you heat the pan up again?"

"Yes, sir," Cormier said, and Maher handed him the pan and the potholder.

The hotel manager, his expression hollow, sleep-walked away, and Grissom followed him, stopping him at the hotel room door. "You do know you can't say anything to anyone about this."

"Yes, Dr. Grissom."

From across the room, Sara called, "That includes Pearl, Mr. Cormier!"

"Pearl," the hotel manager said numbly, " 'specially."

Grissom said, "Mr. Cormier?"

Seeming to snap out of it a little, Cormier looked at Grissom.

"If you give Amy a heads-up," Grissom said, smiling his pleasant smile that was not at all pleasant, "I'd have to construe that as aiding and abetting."

Cormier came fully awake. "Wouldn't do that, sir. Amy's just an employee. . . . I only . . . it's just . . ."

"People are a disappointment?"

Cormier swallowed. "Yes, sir."

Grissom made a clicking sound in his cheek. "I find insects are much more consistent. . . . Go."

"All right," said Cormier, then he walked out the door, a little of the zombie creeping back in.

While they waited for the hotel manager to come back, Grissom and Maher sat at the table by the window and, using the magnifying glass, compared the prints from the coffee cup and the ziplock bag.

"I think that's a match," Maher said, frowning.

"Tough to tell in conditions like this," Grissom said. "But it does look close—statistically, prints from such a small sample of people, appearing this similar, would just about have to be a match."

When Cormier returned with the heated pan in hand, he said, "I need to get back downstairs."

Still at the table, Grissom, not exactly suspicious—not exactly not suspicious—glanced over at Cormier, poised at the doorway, and asked, "Why is that, sir?"

"Pearl got through to the sheriff once," the hotel man said, "but got cut off. I'm gonna take another crack with my ham radio."

As the hotel manager was leaving, Sara got her cell phone out of her purse and punched in Catherine's number. This time she heard nothing, not even the robotic voice. She put the cell phone away and went back to work.

Grissom and Maher returned to their bathroom crime lab. Grissom attached the pistol to the hanger, placed the bullets into a glass wrapped in one of the hangers, dripped more Super Glue on the reheated pan, then placed the lid on top. Again they waited and again they were rewarded: good prints revealed themselves, from several of the casings and the bullet. The gun had been mostly wiped clean, but a glove print appeared on the barrel, and Grissom felt sure it would match the wear patterns on the gloves Sara was processing.

Grissom sighed in satisfaction, and gave Maher a businesslike smile.

"What say we go find Amy Barlow?" Grissom said.

"And her boots," Maher said.

The trio of criminalists went to the waitress's room, and Grissom knocked on the door, but got no response.

"We could pick the lock," Maher said.

"Not and have what we find hold up in court," Grissom said. "Not in this country."

Maher frowned. "What about getting Cormier to give us permission? I mean, he's the manager."

Sara said, "Supreme Court ruled in 1948 that, under the Fourth Amendment, a hotel room counts as a person's home."

Grissom added for the constable's benefit, "Even if our buddy Herm gave us his permission, whatever we found would still get thrown out."

The three tried the dining room, on the second floor, but the waitress was not there. They split up and looked around the main floor, but couldn't find her. They met at the front desk, to track down Cormier and see if he had any notion where Amy Barlow had gone.

Through an open doorway behind the desk, they could see the hotel man in a small office, seated at a desk, bending over a microphone, fiddling with knobs on his ham radio set.

"Tom," Cormier was saying into the mike, "can you hear me?"

Static was the only response.

Grissom slipped behind the desk, the others following him. He stood in the doorway and said, "Excuse me . . . Herm?"

The hotel manager jumped and swung around. "Judas H. Priest! You have to scare me like that, with a murderer on the loose?"

Grissom smiled. "Just the kind of discretion I was counting on, Herm."

". . . I'm sorry. Really, Dr. Grissom, I haven't told a soul. . . ."

"Have you seen Amy?"

He nodded. "Just a few minutes ago."

Grissom's eyes tightened. "Where?"

Cormier gestured vaguely. "Out in the lobby. Said

she was wondering what was wrong with Tony. Said she hadn't seen him since he came draggin' in, looking all depressed, and since it was almost time for the dinner rush . . ."

Grissom turned to give Sara and Maher a concerned look, even as he said to Cormier, "And you didn't think maybe you should've called that to my attention?"

Sara was shaking her head, eyes wide with dread. "Oh, she wouldn't . . . would she? With us around?"

"With her people skills," Grissom said, already on the move, "she just might."

The trio sprinted across the lobby, eyes of the scattered guests popping up from books and magazines, responding to the unusual commotion in this quiet place. Grissom punched the UP button and they waited as the ancient car made its slow descent.

When the bell dinged and the doors groaned open, Grissom was about to rush in, when he found himself nose to nose with . . .

. . . Amy Barlow.

This gave the slender but bosomy waitress a start, and she jumped back, dark ponytail swinging, eyes wide in shock, her hands coming up in a defensive pose.

Recovering quickly, Grissom held the elevator door open and looked in at the woman, in the cell-like space, and said, "Amy Barlow, you're under arrest."

As he recited her rights, Amy made a face—part confusion, part disgust. "What the hell for? You're not a cop!"

"Call it a citizen's arrest . . . for the murder of James Moss."

Her eyes widened more. "What? . . . Is that who was killed out in the woods? Jimmy?"

Sara stepped up beside Grissom, further boxing the woman in. "This is where you try to summon up some tears. I'd save the indignant act for later."

The waitress just stood frozen for several long moments; then she said, "I'm shocked, that's all. He was my boyfriend. . . . Everybody deals with grief, different."

"I heard you two broke up," Grissom said.

"That's a lie! Who told you that? That queer?"

Grissom sighed, then stepped aside and gestured with mock gallantry for her to step out of the elevator. "Why don't you come with us . . . for a little grief counseling?"

She glared at him, slouching out into the lobby.

Grissom took her firmly by the arm, and turned to Maher. "Constable, go get a passkey from Cormier and get upstairs, and check on Tony Dominguez."

"I thought Cormier couldn't open a—"

"I'm not worried about evidence," the CSI said. "I'm concerned for that kid's life."

Amy sneered at them. "Why? He isn't!"

"Charming," Sara said.

But Cormier, to his credit, had anticipated this, and was right there with the passkey, which he handed to Maher, who got onto the elevator.

"Sara," Grissom said, "hold the door! . . . Herm, you need to accompany the constable."

Cormier joined Maher in the elevator and, before the doors closed, Grissom—still holding on to his sullen suspect's arm—said, "Mr. Cormier, could we use your office?"

The hotel manager nodded as he gazed at the waitress in disbelief. "I just can't fathom it, Amy, you doing this."

"I didn't do anything, you old fart," she said.

Cormier's eyes showed white all around, as the elevator doors shut over him.

Grissom and Sara each took an arm and guided Amy behind the front desk to the larger of the offices back there, which was still fairly small, just a wooden desk, a couple file cabinets and a big calendar of Hawaiian scenery—people who ran resorts longed for vacations, too, Grissom figured.

He ushered the waitress to the desk chair, as Sara closed the door.

"I didn't do anything to anybody," Amy said. Superficially, she seemed calm, but a tiny tremor underlined her words. "You should be after that faggot, Tony—he's been, like . . . stalking Jimmy. What musta happened is, Jimmy spurned his pervert advances, and that sick creep went ballistic."

Grissom said, "That's your theory, is it?"

Sara, leaning against the door, arms folded, said, "Somehow you don't seem very upset, or surprised, for a woman who just lost the love of her life."

She shrugged. "I'm in, like . . . shock."

Sara smiled a pretend smile at the waitress and said, "You might want to, like . . . work on that before your trial."

Amy's eyes got huge. "I'm telling you people—it's Tony. He's a fag! Can you imagine? Trying to steal Jimmy away from me? . . . Guys are after me all the time. I can have my damn pick."

"Tony didn't just try to steal Jimmy away from you," Grissom said. "He succeeded. Didn't he?"

She shook her head, emphatically. "Jimmy didn't want anything to do with that deviant shit."

A knock at the door startled Sara; she opened it and Cormier—his face deathly pale—staggered in a step, then leaned against the doorjamb.

"We . . . we were too late," the hotel man said.

"For what?" Sara asked.

"Poor kid . . . he's dead."

The waitress did not react.

Grissom, not leaving his position by the suspect, said gently, "What happened, Herm?"

The old boy swallowed; his eyes were moist. "Found him in the tub . . . slashed his wrists." The hotel manager shook his head, his eyes haunted. "It . . . sprayed everyplace. Goddamn mess . . . never seen the like."

All eyes went to Amy.

Her expression went from bland to aggravated, as she realized what they were thinking. "Hey, I had nothing to do with that."

Grissom noted the inflection.

"Sounds like he killed himself," she said, with a shrug. "Fags do that every day."

His voice calm, Grissom said, "You told Mr. Cormier that you were going up to Tony's room to check on him."

Amy started to rise, but a firm-jawed Sara lurched forward and put a hand on the suspect's shoulder.

"If you're not growing," Sara said, "sit down."

And shoved her back in the chair.

Amy straightened herself and said, "Let's not all get our panties in a bunch. . . . Yes, I went up to his room. Just 'cause he's a swish don't mean he's not a co-worker who I gotta work with and, like . . . respect."

Sara rolled her eyes.

"But the asshole didn't even answer me," she said. "I know he was in there."

Grissom asked, "How?"

She shrugged. "I heard him bawlin'."

Silence draped the small room.

Then Amy plunged back in: "Anyway, when he wouldn't open the door, I tried the knob; but it was locked. I was worried about him."

Sara almost laughed. "Worried?"

"Yeah. We needed his help in the dining room. So I came downstairs to get Herm, to try to get Tony outa his room. That's why I was on the elevator—remember?"

Grissom had a sinking feeling: how close they'd come to preventing this . . . if she was lying, and if she wasn't lying.

The phone on the desk rang, and Cormier excused himself past Sara and picked up the receiver. His voice was shaky as he said, "Hello?"

Several moments later, the old man handed the phone to Grissom, saying, "The constable—wants you."

Grissom took the phone and heard the Canadian say, in a somberly professional manner, "I've locked myself in the room to protect the scene. We can work it whenever you're ready."

"We're interviewing Amy on that subject now," Grissom said. "She claims she went to the room and he wouldn't answer. Says she didn't do this."

"She have any blood on her?"

"No."

"What's she wearing?"

"Standard waitress uniform."

"Unless she dumped her clothes somewhere and switched into a spare uniform, she's probably telling the truth. The bathroom walls are red. Dripping from the damn ceiling. Hit an artery—incredible spray."

"I've seen it often," Grissom said grimly.

"If Amy Barlow was in that room, she'd have blood on her somewhere."

Grissom said, "Yeah. Okay. Thanks." He hung up. "Amy, we'd like to look in your room. You say you're innocent, and the only way we can help you prove that is—"

"Help me? Right."

"We need your permission."

"What, so you can try to find evidence to lock me up?" She thrust her middle finger at him.

"I'm going to take that as a 'no,' " Grissom said.

He picked the phone up, got an outside line, a dial tone, and—after punching the numbers—was pleasantly surprised to hear the voice of an operator.

"Nine-one-one," the crisp female voice said. "Please state your emergency."

"I need to speak to the sheriff—we have another suspicious death at the Mumford Mountain Hotel. At least one is a murder."

A long silence ensued and Grissom wondered if the woman had heard him. He was about to repeat himself when she intoned, "Transferring."

Covering the mouthpiece, Grissom asked Cormier, "Who will I be talking to?"

"Sheriff Tom Woods."

When Sheriff Woods came on the line, Grissom introduced himself and began to explain the situation. He wasn't very far along when the husky-voiced Woods asked to speak to Herm Cormier.

Grissom handed Cormier the receiver; the hotel man held it in a hand as shaky as his voice, saying, "Hello, Tom—this is Herm. . . . No, he's for real, a forensics man from Vegas who made it in for that conference 'fore the storm hit. . . . Yup, happened just like he was saying. You better hear the rest."

Cormier listened again, then handed the phone back to Grissom. "Wants you, Dr. Grissom."

"This is Grissom, Sheriff."

"Would you continue, please," Woods requested.

Grissom finished filling him in.

"We're damn lucky to have you there, Mr. Grissom. But the fact is, you're not a peace officer in New York State. You have no jurisdiction. What do you propose we do?"

"I would happily turn this over to you," Grissom said.

"Lord knows I'd love to help, but the roads won't be open today, for sure . . . and maybe not tomorrow. Record snowfall, y'know."

"Right now, I need a search warrant for our suspect's room."

Amy, sitting with her arms folded, sneered at a wall.

The line crackled while Woods thought about it. Then the deep voice said, "Here's how we're going to handle this, Mr. Grissom. Would you raise your right hand, please?"

". . . Are you deputizing me?"

"I'm appointing you a special deputy for Ulster County. That allows me to get a judge to grant you your search warrant—and allows you to serve it. Your hand in the air?"

Sara grinned as Grissom, feeling a little foolish, switched the receiver to his left hand and raised his right. Over the phone, Sheriff Woods read him the oath, at the end of which, Grissom said solemnly, "I do."

"Deputy Grissom, I'll fax that warrant to the hotel as soon as Judge Bell grants it. Put Herm on so I can get the number."

"Thanks, Sheriff Woods. I appreciate this." And he gave the receiver to Cormier.

Half an hour later, a fax warrant in hand, Grissom served it on Amy Barlow. Maher stayed behind in the manager's office, watching the prisoner, while Grissom and Sara searched the room. Sara found the boots in a closet; not only did they match the castings from both the crime scene and the lake, multiple dried drops of blood were visible on the upper portion of both boots.

They searched the room carefully but found no sign of bloody clothing that would tie the waitress to Tony Dominguez' death. The hotel would have to be searched, but the likelihood that the boy had taken his own life seemed strong.

Back in the office, Grissom confronted the young woman with the bloody boots. Amy remained adamant about her innocence. "I still say Tony did it, and a couple boots with a couple flecks of blood ain't gonna convince anybody otherwise." She gave him a satisfied smile, saying, "And looks like Tony won't be around to defend himself, either."

"He won't have to be," Grissom said. "We have your boots. We have matching footprints at the crime scene. We found James's . . . Jimmy's . . . knife, with blood on it, which I'm confident will match yours. Oh, and we found your bloody gloves and the gun you threw out on the lake. . . . Next time, Amy, when you throw evidence in a lake, better that it not be frozen over."

She paled.

But Grissom wasn't through: "We've got your fingerprints on a coffee cup you served me this afternoon . . . remember? . . . and they match the prints on the ziplock bag . . . the one you put the gun and gloves in, when you tried to hide them in the lake?"

The weight of the evidence seemed to sink her deeper and deeper into the chair.

"Anything you'd like to tell us, Amy?" he asked.

Her voice seemed small, childlike, and not as cruel. "I loved Jimmy. I gave him everything . . . I was a lover, a friend, a mother to him . . . and he throws me over for . . . a guy?" She shook her head, swallowed, and finally some tears came—no sobs, just crystal trails dribbling down her cheeks. She looked at Sara and said, bitterly, "Try that out on your self-esteem, honey."

Sara asked, "Was it self-defense?"

Now the usual Amy reasserted herself. "Fuck no! Jimmy was weak . . . weak in a lotta ways, I see that now. What I was gonna do was beat the shit out of him, for what he did to me. I only took the gun along to scare him, humiliate him like I was humiliated. . . ."

Sara said, "He hurt you."

The tears began their gentle trail again; her voice trembled. "He didn't hurt me . . . he killed me. He ripped the woman part of me out and stomped on it. He made me feel like a useless, worthless, unwanted skank."

Grissom asked, "What happened, Amy?"

She shrugged, taking the tissue Sara handed her. "I was yelling at him, beating on him. He couldn't feel the kind of . . . inside pain I felt, but I could at least hurt the outside of his sorry ass."

"Is that when he pulled the knife?" Grissom asked.

". . . He pulled that damned knife and I just looked at him. You know what I said? I said, Well, faggot— looks like you still wanna stick somethin' in me after all! . . . And he did. Got in a lucky one." She gestured with her wounded hand. "So I pulled out the gun and . . ." She laughed. "He ran . . . ran like the scared little girl that he was."

Sara asked, "When you hit him, was that a . . . miss? A mistake?"

"Knowing Jimmy, *that* was the mistake. No, honey, I meant to shoot the son of a bitch, and I did. He wasn't gonna hurt me no more."

Grissom asked, "Amy . . . why did you burn him?"

She wiped the tears off her face, drew breath in through her nose. "I turned him over and he was looking up at me. He was dead, and he was still fuckin' mocking me." She swallowed. "And I still hurt inside. So what else could I do? I went back to the toolshed and got the gasoline."

She folded her arms, as if trying to warm herself; she smiled—a terrible smile.

"When he was burning," she said, "finally . . . I felt better. I felt like I was a woman again."

Grissom glanced at Sara, who said, "Then you heard someone coming, right? Heard someone and ran?"

"Yeah." She looked from one CSI to the other. "What, was that you two?"

Grissom nodded. So did Sara.

Her eyes narrowed and she bared her teeth, a vicious animal. "Well, go to hell, both of you . . . go to hell for spoiling my fun. I wanted to see that prick turn to ashes."

Grissom looked at Sara and shrugged; she did the same—neither had any more questions for the suspect, who sat, eyes glazed, sinking into the chair, arms tight across her chest, her face as blank as a baby's.

"Herm," Grissom said. "Keep an eye on her for a second."

"Sure thing, Dr. Grissom."

Grissom and Sara stepped out of the little room, behind the front counter.

"What now?" Sara asked.

"We still have plenty to do. We should process that scene upstairs. Try to determine whether Tony committed suicide or Amy did it."

"I'm betting Amy."

"We'll wait for evidence. Oh, and another thing . . ." Grissom nodded toward the open doorway of the little office, where dead-eyed Amy sat. "We'll need to keep tabs on our perp till the police arrive."

Sara said, "I'll take first watch, if you don't mind. I'm not anxious to work that red room upstairs."

"I don't blame you. Could be another long night."

A pretty half-smile dug a dimple in the young woman's cheek. "Could be worse."

Grissom huffed a laugh. "How?"

She grinned. "Could be outdoors. . . ."

12

Jim Brass was in no hurry.

Jim Brass was in no hurry.

The Taurus was in a late-morning line of residential traffic consisting of churchgoers bound for home or maybe brunch, as opposed to salvation. Getting a judge to sign a warrant for DNA on a Sunday was never an easy assignment, and he'd delegated O'Riley to track down a magistrate who owed Brass a favor.

But cell phone reports from the crew-cut detective indicated the judge was proving elusive, and Brass had no intention of sitting outside the Mortenson home, waiting for a warrant. If Regan Mortenson proved to be guilty—which with the evidence the crime lab had amassed seemed a dead certainty—she was a cold-blooded murderer, possibly psychotic and capable of God knew what; so the homicide captain preferred not to announce his presence in advance by sitting in an unmarked car on Goldhill Road, about as inconspicuous as a Good Humor truck.

Next to him as he slogged through Sunday morning traffic, Catherine sat back, her eyes closed, her breath not heavy—not asleep, just relaxing. Brass felt fairly alert, though he, like Catherine, had been up forever. They both knew that Sheriff Mobley would be apoplectic over the OT, but graveyard was so close to breaking the Missy Sherman case, they couldn't bear to pass the ball to Ecklie's day-shift crew, who had screwed it up in the first place. The eventual media attention would salve any wounds the overtime created, anyway.

A cell phone ring gave him a rush—Brass was surprised by how eager he was for that warrant—but he settled back behind the wheel when he realized it was Catherine's phone. Her eyes opened slowly and she answered it on the third ring.

She identified herself, then listened for a long moment. "So they were already looking into it? . . . But they hadn't gone to the authorities yet?"

Brass took an exit ramp off 215, easing down to a stoplight. He took a quick right and pulled into a gas station. He'd worked up a thirst, waiting for O'Riley's call.

"Water?" he mouthed to her, as Catherine continued on the phone, and she nodded.

About five minutes later, when Brass returned with two bottles of Evian, Catherine was still on the phone. He got in, handed her a bottle, removed the cap from his and took a long pull.

"All right, then," Catherine said, finally. "Keep me posted, Nick, will you? . . . Thanks." She clicked off.

"What did Nick have?"

"Plenty," she said, and unscrewed the cap on her water. "He got hold of Gloria Holcomb, the accountant for Las Vegas Arts. She agreed to meet with him in her office."

"On Sunday morning?"

She lifted both eyebrows and gave him a wry look—nobody did wry looks better, or prettier, than Catherine Willows. "Seems Ms. Holcomb needs the LVMPD as much as the LVMPD needs her. She has strong suspicions that the Arts council has an embezzler in its midst . . . more than suspicions, really."

"Why hasn't she gone to her boss?"

"She reports to the suspected embezzler—Regan Mortenson."

Brass grunted a laugh. "Versatile girl, our Regan. But I thought she was just a volunteer worker."

"Seems Regan started out that way. Made such a strong impression, she was offered more responsibility. But the council could only provide her a nominal salary, which she said was fine with her—she just wanted to help out."

"Or help herself."

"I should say—about six figures worth."

"Which, end of the day—not that nominal," Brass said. "Is that our murder motive?"

"You mean, friend Missy found out Regan was embezzling? Probably not—Regan only moved from volunteer status to 'nominal' salary maybe a month prior to Missy's disappearance."

"It's possible, then," Brass said. "It does predate Missy camping out in that Kenmore."

"But not by much—Regan would have to be knee-deep in pilfering during her first month on the job, and Missy would somehow have to stumble onto it.

And I never heard that the Sherman woman was even active with the Arts council."

Soon they were headed back for the interstate. They were barely back on the expressway when another phone ring got Brass's hopes up—his own cell, this time.

And it was O'Riley, beautiful O'Riley, saying, "Signed, sealed and 'bout to be delivered . . . on my way."

"What's the deal? Stop at Denny's for a couple Grand Slams?"

"Hey, I deserve better—Judge Hewitt was playing golf. I had to rent a cart."

"What the hell's he playing golf for?"

"I know, it's a dumb sport."

"No, I mean it's like forty-five degrees out."

"Temperature does not seem to be an issue for his honor. But getting interrupted when he's playing golf . . . that is. An issue, I mean."

"You did good. How long?"

"Ten minutes."

Brass thanked O'Riley and clicked off.

He hit the lights, but not the siren. They whizzed along 215 toward Eastern Avenue.

"I take it we've got the warrant," Catherine said.

"A calligraphy class couldn't've taken longer coming up with one." Then he laughed abruptly.

"What?" Catherine said, Brass's laughter infectious enough to put a smile on her face.

"Just thinkin' about the sight of O'Riley riding the golf course in a cart, chasin' that judge."

Less than five minutes later, they drew up in front of the Mortensons' mission-style house. As a precaution, Brass parked his Taurus at an angle blocking the driveway.

"Wait for O'Riley?" Catherine asked.

"No. He'll be here."

They strolled to the front door, keeping their manner as low-key as possible—Brass in front, Catherine a step behind and to his left, both conscious that in a matter like this, a detective never knew when he might have to draw his gun, the CSI knowing better than to be in the way. His badge was pinned to his sport-coat breast pocket; this would be all the credentials he'd need. He rang the doorbell.

Regan Mortenson, her blonde hair pulled back in a loose ponytail, peeked out the window next to the door, forehead crinkled, as she studied her callers.

Brass tapped his badge. He stopped short of yelling, but tried to make sure his voice would be heard through the glass: "We need to talk to you, Mrs. Mortenson!"

She nodded, and seemed about to leave her lookout to let them in, when a screeching sound froze her, and she—and Brass and Catherine, turning—watched as O'Riley's Taurus jerked to a stop in front of the house. Then the big detective jumped out and charged the house, warrant in hand, like a pro football tackle bearing down on a quarterback.

Brass and Catherine looked back at the window and Regan was gone.

Huffing, O'Riley was next to Brass now, proffering the warrant. "Got it!"

"You forgot the bullhorn," Brass said to him, and O'Riley just looked at him.

They gave it a few seconds, until it became obvious

Regan Mortenson had not left the window to answer the door.

"She's ducked back inside," Brass said.

O'Riley said, "I've got the rear," and went hustling around the garage.

Catherine was shaking her head. "What does she think she's accomplishing with this?"

"Either she's making a break for it," Brass said, "or getting ready to hole up."

He tugged the nine millimeter from its hip holster, held it with barrel pointed down, per safety regs. With his left hand, he checked the door—double-locked . . . lock in the knob and a dead bolt. No kicking this sucker in; no shooting the lock, either—why risk a ricochet?

"Catherine," he said, his voice tranquil, eyes on the door, "battering ram in the trunk—go get it. Cover you."

She huffed out a little anxious breath. "Keys?"

Pistol still pointed downward, Brass—feeling that strange calm that came over him, in such potentially violent situations—reached into his sportcoat pocket, withdrew the Taurus keys, and tossed them toward the sound of her voice, eyes never leaving the door.

He could hear Catherine's low heels click on the concrete for a couple of steps, then she must have cut across the lawn. Standing staring at the door, he was wondering which way to play it when Catherine returned. The manual said he should call in SWAT, but hell with that—this wasn't a bunch of holed-up gangbangers or some heist crew, this was a suburban housewife with ice water in her homicidal veins, and moreover this was an important bust. His bust.

His immediate concerns were more concrete. Was Catherine strong enough to bust the lock with the ram? The Thor's Hammer battering ram resembled a giant croquet mallet, a nonsparking and nonconductive ram, perfect for entering, say, the meth labs that seemed to be springing up everywhere. But it was a heavy mother, and not equipment a CSI often handled.

If Catherine wasn't up to it, Brass would have to trust her to cover him while he broke the door. Not really a problem, though. Of the night-shift CSIs, Catherine was the most skilled with her weapon and had, in recent years, taken two perps down in clean kills that passed the Shooting Board with flying colors. She might be a scientist, but at heart she was all cop and there wasn't a man or woman on the LVMPD who wouldn't trust Catherine Willows with their lives.

Catherine appeared beside him, hefting the big, black hammer like a lumberjack, despite her fashion-model looks. She gazed at him with an admirably flinty-eyed expression—she was ready. He was about to give her the go-ahead, when the latch suddenly clicked.

The nine millimeter swung up automatically and, as the door opened, Brass pushed through, moving inside, pistol in the lead.

Regan Mortenson stood before him in the stucco entryway—small, blonde and very pale. She looked like a teenage girl in a Dali-print black tee shirt and blood-red sweatpants, her feet bare, toenails painted red, fingernails, too.

"Las Vegas Police," Brass barked. "Show me your hands."

But her hands were empty, and so were her eyes,

staring at the black hole of the barrel without fear or apparent interest. Behind Brass, Catherine had set down the battering ram and filled her right hand with her automatic. She followed Brass in, as Regan backed up, her hands high, palms open, head bowed, the stairway to the second floor at her back.

Clipping the words, Brass said, "Hands behind your head—now."

She was doing that when a shattering noise shook them all—from the rear of the house!—the brittle music of breaking glass.

Regan flinched, her raised hands covering herself, as if that glass might be raining down on her.

"Easy," Brass told her, as he kept his pistol trained on the young woman. "Catherine, check that out."

But Brass had the sinking feeling he knew what it was already. And indeed, before Catherine could respond to Brass's request, O'Riley came barreling into the hallway.

"Police!" he shouted, as he leveled his pistol at Regan.

"Sliding glass doors?" Brass asked.

"Yeah," O'Riley said, breathing hard.

Brass was just thinking the city could afford the price of a little glass, considering, when another noise shook the house.

Brian Mortenson came tromping down the stairs, his eyes wide and indignant, the close-trimmed goatee looking smudgy on his chin, like he'd been eating chocolate cake by sticking his face in it.

About halfway down, he yelled, "What the hell is going on . . ."

His voice trailed off as he saw Catherine—in shooting stance at the bottom of the stairs—aiming her pistol up at him.

"Las Vegas Metro Police," she said, not yelling, but there was no mistaking the no-nonsense meaning.

He stopped with one foot on one step, the other on another, hands shooting skyward, a pose that vaguely recalled his college basketball background.

Brass said, "Walk slowly down the rest of the stairs, sir, and please keep your hands where we can see them."

Mortenson obeyed the command, and Catherine gave him a quick frisk. Then she told him he could lower his hands. The tableau consisted of Brass holding his nine millimeter on the woman of the house, just beyond the entryway, and Catherine training her automatic on the man of the house, at the bottom of the stairs. O'Riley stood in the archway of the living room as if on guard, his weapon in hand.

It only took Brian Mortenson a few moments to regain his composure. "What is going on here?" he demanded. "You better have a warrant or I'll build a parking lot where the police station used to be."

"We're here to serve a warrant," Catherine said. "Specifically, to serve your wife with a warrant for DNA and fingerprints . . . but she decided not to cooperate."

Mortenson frowned. "So you people decided to dismantle our house?"

"Your wife resisted," Brass said.

The childlike Regan finally found her voice. She turned on Brass with indignation: "You scared me! I was going to let you in until . . ." She turned toward

O'Riley, who was standing on the periphery like an oversize garden gnome with a gun. "That big brute came running across our lawn, and I thought . . . I thought . . . I don't know what I thought! I was just scared."

"Mrs. Mortenson," Brass said, "we properly identified ourselves—and I'm sure you recognized me."

"How could I forget you?" she asked.

Mortenson gestured to Catherine's weapon, still trained on him. "Do you mind? . . . You searched me. Could I go to my wife?"

Catherine nodded; and she holstered her weapon.

Before she allowed the husband to stand at his wife's side, she quickly but thoroughly frisked the young woman, too.

She glanced at Brass—clean.

Mortenson slipped an arm around his wife and brought her to him; somehow, she didn't seem terribly interested.

He asked, "Regan, honey . . . are you all right?"

She nodded.

But Brass wasn't so sure—something didn't look quite right about the petite blonde, and he could tell Catherine was concerned, too, flicking little glances Regan's way. Missy Sherman's "best friend" had claimed to be scared, and maybe she was; but did that explain why she was sweating so profusely, and why her skin had lost its color?

One arm still looped around his wife's shoulders, Mortenson said, "Let's see your warrant. What's it all about, anyway?"

Finally Brass holstered his weapon, and nodded to

O'Riley to do the same. Then the burly detective came over and handed the warrant to Brass, who, in turn, passed it on to Mortenson.

"This warrant," Brass said, "gives us the right to fingerprint your wife and for CSI Willows, here, to swab Mrs. Mortenson's mouth for DNA."

Mortenson, forehead taut as he quickly scanned the document, said, "That still doesn't tell me what this is about." He drew the blank-faced Regan even closer. "Now explain yourself, or I call my attorney, right now."

"That's your prerogative, Mr. Mortenson," Brass said. "But the purpose of our visit? Your wife is the primary suspect in the murder of Missy Sherman."

". . . What?" Mortenson was astounded; they might have told him Martians were on the rooftop. "What kinda ridiculous bullshit . . ."

Regan's eyes were huge; she seemed to be in shock, kind of weaving there, Stevie Wonder–style, under his wing.

Meanwhile, her husband was going strong. "Is that what my tax dollars go for? So you can come up with some wild-ass asinine theory that Regan killed her own best friend? Jesus!"

"Mr. Mortenson," Catherine said, "it's best you just comply."

He stepped forward, and Regan slipped out from his shielding grasp. "It's not enough she's lost her best friend . . . now you have to go and say she killed her? Shit!"

"Mr. Mortenson . . . ," Brass began.

But the husband was off and away on his rant. "This is how you treated Alex, isn't it? He cooperates, and then you accuse him! You put him through this same shit, I heard all about it. What, are you just going door to door, accusing people? Maybe it's a conspiracy! Maybe we all did it!"

Finally Mortenson paused to take a breath—Brass had decided to let him blow off some steam—but now the homicide captain waded in.

"Sir," Brass said, "let me explain why your wife is our primary suspect."

"Please! Enlighten me!"

"A blonde hair was found inside the freezer where Missy's body was hidden away; it matched a blonde hair we got from Missy's Lexus."

Mortenson's mouth was open, but no words came out; and confusion tightened his eyes.

Brass continued: "We also believe that fingerprints from the freezer and the SUV will match your wife's."

Mortenson turned to his wife. "You don't know anything about this, do you, baby? . . . They're fuckin' crazy. Tell them they're fucking crazy, baby."

She stared at him. He slipped his big arm around her again, drew her to him. "This'll go away, baby. We'll make it go away. This is just circumstantial bullshit they're misinterpreting. Don't you worry one little—"

"Let me go!" She wrenched away from him. Then she looked at Brass, her icy eyes huge, wild. "You have to protect me!"

Her husband winced, as if he were trying to see her through a haze. "Baby . . . honey?"

She pointed at him, shaking. "I won't lie for him

any more! . . . He admitted it, months ago, and I've had to live with it! He did it!"

Mortenson's mouth hung open.

"Don't deny it, Brian. You did it, you know you did it!" She turned pleadingly toward Brass. "You have to believe me. . . . He and Missy were having an affair, and he tried to break it off—"

"What?" Mortenson said, apparently bewildered.

"And when Missy threatened to tell Alex, he killed her! That's his blonde hair!"

Her husband looked like an actor who'd walked into the wrong scene in some strange play. "My . . . ? What . . . ?"

Regan moved from Brass to O'Riley to Catherine, searching their eyes for support, coming up empty.

Finally, standing before Catherine, she said, "You have to protect me—he said if I ever told anybody, he'd kill me, too! Put a plastic bag over my head and suffocate me!"

"Regan," Mortenson said, "what are you saying? What is wrong with you? . . . She's sick, Officers. Something's wrong with her. . . ."

"She's sick, all right," Brass said.

Looking at the pretty blonde, blue eyes to blue eyes, Catherine said, "I'd call your husband's hair more a light brown, Mrs. Mortenson. And, anyway, the hairs we got from Missy's Lexus and the freezer belong to a blonde . . . woman. A long-haired blonde woman."

"No . . . it's not true!" Regan screamed. "He'll kill me if you don't—"

"Regan," Brian Mortenson said. He stared at his

wife as though he didn't know whether to embrace her or slap her. This seemed to be moving way too fast for him. Finally he managed, "You're trying to blame me . . . for your friend's death?"

"She can try to blame you," Catherine said, "she can try to blame the Boston Strangler . . . it's not going to help. You see, your wife doesn't think we know about Sharon Pope." Catherine turned toward Regan with a tiny smile. "Lavien Rose?"

Regan's lovely features seemed to wilt. "No . . . I . . ." The woman teetered for a moment, losing her balance, as if the room had begun to spin . . .

. . . and then dropped to the floor.

"Regan!" Mortenson shrieked, and he dove to her side, and held her, tenderly, as if she had not, moments before, tried to fit him in a frame for murder.

Brass knelt. "What's wrong with her? Has she been ill? Does she have a medical problem, a condition?"

"Nothing . . . nothing serious. . . . What have you people done to her? . . . You saw her, she had some kind of mental breakdown. . . ."

Catherine ducked into the first-floor bathroom, then called, "Jim!"

Brass said to O'Riley, "Watch them," and joined Catherine in the bathroom, where she had found the answer on the counter: a small white bottle.

"Ambien," Catherine said, reading the label. "Dosage, ten milligrams. If Regan had a full month's supply, that means three hundred milligrams."

"She killed herself?"

"Maybe. But people've been brought back after taking as much as four hundred milligrams. Ambien's engineered to make it difficult to use for suicide." Catherine tucked the bottle in her slacks pocket, and they rushed back to the hallway.

"Overdose," she said, mostly for O'Riley's benefit, dropping to her knees and pushing the husband out of the way. "Sleeping pills."

"Oh my God," Mortenson moaned. "She has sinus headaches . . . can't sleep."

She was having no trouble sleeping now.

Catherine began CPR. "Let's take her in your car, Jim. Label says it was refilled yesterday, and if she took the whole thing, we don't want to wait for an ambulance—she could be gone."

But Brass was already halfway out the door.

O'Riley and Mortenson carried Regan, racing to the Taurus. Brass cranked the key as the men loaded the blonde in the back with Catherine. Mortenson tried to climb in back with them, but Catherine pushed him away.

"Hey, I'm her damn husband! I'm going with her."

"Ride in front, then!"

"I have a right—"

Catherine snapped, "Do you want to waste time?"

Mortenson climbed in front.

O'Riley gunned his Taurus and pulled up next to Brass. "I'll lead," he said. "That new hospital, St. Rose Dominican, Siena Campus? That's closest."

Before Brass could answer, O'Riley hit the lights and was off. Brass hit his lights and siren as well and tore off after O'Riley.

Mortenson leaned over the passenger seat, his eyes moist and focused on Regan. Catherine kept up with the compressions, but things did not look good. She gave Regan mouth-to-mouth—once, twice, three times. Then she resumed CPR.

The woman's skin was the color of an overcast sky. She was limp and lifeless, and when Catherine checked, Regan's pulse was weak. Though the young woman still took the occasional breath on her own, those seemed to be coming more and more infrequently.

O'Riley served as lead blocker as Brass twisted the Taurus through traffic. He sawed the wheel and turned onto St. Rose Parkway—former Lake Mead Boulevard—and slammed down the gas again.

The Siena Campus, the second St. Rose Dominican facility, was mission-style—like the Sherman and Mortenson homes—white stucco with a red tile roof. O'Riley slid to a stop in front of the emergency room entrance and was out of the car and through the doors before Brass even had his car stopped.

A crew dressed in scrubs came running out with a gurney, and Catherine handed Regan over into their care; they wheeled the woman inside, with Brass, O'Riley and Brian Mortenson in hot pursuit. Catherine remained behind, sitting in the backseat for several long moments, letting the adrenaline rush subside.

She was quite sure Regan Mortenson had killed Missy Sherman and Sharon Pope—cold-bloodedly, for reasons as yet undetermined. There could be little doubt that Regan was a sociopathic monster. And yet Catherine had just tried her best to save the woman's life.

If a cop asked her why, she might have said, to

make sure that bitch didn't have an easy out, so that a murderer would live to face justice. But Catherine knew it was something else that had driven her. Let the sociopaths take life lightly. She would choose to save a life, if she could.

And if Regan Mortenson lived today, to die via lethal injection tomorrow, that would be another's judgment, not Catherine's.

She went inside to join her colleagues.

Better than an hour went by before a young doctor came out to tell Catherine and Mortenson that "it had been touch and go," but Regan would be fine. While the woman was still unconscious, Catherine got her DNA swab and she already had Regan's fingerprints on the Ambien bottle.

Catherine Willows went home to spend some of what remained of her Sunday with her daughter, and to sleep a few hours, before going in to CSI HQ to process her new evidence. And toward the end of shift, not long before sunup, Catherine found herself back at the hospital with Brass, Nick and Warrick.

They stood at the foot of the bed where Regan Mortenson lay like a tiny broken doll; tubes ran in and out of her, and she looked frail, and had as yet said nothing. But she was not in a coma. The doctor assured them of that.

Brian Mortenson stood next to his wife, two hands holding her limp one. No explaining love, Catherine thought. This woman had killed two people, tried to frame her husband for the crimes, and still, several times he had mentioned that he was convinced his wife was suffering from a mental condition; that these things, if she did them, Regan could only have done if she were not in her right mind.

Brass said, "Mr. Mortenson, we've matched Regan's fingerprints to the freezer and Missy's Lexus. Her DNA was inside the freezer, in the car and on Missy's clothes."

"No way," Mortenson said.

The detective shrugged. "Believe what you like, but the facts tell us your wife killed her best friend."

"It's a lie," Regan said.

Her voice was small and cold. Her eyes, finally open, were big and cold.

Her husband beamed at her. "Baby . . . darling . . . you're going to be fine."

"Welcome back to the world, Mrs. Mortenson," Brass said, and read her her rights.

Regan stared at the ceiling, the icy blues unreadable; her husband, grasping her hand, might well have not been there, for all she seemed to care.

"Do you understand these rights, Mrs. Mortenson?"

"I understand."

"Would you like to tell us anything?"

She turned toward Brass. "I'd like you to tell me something, Detective."

"What?"

"When are visiting hours over?"

"Why did you do all this, Regan? Why did you kill a woman who was supposedly your best friend?"

"Is that Old Spice, Captain Brass? Tell me you don't wear Old Spice."

"Why Sharon Pope?"

"Have you ever seen a performance artist?"

"Why did you freeze Missy Sherman's body?"

"How do you like my responses so far?"

Brass looked toward Catherine, who shrugged. Mortenson, at his wife's side, continued to hold her hand; but he was looking at her oddly now, as if this were a person he'd never seen before, as if perhaps his wife had been replaced in the night by a pod person.

"Brian!"

Everyone looked at the man who'd just appeared in the doorway: Alex Sherman.

The late Missy Sherman's husband—unshaven, in slept-in-looking dark-green sweater and brown slacks—looked distraught. "Brian, I got here as soon as I could." He went to his friend, seated at Regan's bedside, and put a consoling hand on the man's shoulder.

"Thanks," Mortenson managed, but didn't look at his friend.

Regan, however, was staring at Alex Sherman. "You . . . you came."

"Of course I came," he said, and smiled, reassuringly. "Worried about you two."

Catherine went to Sherman and drew him away from Mortenson. She whispered harshly, "What in the hell are you doing here?"

Confused, perhaps even a little hurt by her question, Sherman said, "Well . . . Brian called and told me that Regan had overdosed on sleeping pills. . . . So of course I came right away."

Catherine's eyes flicked to Mortenson, then back to Sherman. "Well, that's sweet all around. . . . Did Brian tell you why Regan took those pills?"

"No . . . It's not like her—she's always so 'up.' I didn't even know she was depressed. What is going on?"

Catherine arched an eyebrow and gave it to him straight. "Regan OD'd because she knew we had evidence proving she killed your wife . . . as well as that woman, the performance artist—Sharon Pope?"

Sherman looked as if the switch on his brain had been shut off—nothing was processing, eyes open, mouth open, but no movement. Finally, the gears started to work again, and he looked toward Regan, searchingly, then accusingly . . . and she looked away.

"She did this?" Sherman asked. "Really did this?"

Catherine said, "We have her cold."

"But . . . why?" Sherman asked.

"She won't tell us."

"I'll tell you," a voice said.

Regan's voice.

Her eyes were on Alex Sherman.

"I didn't do it for myself," she said. "I did it for you . . . Alex."

Dumbfound, Sherman staggered to the bedside opposite the seated husband, who wore a similarly poleaxed expression. With the tension in the air, Warrick moved into position, nearby.

Sherman said, "What . . . what do you mean . . . ? For . . . you killed Missy for . . ."

"You. That's how much I care."

"You care? About me?"

Regan shook her head and looked lovingly up at him. "She wasn't good enough for you, Alex. She was never good enough for you. Not smart enough, not funny enough, not sexy enough, not pretty enough.

Don't you know who you should have been with, all along? . . . Me, of course. Because I love you, Alex—I've always loved you."

Brian Mortenson dropped his wife's hand.

Regan glanced at him. The loving expression she'd shown Sherman fell away. And she laughed.

Her husband's face reddened and he drew back a big fist.

Brass shouted, "No!"

Warrick threw himself over the woman as Mortenson's fist arced down, but at the last moment, the big man caught himself, punch glancing off Warrick's shoulder as Nick sprang around and grabbed Mortenson from behind, in weight-lifter's arms. The big man struggled for only a second, then settled down—all the air, all the fight, all the life, out of him—as Nick dragged him out of the room. Regan's husband didn't start crying till he got out in the hall, but it echoed in.

Regan was still laughing, lightly, but laughing.

Warrick pushed up off Regan, and she looked and blew him a kiss. "My hero."

Warrick twisted away from her and stood, appalled. "Been at this a long time, lady . . . and you win the prize."

Brass asked Warrick, "You all right, Brown?"

The CSI nodded, glared at the woman and walked out of the room, to join Nick and Mortenson in the hall.

Sherman staggered around into the chair Regan's husband had vacated. He didn't seem angry, exactly; more stunned, confused, just trying to understand.

"For me?" Sherman said. "You did this for me? But

you knew I loved Missy. There was never a damn thing between us, Regan!"

"But there could have been, and there should have been." Regan shook her head again, her eyes wild. "You stupid, sad son of a bitch! I am the great missed opportunity of your life! Why do you think I came to Vegas—to be near my 'friend'? Missy was all right. But nothing special. I came out to Vegas to be near you. To be where you were. I wanted to be with you."

"But . . . Brian?"

A tiny shrug from a tiny woman. "To make ends meet . . . till you came to your senses."

Catherine knew she would never forget the look of horror on Alex's face. But he did not cry. Something inside of him kept him alert—he'd said he wanted to help them find his wife's killer.

And now he helped.

"Why did you hide her body away like that?" he asked.

Catherine glanced at Brass; they both knew the man would have liked to either strangle the woman, or run from the room in tears. But Sherman had the presence of mind to keep her talking.

"I kept the body as a sort of . . . back-up. A prop."

"A . . . prop?"

"I thought when Missy 'ran off,' you'd finally see, Alex . . . see that I was the one who really cared about you. And wasn't I there for you?"

"Oh yes," he said. "You came over all the time."

"Yes—trying to help you get past this . . . terrible tragedy . . . but you're such an idiot. All those times, me sitting next to you, alone in that house, you could have had me. . . . Instead, you just went softer and softer over that dumb dead little bitch. For a year I throw myself at you, and all I hear is Missy, Missy, Missy . . . and that's why it was so smart of me to hold onto her body.

"You see, I anticipated that you might need closure . . . that the disappearance might not be enough. That you might be holding out hope, longing for the missing Missy."

"Closure . . ."

"I had hoped that her disappearance would make you think she'd left you—that you'd fall into my arms, desolate, needing the solace only someone who really loved you could provide . . . but no. You needed further convincing. So Missy had to come out of cold storage."

Alex Sherman stood. He looked down at the beautiful young woman, who smiled up at him, adoringly, with ice-blue eyes that to Catherine, frighteningly, did not appear at all crazed.

Regan said, "Do you see now, Alex? Do you see who has really loved you, all these years?"

Alex nodded. He walked slowly to the door, paused and looked back—not at Regan, but at Brass.

"It's lethal injection in this state, isn't it?" he asked.

"Yes," Brass said. "And family members of victims can attend."

Again Alex nodded. ". . . See you later, Regan."

He slipped out.

She frowned, staring at the empty space where he'd been.

Now that Regan was talking, Brass tossed in his own question. "Where does Sharon Pope fit in?"

She brought those cold eyes around and they landed on Brass like a pair of bugs. "Are you still here?"

Catherine stepped up beside Brass. "Figuring the Pope woman's part, Jim . . . it's not that hard."

A starving performance artist hits up the new Arts council fund-raiser, and offers to make kickbacks, if grants come her way. Regan now knows that Sharon can be bought, can be used, and when she needs someone to rent an apartment for her, Regan finds the starving artist is the perfect front.

But when Missy Sherman's body brings the case back to life, Sharon becomes a loose end. Possibly "Lavien Rose" discovered what that apartment she's been renting has been used for— and has begun blackmailing the patron of the Las Vegas Arts, who in turn embezzles to pay off the performance artist . . . deciding, finally, to tie off the loose end as well as stop the extortion, all with one plastic bag over one spiky-haired head. . . .

"By the end of our next shift, Jim," Catherine assured the cop, "Warrick'll have matched the tracks from Charleston Boulevard with the casts from Lake Mead."

A jury might see the evidence as circumstantial, but they had a mountain of it. The actual murder weapons—two cinch-top plastic bags—were long gone; but the CSIs had everything else—the tire tracks, the fingerprints, the DNA, the motive and now Regan's own lovestruck confession.

Back at HQ, with the shift winding down, Catherine sat in the break room with Nick. She'd had only occasional sleep over the past forty-eight hours, and there wasn't much left to do now except go home, get some rest and come back tonight to start over.

Monday nights were sometimes slow, or as slow as Vegas ever got; so she hoped next shift she'd be able to take it easy. She gulped the last of her coffee and pushed her chair back, but before she could rise, Sara Sidle straggled in, also looking less than fresh.

"Didn't you used to work here?" Nick said, leaning back on two legs of his chair.

Before Sara could reply, Catherine tossed in her own question. "You're not due in till next shift—miss us that much?"

Sara staggered over to the counter where a mixture suspected to be coffee awaited. "Wanted to get rid of the equipment we took, so we didn't have to drag it all home and back again, tonight."

"So?" Nick said. "Give!"

"Yeah," Catherine said. "How was the vacation with pay?"

"Don't ask," Sara sighed, pouring herself a cup of coffee and dropping into a chair. "Murder and a suicide."

Nick looked skeptical. "You mean, one of the workshops was on murder, and another was on suicide."

"No," she said, "I mean, we were snowbound, no cops, and had a murder and a suicide to work."

Sara's story seemed to reenergize Catherine, who sat up. "That phone call—when we got cut off, that was about a homicide, there?"

Sara nodded, smirked humorlessly, and in a monotone rattled off the following: "In the woods behind the hotel. Waitress killed a waiter for having a gay affair. Then waiter number two, who was having the affair with waiter number one, killed himself, and it looked like the waitress had done him, too. Only it came up suicide. A Canadian CSI helped us—eh?"

Grissom stuck his head in the door. "I see the place didn't burn down while I was gone."

Catherine simply nodded. "Sheer boredom without you."

Grissom—leaning against the jamb—nodded back, as if that sounded like the most reasonable response.

"So, Gris," Nick said, grinning his boyish grin, "did you teach the yokels all about big-city high-tech crime scene investigation in the twenty-first century?"

Grissom lifted his eyebrows. "More like nineteenth century. Right, Sara?"

With a weary smile, she revealed, "Grissom is an Ulster County Deputy Sheriff now."

Their boss smirked. "And for that singular honor, I get to go back to New York, one of these days, and testify at the trial of a woman who you would not wish on your worst enemy."

"I know the kind," Catherine said.

"Did they give you a bullet to keep in your breast pocket, Deputy?" Nick asked.

Grissom frowned. "Is that a movie reference? Books, Nick. Stick with books."

Their supervisor gave them a little grin, then was gone.

"So the trip turned into one big crime scene?" Catherine asked. Struggling to keep the glee out of her voice, she added, "That's just terrible."

Sara shrugged and rose. "Most of it was pretty hard, actually. Snowed in for two days. Froze our butts off guarding, then working the crime scene, had gallons of blood at the suicide, had to find the killer and watch her till the local cops showed and then catch a redeye to get back, so we could be home to work tonight."

Catherine said, "Tough," but couldn't repress the smile any longer. And Nick, arms folded, rocking back, was grinning openly.

Sara paused at the door. "Last day—Sunday? That was nice and cozy, though. We spent the day reading by the fire."

She slipped out, leaving behind two co-workers who were looking at each other with wide eyes and open mouths.

"No," Catherine said.

"No way," Nick said.

In the hallway, Sara was smiling to herself. Nick and Cath didn't know that she and Grissom had separate fireplaces in their separate rooms.

And they didn't need to know.

Let them wonder.

Author's Note

I would again like to acknowledge the contribution of Matthew V. Clemens.

Matt—who has collaborated with me on numerous published short stories—is an accomplished true-crime writer, as well as a knowledgeable fan of CSI. He helped me develop the plot of this novel, and worked up a lengthy story treatment, which included all of his considerable forensic research, for me to expand my novel upon.

Criminalist Sergeant Chris Kaufman CLPE—the Gil Grissom of the Bettendorf Iowa Police Department—provided comments, insights and information that were invaluable to this project, including material from his own forthcoming book on winter crime scenes. Thank you also to Jaimie Vitek of the Mississippi Valley Regional Blood Center for sharing her expertise.

Books consulted include two works by Vernon J. Gerberth: *Practical Homicide Investigation Checklist and Field Guide* (1997) and *Practical Homicide Investigation: Tactics, Procedures and Forensic Investigation* (1996). Also helpful was *Scene of the Crime: A Writer's Guide to Crime-*

Scene Investigations (1992), Anne Wingate, Ph.D. Any inaccuracies, however, are my own.

Again, Jessica McGivney at Pocket Books provided support, suggestions and guidance. The producers of CSI were gracious in providing scripts, background material and episode tapes, without which this novel would have been impossible.

Finally, the inventive Anthony E. Zuiker must be singled out as creator of this concept and these characters. Thank you to him and other CSI writers, whose lively and well-documented scripts inspired this novel and have done much toward making the series such a success both commercially and artistically.

MAX ALLAN COLLINS has earned an unprecedented eleven Private Eye Writers of America "Shamus" nominations for his historical thrillers, winning twice for his Nathan Heller novels, *True Detective* (1983) and *Stolen Away* (1991). He received the 2001 "Herodotus" Lifetime Achievement Award for Excellence from the Historical Mystery Appreciation Society.

A Mystery Writers of America "Edgar" nominee in both fiction and nonfiction categories, Collins has been hailed as "the Renaissance man of mystery fiction." His credits include five suspense-novel series, film criticism, short fiction, songwriting, trading-card sets, video games and movie/TV tie-in novels, including *In the Line of Fire*, *Air Force One* and the *New York Times*–bestselling *Saving Private Ryan*.

He scripted the internationally syndicated comic strip *Dick Tracy* from 1977 to 1993, is cocreator of the comic-book features *Ms. Tree*, *Wild Dog*, and *Mike Danger*, has written the *Batman* comic book and newspaper strip, the miniseries *Johnny Dynamite: Underworld*, and a CSI graphic novel published as a serialized miniseries. His *New York Times*–bestselling graphic novel *Road to Perdition* is the basis of the acclaimed feature film starring Tom Hanks and Paul Newman, directed by Sam Mendes.

As an independent filmmaker in his native Iowa, he wrote and directed the suspense film *Mommy*, starring Patty McCormack, premiering on Lifetime in 1996, and a 1997 sequel, *Mommy's Day*. The recipient of a record six Iowa Motion Picture Awards for screenplays, he wrote *The Expert*, a 1995 HBO World Premiere; and wrote and directed the award-winning documentary *Mike Hammer's Mickey Spillane* (1999) and the innovative *Real Time: Siege at Lucas Street Market* (2000).

Collins lives in Muscatine, Iowa, with his wife, writer Barbara Collins, and their teenage son, Nathan.

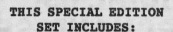